CHAPTER ONE

Tonight is the night!

It was just before twilight as Lisa began to prepare
for a night to remember. She felt as if this was the
night she had waited, planned, even hoped for all her
life. It wasn't the event itself that she was so excited
about, and she didn't even have a date; this was
something much deeper. Every nerve in her body
seemed to be tingling with excitement and
anticipation of what was to come. Now there she
stood in front of the mirror that she used to dread,
putting on her attire; first her pearl necklace, a
decorative lace that lay flat draping down her chest,
then the chandeliered pearl earrings. Her hands down
to her side, she looked at herself and admired her
curves as she began to caress herself with her own
hands, starting from her thighs, slowly sliding up her
hips, then up to her breasts as she pushed them up a
bit wondering as she often did, how she would look
with bigger ones. She giggled and thought to herself,
"that's all I have and if it is good enough for God,
then it's good enough for me, but he could have given
me a little bigger breasts to even out the score," as she
looked at her pear shaped body once more. She shook
herself and thought; "I've got to get ready!" She
grabbed her black silk stockings, and carefully

gathered them in her fingers just as her mother had taught her; slowly pulling and smoothing all the way up her legs carefully, as not to cause a snag or have elephant ankles. She giggled again, and said "chocolate thunder...no chocolate thunder thighs!" She remembered her grandmother used to say; "that girl ain't nothing but butt and thighs." She giggled again as she thought of how that would look, just butt and thighs walking around. She shook herself again and even said out loud, "okay I've got to hurry up and get ready!" She paused as she looked at the final piece lying on the bed. "That's a b-a-a-a-d black dress right there!" It was a sleek little number that she purchased about a year earlier but never wore; but tonight was the night. Tonight was special. She had always wondered how it would feel to wear it, and tonight was it!

She remembered the day she laid eyes on it as if it were yesterday. She first saw it in a shop window. She remembered thinking; "that dress looks like it was sprayed on the mannequin," because it was so form fitting. It wasn't fancy, it had no sequins, no real distinctive design, and while it would show off the little bit of cleavage she had it wasn't even low cut. She knew however, that once she put that dress on it would change her world forever and maybe rock someone else's too. She picked it up and held it up in front of her. It was short, mid-thigh, which was really short for her. In fact, it was shorter than anything she had ever worn before. "Oh well!" She thought. "Here

6

we go." She carefully slipped it over her head, slowly smoothing it as she tugged it down past her waist as she thought; "it feels like this is going to be a little tight." No matter, it made it past the point of no return; those voluptuous hips of hers. "It fits!" She said in disbelief as she smoothed it down around her hips and stomach. Lisa giggled gleefully as she remembered the store clerk's face the day she picked it out off the rack.

"Would you like to try it on?" The store clerk asked in a very condescending tone.

Lisa knew what the store clerk was thinking. "How dare you pick that dress!" She simply smiled and said; "No, I'm sure it will be a perfect fit." Man! Lisa remembered the look on her face was priceless as she approached the counter with her size 16 self with a size 6 dress as if she hadn't a second thought. Lisa slid her feet into her stilettos and thought; "these are probably half-hour shoes." She had never worn those either but she just knew that a four inch heel shoe with pointed toes couldn't be comfortable for too long. She playfully did a short step wiggle up to the mirror and said out loud; "you sure are one fine and sexy black woman!" "Why thank you, I know." She winked, did a spin, and then stopped. Posing now in a side profile, being careful to make sure that everything was tucked in, pushed up, and looked just right. She took a deep breath and said "Let's do this!" She cocked her head to the side, and still looking at herself in the mirror, winked once more then dashed off down the hall grabbing her clutch and wrap.

As she stepped into her parking garage and looked at her car she thought, "that's what I forgot; I meant to wash the car. I probably could have gotten Tony to do it for me."

Just then she thought about Tony and his red car. She hated that car; in fact she even hated the color red. Red reminded her of the man with the red shoes from her childhood and of the horrible things he had done to her. "That's funny," she thought, "it doesn't bother me anymore; it's still there, I remember it, but it's not the same." She exclaimed out loud, "I purposely remember." It was one of the many sayings she had learned from Tony. She smiled as she wondered how he was doing.

Tony was a guy she had met about a year ago. She could never remember exactly when it was, but Tony did and that's one of the many things that always bugged her about him. He remembered stuff that she couldn't. Tony was a little too ghetto for her taste and a bit of a roughneck, yet at the same time she had always found that attractive about him. She knew she wasn't supposed to, but she did, and tried hard not to let it show. She always wondered if he knew it. She could never quite figure him out. She remembered how he used to just stare at her; at least she thought so. It wasn't really a lustful look; it was more like a curiosity of sorts. That always made her paranoid. She'd ask "Tony, what's wrong?" She was sure he'd noticed a blemish or something that she'd missed and hadn't covered up. She'd always had trouble with her skin, and on top of that, she would pick at it and make it worse, and then try to cover it up with her makeup. He'd just laugh and say "nothing that can't be fixed." In horror Lisa would then ask Tony, "What's wrong with me, what needs to be fixed?" Tony would laugh and say, "that's a good question. I don't know. How do you fix what's already perfect, but when I figure that one out I'll be a millionaire." Lisa never knew what he meant by that.

That was another one of the many things that frustrated her about Tony; it always seemed like he spoke in riddles or something. She shook herself and said, "No, I am not going to think about him tonight. This is *my* night." Lisa started her car, turned on her radio and the *Average White Band* was singing *A Love of Your Own.* "Oh, I can't believe they're playing *AWB*; I haven't heard that one in years! I know it's about to be a good night now!"

Lisa flashed back to the day Tony walked into her life. Lisa was an usher in the church. It was her Sunday to work the center aisle and seat people and in walked Tony. She was immediately disgusted with how he looked but she was good at not letting it show. She had actually asked God to help her to become stoic and not let things show on her face. She had actually gotten pretty good at it, but had become a little cold in some respects. She cared for people, but she realized that if she didn't learn to guard her emotions and protect her feelings she might get hurt again, be viewed as being weak, or even worse a punk. Lisa hated more than anything being thought of as, or called, a punk. You could just about get away with calling her anything else, but she was no punk, and she'd fight you if you called her one. And don't even think about treating her like one. Tony had on a cream colored suit and gold shoes. If there was anything she hated more on a man, it was those ghetto suits as she called them, and colored shoes. "It looks like a pimp suit." Lisa thought. It was a cashmere cream colored suit. Lisa thought it was awful. She quickly shook it off as she looked into his face and thought this light-skinned man with long black hair has got to be Latino or something, cause he didn't look black and he looked angry. "It figures", she thought, "he's probably abusive too." The only experience she ever had with a Latino male was her cousin's boyfriend, and he was possessive and abusive. She had always been afraid of Latino men since, and vowed never to date one. She seated him. He said "thank you,' glanced at her for a moment as if he had something to say and then quickly looked away.

CHAPTER TWO

Tony

Now Tony had not too long ago been released from a program that he was ordered by a judge to complete as part of one of the conditions of his probation. He had a host of legal problems and a long ugly rap sheet.

Tony was invited to the church by a lady friend he had met while coaching youth football. She invited him to come to her church. She told him that they had a great men's group that met on Thursday nights, and she assured him that he would love it.

Tony was angry at the church and didn't care much for church people either; he even used to say that he hated church people. Whenever one of them would ask him if he was saved or if he would like to come to church, he'd reply; "Who wants to be saved like you? You're bitter, angry, and you don't have love, and on top of that you're broke." Tony always wondered how you could attract someone to be what you appeared to hate to be. Tony believed that there was a difference between God stuff and church stuff. Just like he believed that there are God's people, and church people.

While most that knew him now found it hard to believe, Tony had in fact, at one time, given a great part of his life to the church. You see, over the years while raising his family, Tony had actually served in several ministries and he had even almost become an ordained minister. Tony had even worked for the church's rehab program as well, which eventually had to close because of funding issues and because they hadn't paid into unemployment. Tony couldn't even collect benefits. He and his family got evicted from their house and he almost lost a van that he had just purchased for his family. Then some years later Tony started having marital problems and began struggling with drugs and alcohol himself. He then found himself seeking help from the same church where he had sacrificed and served all of those years. *And* after having spent all that time working long days, even working overnight and weekends, spending hours, and days, away from his wife and children, believing that he was doing "God's will and God's work", there was no help for him there. Worse, his wife at the time would always complain about it and say "that church is just using you." But Tony always sided with the church and excused it as ministry; besides, he was doing God's work. One time, his wife told him the only difference between him now and then, was instead of always being in the streets, he was always at THAT church. So now here he was after all of that service and self-sacrifice, struggling with drugs and alcohol, and headed for divorce. It seemed that the very church itself, for which he had labored and served, had no help for him.

He did go to them for help once and he was told: "Brother Tony, Holy Spirit told me you need to quit drinking." "REALLY?!", Tony answered, "Now, here I stand bleeding all over the place, hurting like hell, and all you've got is I need to quit drinking?" "Man! the Holy Spirit ain't told you nothing like that. You smell beer on me because I do drink. I drink because I'm angry. I'm angry because I hurt. I hurt because I'm losing my marriage. So why don't you deal with the gaping wound in my heart that you can't see before you deal with the obvious. Oh I know, its 'cause you ain't gotta a clue as to what's really going on!"

One night he decided to go to a men's group thinking maybe he'd find some help there. Only to hear one of the leaders say right in his face to the rest of the group; "Don't waste any more time on Tony, because he's immature and behaving like a baby. Only babies cry and whine all the time." He said that in response to Tony having poured out his heart about all that he was going through. That same night they went and got the pastor and brought him into the group to deal with Tony. At first Tony thought "finally, now he's going to see how these clowns have been behaving." He proceeded to tell the pastor of all of his problems and how it pissed him off that he only came in for help and was being mistreated by the people he thought were there to help. The pastor listened to all that Tony had to say and then flatly told him that the church was not a hospital. Tony said, "Well, that may be true, but there should at least be a MASH unit around here to patch a brother up before you send him back to the front lines; instead, it feels more like I stepped into the enemy's camp." "MAN!" He exclaimed. "This is the only army I know that shoots its wounded!" Now the straw that broke the camel's back was when a brother told Tony that a group of brothers had decided to get together to confront him and rebuke him for his lifestyle and behavior. The brother told Tony that the men went over to Tony's apartment looking for him.

Tony was living alone in an apartment, but he wasn't there that evening. It was a good thing, too. Tony told him; "I've been carrying a pistol lately, because my wife's boyfriend and his boys keep trying to jump me, and if I would have been there that night somebody might have got lead poison!" He wouldn't have shot anyone, but he was angry enough that he felt like he could have. He felt like at the time when he needed them the most, the church not only abandoned him, they wanted to crucify him.

So you see when Tony walked into the church that day he was angry, he was bitter, hurt, and guarded, like a wounded animal ready to attack to keep from ever getting wounded again.

Mitch, one of the men he had become friends with, asked Tony to come and check out the Sunday service. Tony didn't want to, but agreed. He did finally start going, but didn't like it. Tony felt like the pastor was arrogant and full of himself. He didn't seem anointed at all. All Tony saw was flesh on display. The other thing that Tony couldn't understand was why there were so many women up front serving. Where were all the men? He knew there were plenty of men there, because he saw them every week in the men's group. The men he did see serving that day seemed soft, and appeared to be afraid of something. "Probably of the pastor." He thought. They hardly behaved like men at all.

As Lisa seated him, Tony looked up at her and thought "cinnamon." The streaks of color in her hair reminded him of cinnamon, and for a fleeting moment he thought, "I wonder if this is my wife?" He quickly dismissed it and rebuked the thought in the name of Jesus and strained hard to pay attention to the service. Up until that point he had only come to the church on Thursdays to the men's meeting. He liked this men's meeting, even though he felt like he was always being attacked by the facilitator most nights, but he didn't mind. Tony liked a good debate and he really liked the guys.

After the first service he attended Mitch asked Tony, "Hey man, so how'd you like it?"

Tony, not one to bite his tongue, answered; "I didn't."

"So you didn't see *anything* you liked?"

Tony thought for a moment, and still being quite carnal, Tony smiled and said "As a matter of fact, I *did*. I saw this sister."

"What does she look like?" asked Mitch.

Tony tried to describe her but he drew a blank. He couldn't remember. It was as if her face had been erased from his memory; no body type, nothing came back. He said "Man, I don't know. I couldn't tell you what she looked like. All I know is that it was just something about her."

"You don't remember anything about her?"

"All I remember is cinnamon."

"Cinnamon?" Mitch asked.

"Yeah, her hair was streaked or something and it reminded me of cinnamon."

For weeks they tried to find out who she was to no avail. It was as if she had vanished into thin air.

Now, one Sunday morning after Tony had been out all night partying, as he had so often done, (Tony just wasn't a drunk; he loved to dance too, so he stayed in the clubs) he found himself on one of those many occasions after he last-called the bar and had also last-called the after-hour feeling empty and tired. He thought. "How can I be in a room full of people and be lonely?" He knew he could go home with someone, or take someone back to his place, but that wasn't what he really wanted. Tony really wasn't the player type, although he could be. Instead Tony was quite the gentleman, and as one of his good lady friends called him - a *hopeless romantic*. Tony used to love talking to her, and even hoped for something more with her when all the mess was over with his current relationship, but he lost her even as a friend due to his alcoholism. Now it wasn't like Tony was any different from any other man. Tony loved the ladies. This just wasn't one of those days. Tony thought since he was still up, and it was Sunday morning, he may as well go to church. He chuckled to himself as he thought about what a comedian said about people showing up to church with the same clothes they had on the night before at the club. So he figured he'd at least go home and shower and attempt to get the smell of alcohol and weed off of him and put on a fresh set of clothes.

Tony was what you might call a 'pretty boy'; he didn't like it when people called him that, even though he knew it was true based on most people's definition. His rags had to be together, his hair had to be just right, and his shoes were his biggest pet peeve. He always thought that you can really measure a man by the quality of his shoes. The shoes had to be some type of animal skin or hide, and they had to be stitched and bound leather soles, not glued-on rubber or plastic.

He went to church that morning and didn't really hear much. The preacher sounded like Charlie Brown's teacher to him. At the end of the service there were alter workers standing in the front of the church with their arms extended, beckoning for folk to come down. "All women!" Tony thought, as he walked down the aisle, deciding that maybe it was time to re-dedicate his life to the Lord. Tony made his way down to the altar; he thought "I've tried everything else, why not try God?" He'd had many of these clichés drilled in his head over the years by well-meaning saints.

The next thing he knew he was being hurried off into an office somewhere and was filling out paperwork and answering a bunch of questions. His head was still in a fog from the night before, so he wasn't even sure what this was all about, and he never even got a chance to say what he had come up to the altar for in the first place. "Humph!" He grunted, as they rushed him out.

Tony remembered going to the altar when he was younger and a bunch of people asking him questions and praying with him and for him, for what seemed like hours. It was really only a few minutes. "They didn't even pray with me," he thought. The next thing he knew, he was back in front of the church. He had apparently just joined and was scheduled to be baptized. He remembered being horrified and thinking "What have I just done?" The last thing he meant to do was join another church. That had never worked in the past. Though Tony wasn't a very religious person, and was even a bit of a hellion; often rebelling when he disagreed, or whenever something just didn't sit right with him, Tony loved the Word, and he tried to love God; yet he still rebelled, and sometimes he didn't even understand why. What he did know is it always seemed like he was fighting. Tony believed the majority of the time that what he really rebelled against was the falsehood and the misrepresentation of God's word as he understood it. Tony talked to God all the time, since early childhood, and he loved to read the Word. He even felt like he knew how to teach it and apply it to everyone's life but his own. Tony believed that you only knew as much word as you could live, and he felt like a failure most days for backsliding. Now he began to wonder if he really ever knew what he thought he knew at all. Now, here he is again.

"Man, I've got to play the church game again." He wasn't looking forward to it. He had always felt like most churches he had attended were all about indoctrination and not education; "Walk like we walk, talk like we talk, think like we think, and *don't you dare* try and get all educated, and think for yourself, and oh, by the way, you can't hear from God; *we'll hear from God for you.* We'll tell you what God is saying to you, and if you step out of line you'll have hell to pay!" Nope, in his mind he was done with all of that. He wanted something more this time, something deeper, a relationship with God. Something he thought he had once, but he felt like he had never known a real relationship in any sense of the word, not with God, not with anyone. He didn't trust people. He'd only had one true friend, and all others had always betrayed him; so the only person Tony really trusted was God. Yet now he felt like there had to be something he had missed, even in the God he trusted, because he still felt so empty. In fact, he was sure of it! So now Tony was on a mission. Exactly what it was he didn't know yet, but he was going to find out what it was, even if it meant dying while trying to figure it out. He felt so strongly about it at times that he felt like he would even fight someone if they got in his way, and he did that too, not physically mind you, but he sure could verbally beat the snot out of folks if he thought they were standing in his way.

Tony was unemployed and decided to start attending noon bible study in addition to the men's group he still attended. The bible study was made up of women with a woman teacher. Again Tony thought, "Man!, Where are all the brothers at in this church?" Then he thought "well, maybe they are all at work. This *is* a noon bible study."

Now, one day in bible study Tony made a prayer request. He asked that they pray that he get a job, and said "I'm a carpenter and a bit of a handyman," going on to say that "I can fix anything but a broke woman; she had to get a job." They all laughed, and one of the ladies said "Brother Tony, you're so crazy, but you just don't know how much of a blessing it is that you should say that, because we need so much stuff done around this church it ain't funny. You need to go into the office and see the church administrator, Lisa; she's the lady at the first desk."

At the close of the bible study Tony did as suggested and walked into the office and there she was. "It's her!" He stood stunned for a brief moment, staring in amazement. He thought to himself "It's my wife! I mean, the cinnamon usher lady."

Now Tony was always a pretty smooth talker, and quite the lady's man; the coolest there was, so he thought. Now here he stood, stuttering and stammering for words; trying to explain who he was, and why he was there, while all she could do was giggle, and the more she giggled the more he struggled. He had never been nervous around women; rather normally he was very confident and enjoyed entertaining them, yet here he stood nervous, and he couldn't understand why she made him so nervous. What was it about this one that made him nervous? Could she really be the one? Tony didn't like being nervous; he liked being in control, and this was anything but control. He began to become frustrated, and wondered what the heck she is giggling about.

CHAPTER THREE

The Handyman

Lisa was tickled; and for good reason too, because just days before, in front of witnesses, one of which was present at the time Tony walked in, she made the statement that she was going to pray that God send the church a handyman. Everyone laughed; believing her to be simple and thinking it was a stupid request to make of God." All the women believed that there were *no* men like that out there, not for the church and certainly not for *them* to marry. Besides most of them felt like they had been waiting for a husband all their lives and either God had abandoned them or it was just never meant to be. Some of the ones who had been married before were now divorced, angry, lonely and miserable and even the currently married felt like they settled and were angry and miserable too. So no; this man she sought could *not* exist!

Now there she sat looking at this light skinned man with long wild hair wondering if he was Latino, black, maybe Native American, she just wasn't sure. But the one thing she knew was he was definitely the answer to at least one of her prayers. She was excited because she had her handyman to work around the church. Now he wasn't appealing to her; he wasn't even her type so it wasn't an awkward moment for her at all. Lisa couldn't understand what was going on with Tony, though she did notice he seemed a little nervous and that tickled her too.

At first Lisa was a little bit apprehensive about Tony working around the church and her safety with him there, because she had been keeping an eye on him and noticed that Tony was always on his cell phone, and that really bugged her. She thought "*who* could this man be talking to all the time, and what man talks on the phone *that much*? It's probably something illegal" she thought. she didn't fully trust that Tony had let go completely of whatever it was he was in to before he came to the church; she didn't hold it against him; she was just mindful of it.   She knew these things took time. She hated cell phones! Lisa didn't have one and barely answered her home phone. Besides, after dealing with phone calls all day at the church, the last thing she wanted was anything to do with a phone, and the last thing she EVER wanted was a cell phone! She had noticed that he was coming to bible study every day and thought, "that's good."

Tony didn't even remember that Lisa was the one who filled out his paperwork for membership and baptism. She was glad that a man was finally helping out at the church, and hoped it would inspire more to come. She doubted it though; she knew that most men with any depth to them at all never stayed there long, someone always made sure of that. It seemed like if you were a man and could think for yourself, and articulate your thoughts, and expound on what you gleaned from God and His word, you posed a threat! She didn't want to believe it, but she knew it was true. She had seen too many good ones leave out of confusion and frustration. Now, no one ever *directly* said it, or did anything, but they did have a way of frustrating things so much that it would drive them right out of the church. If they didn't want one person to serve in a function who had signed up to help out, they then would just postpone or cancel the whole thing; even blaming it on God, saying something like "the Lord is redirecting us." "Here comes another one", she thought, "I wonder how long this one will last?"

Lisa knew from firsthand experience that many times it wasn't the devil that prevented God's work from being done in the church, and destroying people's lives and ministries; it was the people!

Lisa sure was happy that God had answered her prayer and sent someone (a man) to do what she and the other women usually had to do at the church. So all she really thought about Tony that day was that the church got its handyman. Lisa was a little confused about God's choice "but if He sent him, he must be qualified," she thought.

Tony on the other hand, was *smitten*. As soon as he turned that corner and saw Lisa sitting there he felt as if he was looking at the women of his dreams. He couldn't understand why he felt so strongly about someone he had never even really met. They had never even spoken to each other before, so he thought. "Why am I trippin so hard?" He felt like he knew her from somewhere, but he couldn't remember where. He studied her face curiously, trying to figure out what it was about her. He couldn't quite put his finger on it, but it was something about her that was different; he wasn't quite sure what it was, but whatever it was, it was *strong*.

The one thing Tony knew for sure was that she was definitely a woman of God; and if it was one thing Tony tried hard to respect, it was God, and what belonged to Him. Tony had a saying, "there are women you 'do', and there are women you say 'I do' to" and in Tony's mind, she was definitely an "I do" woman, and not one to be messed with.

Now as soon as Tony got back to his car he called Mitch. It was a red Camaro with tinted windows, "T" top, and chrome rims, and Lisa hated it; for one it was red, and it looked dangerous "Just like him". "It fits", she thought, and she bet he drove too fast.

"MAN, I found her!"

"Who?" Mitch asked.

"That girl, I mean, that lady at the church I was telling you about."

"Well, who is it?" Mitch shouted.

"Her name is Lisa."

"Man, I told you!"

Mitch had told him that it was probably Lisa, the church administrator, but Tony couldn't see it, besides, he didn't even remember what she looked like, but he was sure it wasn't Lisa; at least not how Mitch had described her.

"Well, what you gonna do *playa*?" Mitch asked.

Knowing what he meant, Tony said.

"Man, who wants to be bothered with a raggedy "A" brother like me?"

"So, what you got to lose? Since your stuff is so raggedy it can't get no worse; what else you got going for yourself?"

"Nothing, I guess." Tony responded.

"Man, Tony, I can see ya'll together."

"I can't" Tony said, "It ain't like I ain't all twisted up inside about her right now, but it's *not* gonna happen so…anyway man, I'll holla."

Mitch laughed and said, "Man I don't know, but okay, holla".

Tony thought about it. He knew that they would be in close proximity to each other every day with him working around the church. Nothing could even be purchased without her approval. He knew he was attracted to her, and that this could cause some problems.

Tony was still married, legally separated but still married; it weighed heavily on his mind too. He couldn't even understand how or why he could even feel for someone the way he did, so soon after all he had been through (and was still going through), but it was as if he couldn't help himself. He used to laugh at men who fell hard like he had for Lisa. Already he felt like he could chase her to the end of the earth if he had to. He knew he had to do something to stop this and he had to do it now. Lisa had given him the number to the church so he called.

"Hello; The church of regular people, Lisa speaking,"

"Lisa?"

"Uh", he struggled, "this is Tony, and well I just," Tony hesitated a second, took a deep breath then just said it.

"I just wanted to let you know that I feel like I might be attracted to you, and I don't want to disrespect God, you, or have people talking. I don't care what they say about me, because whatever they say about me will most likely be true, but I swear if somebody were to put your name in their mouth in a bad way I'll..." Tony stopped because he could hear Lisa giggling.

Lisa just sat too tickled by all of this as she thought "oh how cute!" as she giggled!

"Listen now," Tony said sternly. "I'm not joking, it looks like we might be working together for a while, and I'm not trying to start no trouble, so if you feel uncomfortable in the least bit, or I come off the wrong way, check me; you hear me?"

Lisa still giggling tried to compose herself, said, "Oh I'm sure you'll do just fine."

"Man, you don't know me like that, I'm telling you right now! I'm not no good, and I'd stay away from me if I were you."

Lisa just giggled and said, "Like I said, you'll do just fine."

Tony hung up the phone; he wasn't upset that she was laughing; he knew she wasn't laughing at him, because he got that a lot. Tony was always told that he was funny and should be a comedian; only what puzzled him is he was never trying to be funny, he was always just telling the truth. It seemed like Tony couldn't even order food without getting a laugh.

Tony loved chicken wings; he always said "Man, I'm about to get me a wing and a biscuit." He went in the chicken house to get some wings, but when he got back to the car and checked his food he found that they weren't wings at all, he went back in and said "Hey man, I asked for wings!" The clerk said "those are wings," and

Tony said "Man, no, they're not," the clerk said "yes, they are, they're boneless."

Tony said "Man, I don't want *this,* I want my chicken *with the bone on it*!" The whole restaurant roared in laughter except Tony; he was serious.

Lisa hung up the phone and thought, "that was cute." She couldn't believe that someone would be attracted to her. "I look a mess, I haven't bought any new clothes in years, and I'm fifty pounds overweight. That man must be crazy, have something up his sleeve or something's wrong with him."

No one had paid any attention to her like that in years. She had always been called homely and even thought of herself as homely too. Besides, it had been years since she felt like any man could even think about looking at her as desirable. Even the other women in the church office thought that she would be the last one to get married, and would probably be an old maid. None of that mattered anyway, there was no way she was going to get hooked up with him anyway, because he wasn't her type, and she still wasn't sure if he was a Latino or not. She did find him to be interesting though, and she had heard the buzz going around about how he was in bible study. They said "That man knows his Word, and he's funny too." If there was one thing she liked, it was a man with a sense of humor. She kind of knew he wasn't trying to be funny, but he sure made her laugh, and that was something she rarely got a chance to do.

Everything in her world was always so serious. Gloom and doom seemed to loom over her like a plague, and it seemed that she could do nothing right. All she wanted was a nice house with a backyard and swing set in a decent neighborhood where she could raise her kids and stay put until they all graduated. She rented a house once, thinking she'd maybe even buy it one day. The owner told her it needed a little fixing up, but it had potential. Lisa even thought it had a lot of character; she loved the woodwork and the wood floors. It didn't turn out as she had hoped; the house was a disaster and it needed some fixing up alright. It was so bad they had to leave because instead of issuing her a permit for rehab, the city condemned it. She also had spent hundreds of dollars trying to keep second hand cars going, and often got deceived by shady mechanics; sometimes leaving with a car that seemed like it was in worse shape than before she took it to them.

She did find a mechanic with compassion once. He helped her out as much as he could, but she had a car that was so bad that he had to tell her; "Miss you shouldn't put another dime into this car, it's not even fit for scrap metal" She abandoned trying to deal with as she called it "anybody else's junk" after that experience, and just took the bus, and walked, and did whatever she had to do to get back and forth. She hated asking people for rides, but she even had to do that too. Finally she was able to purchase a new car (at a high interest rate of course), but even that one turned out to be a lemon; something was wrong with the suspension that caused her to lose control. It was totaled in an accident and she still had to pay it off. She finally ended up with an old dependable car given to her by one of her family members.

So you see, the last thing on Lisa's mind was trying anything else that would end in disaster; especially a relationship --- *that* was *definitely* out.

Lisa got to work the next morning at her regular time, which was barely on time. "Oh no" she said as she turned into the parking lot. It was Tony and that red sports car! "I wonder how long he's been here?" She thought.

Tony was a morning person, up at the crack of dawn every morning. It seemed to him like he had been sitting there waiting for *hours,* but it was more like a few minutes.

"Good Morning Lisa, - Man! What time do you start work?" Tony asked. Lisa had told Tony the day before to be there at 8:30am. "8:30am sharp" she said. She was used to people not keeping their word; showing up late, if they even showed up at all.

"When I get here" Lisa replied.

"Aw, it's like *that*?" Tony said.

"No, I try to get here around 8:30 or so."

"8:30 or so?" "You said for me to be here at 8:30 a.m. SHARP! "On time' to me is anywhere 15 minutes to a half hour early!"

"That's excessive; work doesn't start until 8:30! Why would anybody do that to themselves?" Lisa exclaimed.

"You can't get to work at 8:30 and start work at 8:30!" Tony said. (Tony looked at his phone) "Man, it's Nine-0-clock; I'm a morning person and the earlier the better for me. I would prefer to get started around 6:00."

"I could never tell that," Lisa murmured.

"What was that?" Tony asked.

"Nothing," Lisa said giggling.

It seemed like she had a ton of stuff in her hands, coffee, a big purse, another big bag of stuff, and a postal tub.

"What's all this stuff?" Tony asked.

"Just some stuff I need for work." Lisa answered.

Lisa fumbled with the keys but once she got inside the building she told Tony to stay outside the door until she turned off the alarm. As Tony stood there he got angry, when Lisa came back to let him in she picked up on it. "What's wrong?" she asked.

"You open this church every morning by yourself?"

"Yes, what's wrong with that?"

"Man, that's crazy as hell - that's what's wrong with that. There should be a man up in here with you."

"We're in a church Tony; watch your language! Besides, there is a man with me!" Lisa giggled.

"Man, Hell is in the bible, plus you know what I mean." Tony exclaimed.

They went inside the church and Tony was agitated. "My God, she is so *slow!*" he thought to himself, as he watched her go through her morning routine. She had to open this, check that, turn on this, close that, and he was ready to get right to work but Lisa had her daily setup ritual she had to complete first. Then she looked at Tony as if she could hear him thinking, and said "I go in the sanctuary and pray every morning before I get started." Tony thought "what the heck is all that about?" Knowing what he was thinking, she answered; "well, I have to turn on my computer, the lights, and all the other machines so that once I get through praying I can get right to work." Now Tony was thinking that having to wait through all of that was work for him.

Lisa walked off to the sanctuary and looked back at Tony and said

"Well?"

"Well what?" Tony answered

"You coming?" Lisa asked.

Tony was embarrassed because he thought she might make him pray out loud, and he didn't want to pray, but he was too scared not to. It was something about the way she looked at him; it was as if she could see his thoughts. They walked into the sanctuary and she held her hands out for Tony to put his hands in hers. He didn't want to touch her but he did. Tony didn't like the thoughts that were racing through his head. He wanted to just grab her and kiss her, and he knew it was crazy, but he couldn't help it. Lisa prayed, but Tony never heard a word she said. He was busy rebuking the devil and asking God to forgive him for what he was thinking. That was another thing he never understood, why he had to repent for being a man, "Isn't this how a man is supposed to think?" he thought. Just then he heard Lisa say "Amen." "Amen" Tony said.

Lisa showed Tony where everything was and Tony was all too eager to get away from her and get to work. Tony loved music and while he worked he listened to music. *Earth Wind and Fire* was playing, and he loved *Earth Wind and Fire*. Tony played the horn with his mouth and sang, and in his mind *Earth Wind and Fire* was one of the best bands *ever*.

Lisa thought she heard *Earth Wind and Fire* playing from a distance, and figured it would be a good time to check up on Tony to see how things were going. As she approached the area where Tony was working, she not only heard *Earth Wind and Fire,* she heard Tony playing the horn parts with his mouth. She had never heard anyone sing the horn parts before. "That's different!" She thought.

Tony didn't see Lisa coming but he could feel her. As he turned, he saw her standing behind him; he knocked over the ladder, and when he tried to grab the ladder to keep it from falling, he kicked over the radio, the radio bumped into the box of nails, and stuff just went flying everywhere. Lisa burst into laughter

"Man, you can't be sneaking up on people like that!" Tony yelled.

"Do I make you nervous or something?" Lisa asked.

"Yeah, no, I mean, you just startled me." Tony said.

Lisa just laughed, Tony laughed too. Lisa did make him nervous, only he still couldn't figure out why.

"It's about lunchtime and I just thought you might want to take a break or something." Lisa said.

"Yeah, I am getting kind of hungry." Tony replied.

"Are you eating?" Tony asked.

"No, I didn't really bring anything."

"Man, you have to eat." Tony said.

"I'm alright; I've got popcorn and coffee." Lisa answered.

"That ain't food; that don't even fit into a food group." Tony answered.

"Man, you are so funny!" Lisa laughed

"I'm serious; I'm going to bring you back some real food."

"Oh, you don't have to do that." Lisa said.

Secretly, though, she thought to herself "how sweet of him," because she knew he couldn't have much money because he wasn't working.

"No problem! I love to cook; I was going to cook something anyway - I got you."

"What are you making?" Lisa asked.

Lisa was nervous now, not wanting to hurt his feelings, but not sure if she was ready to try his cooking either. "I hope he at least washes his hands," she thought. One thing that bugged her that she noticed about guys was that they simply will not wash their hands for nothing.

"I'll be back." Tony said as he hurried off down the hall.

Lisa heard Tony peel out of the parking lot. "I knew he drove fast."

Lisa picked up the phone and called Angel.

"Girl, guess who's here?"

"Who?" Angel asked.

"Remember that guy with that cream colored suit?"

"Girl yeah, the thug!"

"I don't know about that, he seems harmless to me."

"Girl you better watch yourself, you know how slick them light skinned Negros are, and they think they soooo smooth, too, so watch it!"

"I don't think he's like that."

"Girl, are you falling for him?"

"No, he's not even my type; I'm just saying he seems like he has the potential to be a good man of God to me."

"Girl, please! You trippin now, and you about as dumb as a box of rocks if you think there's any good in that thug at all! That Negro might look like a black Jesus with that hair and beard of his, but ain't nothing holy about that brother, but maybe his drawls."

"Angel, be nice." Lisa said.

"No, the problem is you *too* nice, that's why you are always getting hurt picking up them strays. Girl, you know I heard he was married and they ain't together. Shoot, he probably cheated on her. I'm telling you, that negro ain't no good."

"That's what he said," Lisa answered.

"He told you he cheated on his wife?"

"No Angel, he told me that he wasn't any good." "Besides, like you always say, three sides to every story, his side, her side..." "And the truth!" they both said together, laughing. "But!" Lisa exclaimed, "he did tell me he 'wasn't no good', as he phrased it."

"Well at least he's an honest dog!"

"Angel!"

"What? I'm just telling the truth, and you know it!"

"Angel, I've got to go, I can hear him pulling back up."

"Be careful girl; watch your back, if I don't hear from you in an hour I'm calling 911." Angel whispered.

"Goodbye Angel." Lisa laughed.

Tony rang the doorbell. Lisa let him in. He seemed agitated. Lisa picked up on it.

"What's wrong?" Lisa asked.

"Are you by yourself up here all the time?" Tony grumbled.

"Most of the time," Lisa said flatly.

"That's just crazy," Tony said in disbelief.

Changing the subject, Lisa said "Wow, it smells wonderful."

"Oh, it is," Tony answered, "And it tastes like some more."

"What?"

"I said it taste like some more. That means it's so good, you'll want some more." Tony answered.

"I'll be the judge of that." Lisa answered laughing.

"Man, my food will make your tongue slap your brain to death continuously."

"Where do you get that from?" Lisa asked.

"What?" Tony asked.

"Those sayings of yours;" Lisa answered, trying not to act anxious but she was really hungry now, and it smelled so wonderful.

"Lisa, man, I don't know; I make them up as I go along I guess, I never thought about it; why?"

"No reason, just curious."

Tony, like a waiter in a fine restaurant, served Lisa. He seemed much more graceful than earlier when he was tripping over things and knocking over stuff. She is impressed by his movement as he placed the plastic fork neatly rolled and folded into a napkin down in front of her with a container of food he had prepared. Lisa thought about what Angel just said about light-skinned brothers and how slick they are. She was still wondering if he even was a brother. She decided to ask him. "Tony, are you black?"

He laughed and answered, "Yeah, why do you ask?"

"I thought you were Latino or something." Lisa answered with a sigh of relief.

"If I was, what's wrong with that?" Tony asked.

"They're abusive." Lisa answered.

"Who told you that?" Tony asked.

"Nobody, I know they are, my cousin dated one and he was a trip." Lisa answered.

"So therefore all Latinos are abusive, right? Tony responded.

"I know it sounds silly, but that's what I thought." Lisa answered.

"Yeah but just because you think a thing don't make it true." Tony responded.

"That means you got the same problem with the truth too." Tony added.

"What's that supposed to mean?" Lisa asked.

"People that think like you let what they think mess with the truth too. Funny thing about it is what we think don't have nothing to do with the truth, yet because we think it, it skews the truth so much so till what we think ends up being our truth. So we never get to the real truth because we are so stuck on what we think."

"I do not know what you just said, and anyway, I've got all this good smelling food in front of me and I only hope it tastes as good as it smells."

Lisa opened the container.

"Oh my god, its cabbage!" she screamed, bouncing in her chair.

Lisa loved cabbage and sausage. She had it before but it never looked like this, and it smelled so good too. She could smell the garlic and crushed red pepper. The cabbage was kind of a golden color; the sausage was slightly burnt just like she liked it. She put a fork full in her mouth and felt as if she'd fall out on the floor, it was *so good.*

"Oh ma gah!" She said with a mouth full, forgetting all manners and etiquette. Tony laughed. He was used to the response.

"What is it?" Lisa asked.

"Cabbage and sausage," Tony answered sarcastically thinking "that's a dumb question."

"I know that, what I mean is what did you do to it? My cabbage never comes out like this."

"And it never will either," Tony answered.

"Okay, now, what did you do?"

"Well, it's just smothered cabbage, I save the stock from my chicken, or whatever I have around, and use that as a base instead of water, then I burn my sausage just a little on both sides, then I bang my garlic to get a bolder flavor, and drop that in with my cabbage just like granny taught me."

"Uh huh," Lisa said still munching.

"But you did something else too, because it's sweet, hot, spicy, salty, and garlicky."

"Man, I can't give away my secrets, or how else would I keep you coming back."

"Oh, I'm in love." Lisa swooned, as she closed her eyes in delight.

Tony is startled and looks in shock.

She looks up and catches his expression and says "I mean with the food, silly."

"I know." Tony answered. "But it still made my heart skip a beat just the same."

"Be good." Lisa scolded.

"I am - this IS me being good. Me, being bad, would have…"

Tony thinks about what he is about to say and realizes that it would be inappropriate, and stops talking. He thought it was so strange that he felt so comfortable with her. It was like he had known her for a lifetime, and he couldn't understand why. He felt like he could tell her anything.

"What?" Lisa said, obviously breaking him out of deep thought.

"Tony, what were you about to say?"

"Nothing, it was just something that I had no business saying anyway.

Lisa let it go, she would love to instigate, but she saw that it was making Tony uncomfortable and nervous again. She did wonder what he might have said.

The day ended, and they both said their goodbyes and went their separate ways. That night Lisa was sitting in her room writing in her journal about the day's events as she normally does, and smiled as she wrote that *Tony brought me lunch today, the best cabbage I have ever had in my life, too!* Just then she remembered, and said out loud "Oh No!" She ran to the closet and began to tear through her old journals. She reached the one that said 1998 and began to flip through it, and there it was.

CHAPTER FOUR

Letters to God

Lisa read what she wrote to God that night. She was *horrified*.

"Lorrrrrrrd" she thought; "he *can't* be the one." "Lord, *please* don't let him be the one. Not now Lord," she thought. She had finally gotten to a place in her life where she was no longer torturing herself. She was at peace; it seemed for the first time in her life. It was not that it didn't still get hard at times; she still got horny from time to time, but it was nothing like it was before; she *wanted* companionship, but did not mourn over it anymore. On those lonely nights she'd lie down and ask God to hold her, and rock her to sleep, and he did.

"How can he be the one; this man is still married, and I don't know anything about him. Not to mention, what would the church think? I have a reputation to keep. I have spent years trying to clean up my name and forget my past. I have finally become a respectable woman of God. If I were to hook up with that man, my name will be drug through mud, and everything I have worked for, the respect I have, my witness, it will all be shot to hell. I'm just trippin! - Calm down! It's just a coincidence, he's not the one." She closed the book and went to sleep.

That night she had a dream that Tony was stalking her. Everywhere she went she saw him watching her; she tried to get away from him, but she just couldn't seem to shake him. Finally she stopped and decided to confront him.

"Why are you following me?"

"I'm supposed to keep an eye on you. I'm protecting you."

"Why?" She asked. "I don't need your protection!"

"Because you are my wife."

Lisa woke up in a panic. "What was that all about? That man did something to that cabbage; I think he put a 'root' on me."

The next morning when Lisa pulled into the parking lot, Tony was already there as usual.

"STALKER!" Lisa yelled at Tony. Lisa got out of the car.

"Good morning! Let's try to get along today, okay." Tony answered as if he didn't hear her, which was beginning to become a pattern. She wondered if he actually had a problem with his hearing. She wouldn't be surprised if he did, as loud as he played his music at times.

Lisa laughed at his response but she was a little troubled in her spirit that morning. She couldn't help but think about the dream she had the night before, and she was a little worried. She was quiet most of the day; Tony picked up on it, and wanted to say something, but before he could, Lisa asked; "What did you do to that cabbage Tony?"

"Nothing." Tony said, seeing the worried look on her face.

"Why, did your grippers come loose?"

"What does that mean?" Lisa asked.

"Well some people don't do cabbage well, and they get the…"

"Oh no, that's not what I meant at all."

"So, you didn't get sick or nothing?"

"No, I'm fine."

"I can't tell, you've hardly said a word all day, and you haven't even snuck up on me today."

"I don't sneak up on you."

"That's not the way I see it. You be floating through here like a ghost. Man, you make me nervous."

"You finally said it." Lisa said.

"What?" Tony answered.

"Well, I knew something was bothering you, because whenever I come around you get to knocking stuff over and tripping over things; what is that all about?"

"I don't know." Tony answered.

"Aren't you comfortable around me?"

"Yeah, I mean, maybe too comfortable." Tony mumbled.

"I can't tell.

"Well, what I mean is it seems like I know you, or like I've known you, or something. I can't explain it; I feel like I can tell you anything."

"Umm" Lisa grunted,

"Man, *that* was loaded."

"What?" Lisa asked.

"That ump sound you just made."

"How can you get anything out of a grunt?"

"Oh, I got a lot out of that?"

"Like what?"

"Well what I heard was 'that's crazy, I have only been around this man for a day and a half and he's ready to tell me his life story."

"Oh, you're good."

"What?"

"That's just what I was thinking but how did you know that?"

"Well I'm not psychic or anything if that's what you're thinking, it's just what I would be thinking if I were you."

After a long pause, Lisa said "Well".

"Well what?"

"Are you going to tell me or not?"

"What?"

"Your life story." Lisa exclaimed, because she was dying to know more about this strange and peculiar man.

"Well, yeah I guess I can, but you might not think of me the same once I do."

48

"Try me." Lisa said, scooting up to the edge of her seat.

"Well, I was raised in the church as a kid and, at one time I even wondered if I was supposed to be a minister or something. I had this dream and at the time I didn't know what it meant, but ah..." Tony paused as he looked up, thinking he didn't want to come off as crazy because he had never shared this with anyone before.

"Man, I guess I must have been about nine or so, and I had this dream that I was up in front of this sea of people. As a kid I thought I was oh, I don't know probably an actor, dancer, singer extraordinaire. I didn't know. I was a kid right? But the older I get, the more I think it may have something to do with ministry but I don't know what..."

"IT'S YOU!" Lisa interrupted. Tony practically jumped out of his skin.

"WHAT?" Tony asked.

Lisa answered, "I had this dream that I was working behind the scenes helping somebody with their ministry, and there was like this sea of people everywhere we went; we were traveling all over the place. I was even making out his itinerary and everything. All this time I thought it was pastor, but I think it's you!"

"Oh, I don't know about that. It is a little freaky that you would have a similar dream and all I admit. At one time I had dreams of doing things

49

like that, but I've got way too much dirt in my past to think that could ever be me now."

"Oh come on, it can't be that bad."

"Bad enough!"

"What did you do?" Lisa asked nervously, hating she ever asked, because now she's thinking she probably doesn't even want to know the answer.

"Well let me put it to you this way; you could get a life sentence for the kind of stuff I been into."

"Lord!" Lisa said as she thought to herself, "Angel was right, this man is an axe murderer."

Now a few months before, Tony had just gotten kicked out of a program for slapping a guy for blowing a kiss at him. He had his best friend Jaxon pick him up to take him home and on the way they talked.

"Jaxon, man, I just wanted to thank you for being my friend. Man, I've had you in some life threatening situations, got you out of your bed at night to come to my aide several times, got money from you to feed my addiction, and you never gave up on me."

"Man, Tony, it really ain't no thang. I'm just glad that I can help. I knew that you had been going through a lot, and I just want to see you come out okay."

"Jaxon, man, I am so glad to see you and I'm not ready to go home yet so can we go get some coffee or something."

"Sure!"

They stopped at a local shop and while hanging out in the parking lot, a young man hollered out "Hey bro- got that fruit!" Jaxon and Tony look at each other and laughed, and said "naw young blood, we're cool."

You see, Tony used to sell, and if anybody knew fruity, he did.

Jaxon said "See, you ain't even home good yet and here they come."

"Yeah, but I ain't on that today, man. I am really trying to get my life back together. Man, she was just crying to me on the phone last week that she's ready to work on us, and how she can't wait for me to be released, telling me we can even start going back to church and everything"

"Man, well I hope it all works out." Jaxon said; trying to sound sincere but he had heard all this before from Tony regarding his wife; she never made good and he was doubtful that she was sincere about it this time either. He couldn't understand how Tony could fall for it over and over again and really wanted to say something, but he kept silent about it for now.

"Man, they are going to be surprised to see me walk in the door, because I wasn't supposed to be home until next year some time.

"Yeah; I can't wait to see the look on their faces when we come walking through the door with all your stuff." Jaxon said expecting the worst, but hoping for the best for Tony's sake.

"Me too!" Tony answered gleefully.

As they approach the house Tony sensed something wasn't right and stopped in his tracks.

"What?" Jaxon asked.

"I don't know, something just doesn't feel right."

Tony always had good instincts; he could always feel if something was about to go down, even if he wasn't quite sure what it was. It kept him out of a lot of things that could have gotten him into even more trouble than he had already gotten himself into. Tony opened the door and the smell of skunk hit him right in the face, WEED! "Man I got to come home to this!" Tony thought.

Tony went to his room expecting his wife to be happy to see him and knock him down in excitement because he was home. Instead she said "What are you doing here?"

"I live here!"

"You know what I mean, aren't you going to get in trouble?

"They kicked me out."

She asked "What did you do?"

"A guy blew a kiss at me," She cut him off. "And you hit him?"

"Yep!" Tony replied.

"Now you violated probation. And now you're probably going to jail."

"I don't know, maybe not." Tony answered.

What weighed more heavily on Tony's mind was the lack of excitement and affection he received for being home. He couldn't quite put his finger on it, but he knew this would not be a good night. He saw Jaxon off and explained to his family that he was trying to stay clean, and that he did not want any drugs or alcohol in the house, and that they would be going back to church. That didn't go over well. Tony and his wife argued because she previously said she would go back to church with him, but had apparently changed her mind. She said "I'm not ready to go to church. I've got some things to get together before I go to church; furthermore, we can't turn on and off like you. Now we going to church, now we're not. You confused your kids, and they not going to church with you either." "Why not?" Tony asked. "Because I said so. Man, ain't nobody 'hopping to' because you say so no more. We never liked that church anyway. They ain't nothing but a bunch of hypocrites. All this stuff we've been through, me struggling with these kids with you being in that program, and they knew you were there, and *none* of them once called, or stopped by to see if we even was okay, let alone needed anything. I *wish* one of them would come and try and tell me about some God. Anyway, I didn't know you were coming, and I gotta go, I got stuff to do!

You acting like you better than us; talking bout what you don't want in this house!" She huffed as she walked off.

Tony yelled out after her. "This ain't no act! I *am* better and I'm gonna *be* better and it ain't gonna be no mess in this house, like I just said!"

"Whatever!" She answered as she slammed the door behind her.

 Tony knew what "she had stuff to do" meant. Sometime during their marriage he had gotten "back doored" (as he called it), and she was seeing someone else. It bothered him, but sometimes he figured that it was what he deserved. He figured she would eventually see the light and forgive him for the stuff he had done, and he was willing to wait, and endure whatever it took to win her back. They had been married for years; since they were both kids and marriage was supposed to be for life, till death do you part, so no matter what it took, it had to work out," or so he thought.

Later that night the phone rang, it was *him*. "Hello" Tony said.

"I got your girl." the voice said on the other line.

"What?" Tony said. "You heard me; I said I got your girl, I *took* your woman."

"You ain't *took* nothin that went freely, and if you got her, she ain't mine, and as far as I'm concerned you did me a favor taking her off my hands; you can keep her!" Tony said.

Tony had pretty much made up in his mind after a few more days and nights like that; his marriage was over. That was hard for Tony. Tony liked to be in control. Now, he didn't mind a good fight, but he liked to win. For the first time in his life he was in a fight he couldn't win, and his life was spiraling out of control. He relapsed after only a few weeks of being released. He was drinking and drugging again, but this time it wasn't the party it once was. This time it was his *cause I hurt* medicine, and his beer was swiftly becoming his best friend!

One sober night Tony finally broke. He started realizing he was fighting a losing battle, and began to accept that maybe his marriage really was over. He also knew he played a part in its death; but that didn't make it hurt any less. That night Tony wrote a letter to God:

Lord, I believe my marriage is over and I don't have anywhere to go. If it is in fact over, show me what to do and where to go, and Lord, I don't ever want to get married again, but if I do, this is what I want my rib to be: I would first of all want her to love You more than anyone or anything else in the world. I would also like her to be smart, and not a punk or a pushover. I don't want anyone that's afraid of me, or intimidated by me. I want her to be secure about herself, and I want someone who will believe in me and support me. I want someone that I can talk to, and who not only just listens, but really hears me. I want someone that I can like, as well as love. I want someone that respects me and accepts me for me. Lord, You know I have always said I like my women like I like my coffee; black, and with an attitude, however, I do want her to look good, too, but that is not as important as... and he wrote down everything he thought a good woman was supposed to be, based on what he had learned over the years through the bible.

You see, Tony wasn't always a bad guy; he had an almost twenty year period where he was a pretty stand-up guy. Tony grew up most of his life without a father; he knew his dad, and everybody told him he looked like him, and he was just like his father. He had lived with his father for a few of his teenage years, and it wasn't good. You see, his dad sold drugs, and had prostitutes around, and ran all kind of scams and hustles, and Tony had seen it all. He saw way more than any young man should have been exposed to at that age, or any age for that matter. Even though Tony found that life alluring, he knew that going into the "family business" was not how he wanted to live his life. When Tony was growing up, he could sense the hurt and struggle that his mom went through trying to raise them alone. Even at a young age, he didn't know how he knew it, but he *knew* she was hurting; and he knew it had something to do with his dad not being there. He often wished that he was a man, and not a little boy, so he could rescue his mom and take care of her so no one would ever hurt her again.

Tony remembered there was this guy his mom was seeing; she had actually met him at the church, but what she didn't know was that he was rotten to the core. This man drank, did drugs, and he was abusive to Tony and his brother when his mother wasn't around. Well, one night he came tipping up the stairs to their place and Tony was waiting for him with a Louisville Slugger. Tony beat him all the way back down the stairs and out the door. Tony swore he hit him so hard that he saw birds flying around the guy's head. That was around the same time Tony made a vow to God; he would never leave his kids or their mom, not realizing at the time that he would get someone pregnant at a young age, and what all that would lead to later on. Once he saw his first child, he realized that his dream had become a reality. While other people dreamt of becoming firemen, policemen, or a doctor, all Tony always wanted to be was a *daddy*.

Now Lisa had been talking to God too over the years. She wasn't raised in the church, but there was a bus that used to come around and pick up kids all over the neighborhood and take them to church. Lisa did believe in God, and talked to him when she was a little girl, but only began to become involved in the church on a regular basis once she got into her twenties. Since then she had spent much of her life devoted to what she believed to be God's work. She had even quit her job with benefits to work full-time for the church, believing that it was God's will; so much so until she was willing to suffer humiliation and loss in the name of God, believing that it was what she was supposed to do. Her dedication was such that she worked over fifty hours a week; at times even being called from home to come and unlock the church so someone could get in.

Lisa was tired of it all, and began to wonder if this is all her life would ever be. She used to have dreams like finishing school and traveling. She once wanted to be married, but she had tried that before and it didn't end well. She now had accepted that she would be celibate and single for the rest of her life, and she wasn't bitter about it either. She had learned to date herself; she went to movies, concerts, even treated herself to dinner. Sometimes she would go out with friends, but she was really okay with being by herself. She had learned to stay off the phone, as she found that it had only caused her trouble in the past. She'd much rather spend time alone at home curled up with a book or writing letters to God.

One evening while up late she was feeling lonely; she thought to herself maybe she *would* like to get married again someday. It had been nine years since her divorce. She was only married for four years, and they were only together for two of those. She thought "if I do get married again, what type of husband would I want?" and she wrote what she wanted her husband to be:

Dear husband, I imagine you to be a six foot five, muscular built, dark skinned black man who is not ashamed to praise the Lord. You are a handyman who loves to cook, and you make me breakfast in bed. You love the arts; you take me to plays and to the museum.

She paused and giggled as she thought of a conversation she had with the ladies in the church office when describing the type of man that she wanted. They said "Girl, you'll have to find a white man to get all of that - there ain't no black man in the world like that."

She proceeded; *we take long walks in the park as we talk. We run and work out together because you are my personal trainer. You only have eyes for me. You listen to me, you hear me, you love me, you are good in bed, and we are sexually compatible. You are my friend, nothing I can do can run you away, and you even tolerate my mood swings. You inspire me to greatness and support my dreams, and I yours. Nothing can ever come between us, because the bond that we have is stronger than a threefold cord that cannot be broken, because our relationship is God ordained.* She paused as she thought to herself. *"This is silly; this man does not exist."*

She then began to write: *Lord if I do get married again it won't be until my kids are grown. I don't want to bring a man into a relationship while I am trying to raise my kids, I don't want to burden anyone with my responsibilities, or with the problems that this conflict can cause. If it is in Your will for me to have a husband, I am perfectly willing to wait on You, and who You have for me. I have chosen wrong so many times for myself, and endured so much pain because of my poor choices, that I would rather be alone than to do that to myself and my kids again, and Lord if it is not in Your will for me to have a husband, then take these desires away from me to want someone, so I don't continue to torture myself like this, time and time again. Lord, I do believe, but You know I have had so many disappointments in my life that it's hard for me even to imagine anything better for myself than my current existence. All my life I have tried to do the right thing and it seems like all I have gotten in return is kicked for it. I serve in the church and even work for the church and I get treated like crap. I thought working for the church would be better, even fun, but Lord it has been hell. I have found that church people can be the cruelest, meanest people that I have ever known. I have gotten better treatment, and been more appreciated, dealing with people in the world, and working a regular job than I do now. Lord, You know I don't even have health insurance, and I am barely making it off of the money they pay. I am not complaining Lord, I just thought things would be different by now and they're not. I am still struggling. I guess that's why I keep coming to this church; hoping some man would come through and sweep me off my feet and take me out of here. I guess that only happens in fairy tales, love novels, and movies, but it would sure be nice if it happens to me. Lord, it looks like it's just me and You, and I am okay with that because You have never let me down, and You are always with me; I know that, but sometimes Lord I just want, and need, some flesh to touch too. I won't bother You with this any longer, but thanks for listening. I love You, -Lisa*

CHAPTER FIVE

Surprise! – Surprise!

On Sunday, Father's Day, a guest pastor was preaching, but before he got up to preach, Tony got up and began to head up to the front of the church. Lisa thought "Oh Lord what's going on. What is *he* about to do?"

Tony, unprompted and uninvited, walked up to the minister holding the mic and whispered something and the preacher handed Tony the mic. Tony began to share how all he ever wanted to be was a father, and how he never saw many men in the positions that he believed they should be in to inspire more young men to not be ashamed to worship God. He challenged the men that day; that if there were any real men in the house, they should stand up and take their rightful place so that their sons and daughters could see them as men worshiping and not ashamed.

Tony sang the song *I really love the Lord.* It was *beautiful.* Every man in that building got up out of their seat and joined him in the front of the church. Lisa couldn't believe her eyes; she had never seen anything like it in her life, and on top of that, it was *Tony.* Lisa couldn't believe it.

Although she had known there was something special about him, she hadn't figured out what it was. She now knew what it was - this man was *anointed* by God, and whatever it was he had done; however rotten he was, it could no longer be denied that he was definitely anointed by God. She had always seen potential in him, but she never imagined this.

That next week when they returned to work Lisa wanted to talk with Tony about Sunday. "Tony, that was powerful."

"What?"

"What you did Sunday."

"I didn't do nothing but be obedient. God did the rest."

"Why are you playing it down?"

"Why are you playing it up?"

"Man! Why do you have be *so* difficult, why can't you just take the compliment?"

"Well, because it's not mine to take, like I said, I didn't do anything."

"You got a problem." Lisa said.

"I got a problem? You are right, I have a problem, and the problem is ain't no men in their proper positions around here, and I just got tired of it, and while I was sitting there thinking about it God said to me 'You can't be too tired about it cause you ain't did nothing about it' and I thought, 'well we can fix that', so I just got up and said what I thought he told me to say. Now, the *bigger* problem to me is when a pastor is micromanaging the flock due to deficiencies in himself; he was abused, so now he himself has become the abuser."

"Tony you are out of line, what would make you say a thing like that? And where do you get the idea from that he was abused?" Lisa asked.

"From him, he said it in his sermon one time, only everybody was so caught up with the flow that they missed it. Okay, remember when he was talking about his relationship with his father?"

"Yes." Lisa, answered

"Do you remember what he said?"

"Not really. I think it was something about his father being drunk and saying something..."

"Yeah," Tony interrupted, "And everybody laughed, only it wasn't meant to be funny, and it wasn't funny, but since people laughed he went with it and moved on. I remember exactly what he said, I remember the hurt in his voice when he said it, and I remember the hurt in his eyes, and the pain on his face. It wasn't funny to him then, and it's not funny to him now, and he's still wounded. Now out of his hurt he attacks, he doesn't mean to, and he isn't even conscious of it, but he does. So now they don't respect him, but they are afraid of him. Man, that *ain't* my Shepherd's voice! So you are right, I do have problem with a leader that's so wounded and insecure that he beats his sheep into bitter submission rather than guiding them to a risen Savior in love. How in the world are young men going to learn how to be men of God if they don't ever see one?"

"What in the world are you talking about?" Lisa asked.

"If you don't know, then I can't tell it." Tony answered.

"What is that supposed to mean." Lisa asked.

"That means you don't have eyes to see or ears to hear, so I'm wasting my time." Tony answered.

"Man, you just don't make sense." Lisa answered.

"You can't make sense out of nonsense or reason with insanity. It's like trying to counsel a demon, it can't be done; you got to bind him up and cast that devil out; then maybe, you can understand something."

"Okay, I am so done with this, now you're trying to say I have a devil?"

"All I was trying to do was to tell you how proud I was of you, and what you did Sunday and you're biting my head off."

"No, not you, but he all up in here somewhere and I apologize. I am angry, but not at you. I'm not attacking *you*, only what you think." Tony answered.

"I just don't get you sometimes Tony." Lisa said.

"That's good because that's all I'm trying to say in the first place. It's not me you need to get but God. Y'all so busy looking at me worried about me; what I'm doing, what I've done, who I've done it to, who or what I'm going to do next, that you can't see Jesus for worrying about me. How do you know that he ain't speaking through me? Everybody here thinks that because I came here all tore up, and I was, that they need to minister to me, and some did that, and I needed that, but how do you know that I wasn't sent here for you to get ministered to as well? Man, you can learn something from a drunk. God even made an ass speak. You can get a message from silence if you can hear. You get a vision while in total darkness if you can see, you feel me?"

"Actually, no I don't I'm afraid I don't, and I guess I never have."

"It's cool, I'm use to that. Anyway, I'll holla."

Tony left that day after their conversation without doing any work and Lisa didn't dare say anything, she could tell he was angry even though he never raised his voice; it was still all a little frightening to her. She couldn't understand how someone could be so angry and yet seem so calm all at the same time.

The next day Tony was in the parking lot early as usual and he was his normal *morning person,* cheery self, as if the day before never happened. Lisa, however, was still very much troubled by it and still pondered what he meant. She still couldn't figure out why he got so defensive when all she was trying to do was give him a compliment, but the one thing she knew was that she would never try to compliment him again.

Lisa and Tony had been spending a lot of time working together and they often had to go out for supplies and talked quite often to each other. One day Lisa got up the nerve to ask Tony what was going on with him and his wife. He answered "Nothing, why do you ask."

"Just curious." she said. (But she was more than just curious; she was trying to get to the bottom of why Tony was so angry at times. He seemed tormented and everybody noticed it but no one ever asked, but they knew it had something to do with what he was going through with his wife.)

"Well," Tony said, "If you mean are we still together, the answer is no."

"Are you still living together?" Lisa asked.

"We're still in the same house if that's what you mean." Tony answered.

"Well then you're still together then."

"Living together yes, but still together no; but I know what you're getting at, so technically," he paused, "I guess you're right." Tony answered.

"Do you still want to be there?" Lisa asked.

"No." Tony answered.

"Then why are you there?" Lisa asked.

"Why do you care?" Tony answered.

"Well it's just that you seem so angry at times."

"What makes you think I'm angry? I'm frustrated most days about it, but I wouldn't call it angry."

"Man, it's written all over your face, half the time you look like you might want to kill somebody or something, and frankly, it's a little scary at times."

"I do?" Tony said.

"I'm serious. And Tony, whether you know it or not, a lot of the guys really like you, and we're concerned about you."

"So am I" Tony answered "And I appreciate the concern and all, but I gotta walk this out alone. But I have to admit it has been hell!"

"Well, if it is that bad then why don't you leave?"

"Well number one, I really don't want to leave my kids, and number two, I don't have anywhere to go, and that's what's messed up about the whole thing. There is all kind of support out there for a woman to get out of an abusive or unhealthy relationship, but ain't no help out there for a brotha. This woman has hit me with her van, thrown stuff at me, her dude is threatened to kill me if he ever sees me. Him and his boys jumped me one night when I was out, and I can't get no help, not even from the police. I even tried to file stalking charges against her because she won't leave me alone, and the prosecutor just laughed at me like *are you serious*, but all she did is just tell them that I hit her and they got a warrant out for my arrest."

"Well, what did you do to make her do all of that?" Lisa asked.

"See, why does it always have to be the man's fault?"

"Because it usually is." Lisa answered.

"Okay, I cheated on her. It was one night, and I was drunk out of my mind. I am not making excuses about it because like sober thoughts from a drunken mind, I only did what was really in me to do in the first place, and being drunk didn't help any. She's involved with somebody, and I thought, okay a fare exchange ain't no robbery if that's what you feel like you've got to do, cool, but then I find out she's been with this guy for almost three years now, and all I'm saying is, it's a big difference between a one night stand and a three year relationship. I was at least drunk when I made my mistake, she made a conscience decision! One night stand, three year relationship; you do the math! Regardless of all that I came to the church for help, but because it's typically always the man's fault I can't get help. I can't receive compassion, and don't even think about the so called "benefit of the doubt." NO, not a man! Specially a black man, he's got to be a dawg! Yet all a woman has got to do is cry wolf, and folks break their neck trying to help them!"

"Okay, okay!" Lisa said.

"You're right, I have seen women come to the church in similar situations and we do bend over backwards to help women out, and what makes it so bad is that half the time they are just scheming and playing on the sympathy of the pastor for attention. I have seen men come in needing help with something and get shown no compassion and get treated like dirt."

"Man, that's messed up." Tony answered.

"I know and I'm sick of it." Lisa answered. "Tony, can I ask you a personal question?"

"What?" Tony answered.

"My husband cheated on me, and to this day I don't know what I did to make him cheat. Since then I have been done so bad by men that I have just come to accept that it's what men are; and what I have always wanted to know is, why do men cheat?"

"Well," Tony answered, "I can't answer for the rest of the men in the world but I can tell you why I did. One thing I can tell you is it didn't *just happen* like you'll hear most men say. It was a process of events that started with my thoughts, helped out by her fears, always saying stuff like I'm going to leave her for somebody else and burning bread on me; talking about I'm gonna be drunk one day and some woman is going to take advantage of me, and then there's a 'man's needs' and that was a problem too.

"See, Lisa, Men have needs too…"

"I know! SEX!"

Tony laughed. "Aah but that's where you're wrong, I mean you're right about the sex thing, but that's a smaller part of it than what you think, and contrary to the fact that some have said that men think about sex every so many seconds, I don't, so either it's something wrong with me, or I'm out of that percentile that they studied."

"I'm gonna give you the four basic needs of a man as I see them. Now, I don't know about nobody else, but over the years these have become important to me!"

"Number one, first and foremost..." "That's an oxymoron", Lisa interrupts. "More like a double positive," Tony laughed. "But I do so for effect of how paramount this is."

"Okay, get on with it!" Lisa exclaims.

"Okay," Tony said. "Respect."

"Respect?" Lisa asked.

"Yeah, respect. If you don't respect me, you don't love me; that's just the way we see it."

"Okay, what's number two?" Lisa asked. "Hold your horses there young lady, now that's where y'all mess up. I haven't even broken down respect yet!" Tony exclaimed.

"I'm not stupid Tony, I know what respect is." "Yeah, but do you know how important it is?" Tony asked.

"Well apparently VERY important to you!" Lisa adds.

"See, again, that's where all y'all women get it all wrong. This is something commanded by God himself..." Tony said.

"AW, HERE WE GO!" Lisa jokes.

"Naw, seriously Lisa!"

"I know, Tony. I'm just joking. I actually know where you're going with this, and I really do get it.

"Okay, what do I mean then?" Tony asked. "Well," Lisa reached out for Tony's hand and said "May I tag in?" They slap hands.

Tony laughed and said "HEY! I like that. We should do a routine like that one day."

Lisa laughed and said, "Well God tells us, women, I mean, that we should obey our husbands as the head, and I sincerely believe that. He is under God as my head? MAN! There's nothing sexier in my mind than a man of God, so you'll get no problem out of me with that!"

"Excuse me?" Tony asks, "I'm just saying Tony, don't get it twisted. Go ahead with your other three."

"Okay," Tony laughed.

"Okay, number two is honor."

"Okay, explain that one." Lisa said.

"Okay, real simple. I take out the trash without being told to; now I know I don't deserve a pat on the back for just doing what a man is supposed to do, but at least act grateful and say thank you. Like when I made that food for you. Man, you must have thanked me and talked about it for

DAYS after that. My chest was stuck out a mile high because of that!" Tony exclaimed.

"Wow, I didn't realize that meant so much to you."

"It does, and it makes me want to do more." Tony continued; And number three is a stable and peaceful environment to come home to. I can't tell you how many times I stayed out, or just around the block, because of the drama I knew I was about to go home to. There was always some kind of mess going on, or about to jump off. I didn't address something that should have been, or could have been, dealt with before I got there. I was the disciplinarian, but you've got to reinforce what I've set in practice for things to work, but when you disagree with what I've set up - then a house divided..."

"Will fall." Lisa chimed in.

"Exactly" Tony said.

"So, what about sex?" Lisa asked.

"Well, that's last on my list" Tony exclaimed. "You can't expect me to wanna poke you if my stuff ain't right."

"*Poke* me?" Lisa laughed.

"Not you literally, you know what I mean."

"I know." Lisa answered.

"Wow, I didn't know men were so sensitive!"
"NOW, SEE!" Tony exclaimed. "You just disrespected me!" he said, laughing.

"We *are* sensitive, but you are NEVER to say it. MAN RULES 101: Don't call our stuff cute, cuddly OR sweet."

Lisa laughed "Okay, okay, I get it. But what does that all have to do with you cheating?" Lisa asked.

"Oh, everything! If I had been able to get my needs met, there would have been no room for the devil to temp me into sin. I think it was Bishop Jakes I heard say one time, 'lust is a temptation to meet a valid need in an unlawful or sinful way."

"YOU LISTEN TO T.D. Jakes? You're not such a heathen after all!" Lisa laughed.

"AW, you've got jokes huh? Yes, I listen to, and read, a lot of great preachers and teachers, some I bet you never even heard of in your search for truth. It was how I really grew up in the faith and learned as much as I think I know now because of them."

"Okay, man; get back to why you cheated," Lisa prompted.

"Okay," Tony said, "So, to be honest, even though I could have resisted a little harder, I had help to fall into sin."

"Because your needs weren't being met," Lisa chimed in.

"Yeah, that was part of it, but the other part was I had started mingling with the people in the break room at work; listening to their stories, and while I thought I was strong enough to handle it, and thought that I'd help to change some of them, and help to change their thinking, that's not what happened. I got invited out for one drink with my co-worker saying 'Aw, come on what's one drink? One drink won't kill you.' Long story short, the next thing I know I'm drinking and, smoking weed, and even selling weed, and now hitting the clubs on a regular basis. You mix all that in with the lust of the flesh, and it just went all bad from there."

"So was it worth it?" Lisa asked.

"What, the sex?" Tony asked.

"Yes, was it worth it?" "Did it meet your needs?" Lisa asked sarcastically.

"Now you just being funny." Tony answered. "And no, it didn't meet my needs."

"Well, was it at least good?" Lisa asked.

"I wish I could answer that." Tony said shaking his head.

"What's that supposed to mean?" Lisa asked. "It means I can't remember what the heck happened that night. I was so drunk I don't remember. All I know is I woke up the next day butt "A" naked on somebody else's couch, in somebody else's apartment, with a woman that didn't belong to me."

"To make matters worse, my wife was always so insecure and always worried about me leaving her for somebody, always worried about me sleeping around, and I could never convince her no matter how hard I tried that I had no desire to ever do that, and now there I was fulfilling her greatest fears."

"Yeah, but she had a hand in that too; and she may have not been 'such the innocent victim' like you think, Tony". Lisa answered.

"What do you mean?" Tony asked.

"Well, I'm not trying to start anything, but just hear me out. Sometimes when somebody is so worried about what you're doing, and you're not doing anything; it can be an indication of what they might have going on and doing. Besides, didn't you say she's been in a relationship with this guy now for three years?"

"YUP, but what's that got to do with it?"

"Everything, just like you said, it didn't happen overnight right? Plus, it's a matter of respect just like you said. Now Tony, this might sound strange coming from a woman, but because I am a woman I can tell what we know that men don't know we know. We know a man can cheat on his wife and still love her and be in love with her, and we'll fight like hell to get you back. We know y'all stupid like that, and as a matter of fact as little girls we compete with each other to try and get that one all the other girls is after. We don't care that they want him too. We just want to win the prize of saying 'yeah I got him.' Now with me, I can tell you; it hurt like hell to be cheated on, and at first I did just like I said; I fought like hell to try and keep him home until I realized that he was never there to begin with. I had to let him go. As a woman, I can tell you from firsthand experience that when a woman steps out on her man, especially her husband, she's lost all respect for him; not just as her man but as a man period!"

"Wow that's deep! That's some heavy stuff right there! I never looked at it like that but that's what I feel like right now about the whole situation. I just never could have worded it like that!" Tony said.

"So, what are you going to do?" Lisa prodded, "I don't know."

"Now Tony, I'm not trying to get in your business. What you decide to do with your wife and kids, and your future, is between you and God. I only brought it up because we're concerned about you, and everyone notices that you're hurting and angry, and wants to help but most are afraid to say anything because you come off so angry. Others just don't know what to say, and then there are some that just feel like it's none of their business to say anything."

"Man, all over one drink!" Tony said shaking his head.

"What?" Lisa asked.

Lisa remained quiet for a moment.

"Well it's a good thing you didn't go into any details." She said sarcastically.

"So how do you feel about it now?" she asked.

"Man, if I knew that one drink would have taken me where I ended up, I don't think I would have even went there. No, that's not true, I can actually go back farther than that. I should have never gone into the break room. I should have just stayed to myself."

"What? So you can never be around people, ever? That seems a bit extreme don't you think?" Lisa asked.

"Extreme?" Tony exclaimed. "Man, I lost my family, my job, my house, my cars, and I almost lost my life!

Today ain't *nobody* that important for me to want to be around just to impress or try to save for me to have to go through all of *that* again."

"That is a lot, and I thought I had it rough." Lisa said sympathetically.

"Anyway, man, I already *been* praying and asking God what to do. He know I don't have nowhere to stay, and no money to really make a move right now, and I feel like if it's His will for me to make a move He'll make a way. At least, that's how I prayed it." Tony said.

"Well, we know we been touched by you, and definitely agree that God can make a way Tony." Lisa answered.

"Well, I'm bout to go outside and get some air. It's gotten way too deep up in here; I really wasn't planning to get into all of that!

"It was good, though, Tony; that's how stuff gets worked out." Lisa said.

"Yeah, if you say so" Tony mumbled, as he walked off.

It was about time for bible study and Tony decided to go outside to get some air. Just then Marcus pulled up; he was one of the men from the men's group.

"What's up big dog?" Marcus said.

"What's up Marcus?"

"Man Tony, I want you to pray for this friend of mine; he used to stay with me, but I don't know what happened to him. I mean, I know he got hooked up with this chick and it probably didn't work out, but he don't have to be ashamed about it, and he is welcome to come back, but I just haven't heard from him. I got this big ole house and I'm staying by myself, so it ain't like I don't have the space."

Tony thought for a moment and asked, "Are you looking for a roommate?"

"Yeah" Marcus answered.

"Well, I need a place to stay, but I'm not working yet, but…"

"Man, I don't care about all that," Marcus exclaimed, "I'm just glad to be able to help a brother out, besides, ain't that what we *supposed* to do?"

"Yeah, but it's just so rare to see someone *actually do it.*" Tony said.

"Well, when you coming?"

"Man, I can move in tomorrow, if that's cool." Tony answered

"Yeah, that's cool with me." Marcus said.

"Can I bring my girl?" Tony asked

"Your *girl*?" Marcus asked

"Yeah, I said before I get married again I'd get me a dog, and that's what I did; I got a little puppy, and that's my little 'girlfriend."

Marcus laughed and said "I hear you big dog, yeah man, as long as you don't mind sharing."

They laughed as they walked into bible study together. After bible study Tony went back to work, but he didn't tell Lisa anything that day because he was still struggling with not wanting to leave his kids.

Tony went home that night and prayed, and then pulled his journal out and began to leaf through it, as he did every now and then, checking to see how many things he had talked to God about and that He (God) had answered. He found a place where he had written to God that if it was time for him to go, make it plain, and give him a way of escape. He remembered when he wrote that; he didn't have a job, and had no place to go. He believed that the conversation that he had with Marcus earlier that day was confirmation. He prayed again, and thanked God and asked that he help things go smoothly with the move, and drifted off to sleep while still in prayer.

The next day When Tony showed up to the church he was excited. Lisa could tell right away that he was extra cheery this morning and asked "What's up with you?"

"Man! I got a place."

"You got a place?" Lisa asked, surprised.

"Well sort of, you see, I was talking to Marcus yesterday in the parking lot, and he started telling me about this brother that used to stay with him, and how he had this big ole house all to himself, and I asked him if he was looking for a roommate, and he said yes."

Lisa knew Tony had just gotten a puppy and asked "What about the puppy?"

"Oh, he said my girl can come too, but that we had to share her." They both laughed.

"Anyway, I wanted to know if I could borrow the 'robber van' to move my stuff" (The robber van was what Lisa called the cargo van that the church used to pick up supplies and stuff).

Lisa said "Sure, as long as you bring it back in one piece."

"Man, I can drive!" Tony exclaimed.

"Too fast!" Lisa answered.

"I will take my time." Tony said.

Tony had met another guy at church, and they worked together from time to time on different projects around the church. His name was Theophilus, but everybody always called him Theo, so Tony didn't know his real name at first, until he saw him sign his name to something. Tony let him have it too! "Who in the world would name their kid Theophilus?" he exclaimed. They'd argue back and forth about it and laugh, and he'd tease Tony about his name too, telling him "Well, who has two first names, plus a first name for a last name?" and he'd say Tony's full name real proper, and with an English accent. Michael Anthony Vincent. Sounds like a rich white boy's name from across the pond to me! They fought like this all the time, but it was nothing serious though, more like brothers. Some people even thought they really were brothers. That was probably because they were both light- skinned and they did favor a little. Now, Theo was older than Tony, but Tony acted more like the older brother, and was very protective of Theo. You see, Theo got treated pretty badly by some of the brothers at the church and Tony didn't like that at all; he even threatened them about it, warning them that they had *one more time* to put him down, or crack another foul joke about him, and he would go off into somebody's mouth. They still did it, but they wouldn't do it around Tony. Theo called Tony his 'little big brother.' Tony always threatened to beat Theo up too, but it was out of love, and Theo knew it. In fact, Theo knew that Tony had a quick temper, and loved to get him going. They'd sit in the car together in the morning waiting on Lisa, with Theo teasing Tony because he knew he liked her. Tony would tell him he'd better shut his mouth before he got hit in it, and Theo would just laugh, and say "the only reason why you're getting mad is because you know I'm telling the truth!"

"Man, Theo said, you two are at Home depot for hours like you are on a date or something."

"We are NOT dating." Tony would respond.

"I can't tell, as *long* as you two are gone." Theo would say. "Y'all be disappearing somewhere around the church and *ain't no tellin* what y'all be doing then."

Tony got angry when he said that; he felt like Theo had crossed the line. Tony said "Theo, I swear to God man, I love you like a brother, but if Lisa's name gets slandered because of that stuff you let come out of your mouth just then..." Theo, realized that Tony was serious. "Okay man, I was just playing. Why you always got to be so violent?"

"Because man, I don't care what these people say about me, but that sister in there is a woman of God, and she doesn't deserve that. Man, I swear, I will *really hurt somebody* if they slander that woman over me!"

"Man, all that ain't called for." Theo said.

"It is to me - I'm cut like that. It should be that serious to them too; maybe if it was, there wouldn't be so much mess around here now. Man, these 'rooty poots' 'round here act worse than the people I used to kick it with in the streets! *Always* in people's business; and man, you know that everybody's business ain't nobody's business."

"Got that right." Theo said, "You and I both know that these people ain't cut like that."

"Shoot," Tony said, "I came to church in the first place because I knew I was 'tow-up from the flo-up'; man. I can look at myself in the mirror and tell myself mo' stuff about myself than they can even make up. I *know* what's wrong with me. I just don't know how to fix it. Now, what gets me is the fact that they actually think that I can't see how they look at me and judge me. Man, I've spent my life looking over my back watching out for people like that. Man, ain't nobody stupid; game know game! 'Bout the only thing they got right about me is I ain't no good. I came here because I ain't no good, and have even said so, so how prophetic is that? Oh, but they can look at me, how I dress, how I talk, what I drive, what I've done, and all of a sudden they've got a word from the Lord for me? Man, I talk to God all the time; and he don't talk to me like they do, so I don't know where they're getting their information from, but it ain't God. Man, one time I ask God, "Why do they trip so hard up here at this church? And do you know what he said?"

"What?" Theo asked.

"He said 'don't ask me, I quit going to that church years ago." They both fell out laughing. Now, Tony had asked Theo if he would help him move, and he said yes, so they jumped in the robber van and headed to Tony's house. When they got out of the van and started loading up, all of a sudden Tony noticed he didn't see the dog. Tony's wife saw him looking and said "Oh, if you're looking for your bitch, you can quit looking; I gave your bitch away."

"What!!!!" Tony said, furious. He couldn't believe it. He knew she could be cold, but this was just too much.

"Why'd you do that? I told you I was coming to get her. I told you that I was going take her with me. Who did you give her to?"

"I don't know - some guy was walking down the street and I asked him if he wanted a dog and he said yeah, so I gave him the dog." she said laughing.

Tony was livid. He felt like punching her in the face he was so angry, he didn't of course, but he was really hurt though. He spent every morning and evening on the porch with that puppy. If he could have, he would have had her with him wherever he went. "How could she be so cold?" he thought. If he had any doubts in his mind about leaving at all, they were all gone now.

"Look at your punk ass daddy running off. He ain't no man; look at him running off as usual!"

"Running?" Tony exclaimed. "I've stayed through a lot of stuff, and YOU know what I'm talking about, so don't make me say anything in front of the kids!" Tony exclaimed. "You can say what you want to," she said "they ain't gonna believe nothing you say, so tell 'em! Tell 'em why you leaving!"

"Are you serious?" Tony said. "You still messin around with dude for number one!" Tony said. "HE'S JUST A FRIEND!!" she yelled. "And they know about him, so AND?"

"Well," Tony said, "you know it's been dead for a long time; we don't sleep together, and it's starting to get violent!"

"Violent? Who's getting violent?" She yelled. "Are you serious?" Tony answered. "You threw the phone at me, you hit me with the van…" at this Tony's kids fell out laughing. Now very angry, Tony said "OH, y'all think that's funny? I can see now I've lost all respect here. I'm out! I ain't got time for this crap!"

He had often felt as if he was all alone in a house full of people. He had been ready to go, but just couldn't find the courage to do it. This thing with the dog, and his kids laughing in his face helped that; he was done.

With all those thoughts racing in Tony's head he yelled out to Theo; "C'mon man, let's do this!"

They put all of Tony's things in the van, everything that would fit, and they drove off. They arrived at Marcus's house and the first thing Marcus said was "Man where's your girl?"

'Man, you ain't going to believe this, the wicked witch of the west gave her away!"

"WHAT!" Marcus exclaimed.

"Yeah man, I can't believe it." Tony answered.

"Man, that's cold," Marcus said, "well, can you get her back. Who'd she give her to?"

"Man that's what's messed up about it, she just gave her to somebody walking down the street." Tony said.

"Man that's crazy." Marcus replied.

"Tell me about it!" Tony said.

"Well, I know you are glad to be out of there." Marcus said.

"You got that right man, I feel like if I would have stayed there any longer, one of us would have ended up dead."

After Theo and Tony unloaded all of Tony's stuff, Tony dropped Theo off at his house and took the van back to the church. Tony parked and leaned back. He was thinking about the look on his kids' faces. He knew that he would have a problem being able to see them because his wife had already told him that if he walked out the door, he would never see his kids again. On top of that, she also threatened to call the police on him if he showed up. He was really hurting, and to make matters worse, he didn't even have his puppy anymore to keep him company. He put his head in his hands and began to cry. Tony didn't like to cry; crying made him feel like a punk, but he couldn't help it, he hurt so bad. On the one hand, he didn't want to leave his kids, but at the same time, he knew he could no longer suffer the abuse he was receiving either. Just then Lisa walked up; he didn't see her but he could feel her. "Oh no," he thought.

"What's wrong?" Lisa asked. "Did something happen?"

Not really wanting to go into it, Tony said, "Man, she gave my dog away. I felt like she was the only friend I had in the world that would love me no matter what. She didn't care about my drinking; she didn't care about my past, and when I was down she knew it. She would just come and lay her head on me. Man, I can't believe she did that."

"Now that's just cold." Lisa said.

"I know, that's what Marcus said too."

"So did you get all moved in?" Lisa asked.

"Yeah," said Tony.

"Well, if it will make you feel any better, I'll be your friend. I may not be able to replace your girl, or lay my head on you like she did, but I'm here if you need me." Lisa whimpered like a puppy.

Tony laughed and said, "Thanks Lisa, I needed that but I'm cool; it just hurts right now."

"I bet" Lisa said. "And Tony; it's *okay* for you to hurt.

"I know, but I just feel like a punk."

"Why? Because you cried?"

"You should be glad you can cry." Lisa said. "I wish I could cry. I haven't been able to cry for years."

"Why not?" Tony asked.

"I don't know. I used to cry all the time over my stuff, and then one night I decided that I had shed my last tear over stupid stuff, and I haven't cried since."

"Wow that's deep." Tony said, not really wanting Lisa to see him like that, and really wanting to go.

"Thanks again for letting me use the robber van. I gotta go."

"Yeah, me too" Lisa said.

She had only come outside because she was headed home too. She was glad Tony made it back in time so she could get the keys.

While at home that night, Lisa found herself thinking about Tony; she felt like she might be falling for him. She asked God, "What is wrong with me?" She couldn't believe that she was falling for a married man.

"How could this, how did I let this happen?" she wondered. She felt horrible, even though they had never done anything sexually, or even kissed, or even hugged, other than the typical greeting. Lisa was so guilt ridden about it, and couldn't understand why because she hadn't done anything. She hadn't even thought about doing anything; yet she couldn't seem to shake her feelings of guilt and shame. That night she wrote:

Lord, I can't believe you sent me a married man, and even though I didn't like him at first, the more I am around him the more I am afraid that he might be the one. Please tell me I'm wrong. Lisa paused. *But Lord, what will people think? I will be the talk of the church if I were to take up with this man. Lord, I have been fighting hard not to like him, but it seems like I can't help it. Everything in me is telling me that it's wrong, but I feel so drawn to him for some reason. The more I get to know him the more he seems like he might be the husband that I wrote to You for. Except, he's not the six foot five baldheaded muscular black man; he's a light skinned five foot ten, slim, long haired dude that is still married. He is also still real rough around the edges. He does seem like he has a lot of potential though. But Lord he's not mine; he's a married man. Plus, he has got way too many issues for me. Please Lord, don't let me do this, help me be strong, don't let me show my true feelings for this man; move him, help him* *find another church or something; he doesn't like this one anyway. Lord, only you can make sense of all of this, and only you can understand what is truly going on in my heart. Lord, you know my husband was on drugs, plus he cheated on me! So you know that the last thing I want to do is to be the <u>other woman</u>, and have to deal with another alcoholic and addict.*

Please help me Lord. I feel like I'm losing control over this, and I do not want to fail and sin against you . - Love Lisa.

That night Tony talked to God:

"Lord, I didn't do a good job of being a husband, and as much as I'd like to, I can't cast all the blame on her. I should have never married her just because she had my son. She told me no, and I kept after her because of a promise I made; an inner vow to you, because my father wasn't in my life, so when I got her pregnant what else was I supposed to do?

I wasn't in love with her, and she knew it too. She even told me that I didn't have to marry her because she was pregnant with my son, and that I could still see him, but that didn't matter to me because I had made a promise to you that I would never leave my kids. Lord, I remember so many people told me not to get married; that we weren't evenly yoked, but I didn't listen. I was in love with the idea of a family; not her. She was right about one thing Lord; I robbed her of the life she could have had, but am I to pay for it the rest of my life, or give her those 20 years back, so she could make me suffer like she said? Lord you know how I feel about Lisa. I really don't wanna bring her into my mess right now, and I'm trying really hard not to disrespect her; but I can't deny the attraction."

Tony paused, in anguish over how much he really liked Lisa, and how he often wished that she was his wife; even dreaming about what his life would be like if they would get together. He shook himself and said: "LORD; I'm not even done with one relationship, how can I even be thinking about starting another one? But, Lord, you most of all know that the bright spot in my life these days is being able to see her face. Lord, please, help me to do the right thing. I have done the wrong thing so many times and I'm okay if I do myself but Lord I don't want to involve someone else's life in my mess."

CHAPTER SIX

Stalker

The next morning Lisa and Tony both arrived at church as usual. Tony didn't say much that morning, remembering the prayer he made to the Lord the night before. At lunch Lisa placed an order for clam chowder soup for herself and some of the ladies in the office, but something came up and they couldn't go pick it up so she asked Tony if he would mind picking up lunch. Tony was all too eager to get away from her for a while. When Tony got back, everyone was gone except Lisa.

"Where did everybody go?" Tony asked.

"Oh they're in a meeting; you can just sit theirs over there."

"How are you doing today Tony?"

"Better, except..."

"Except what?" Lisa asked.

"Well, I am having a little problem right now, and I was taught that if you hide it, then it is easier for you to fall; but if you confess it, you take its power away."

Lisa, not sure where this was going, but hoping that it was not going where she thought it was, started squirming in her seat. "It's you." Tony said.

"Oh, no, I knew it!" She said.

"No - just listen. I know this is going to sound strange, but I think you are the woman of my dreams, and I mean literally. I've kept thinking ever since I first saw you, that I know you from somewhere. Then, when I was praying last night asking God to help me to stay away from you, because, well, you know how I feel about you, and I know it's crazy, and I know you don't feel the same way about me, and that's cool because that helps.."

"Man, get back to how you know me!" Lisa interrupted.

"Well anyway, I remember this dream that I had, and it was you."

"Oh no!" Lisa said.

"No wait, listen, it wasn't a sex dream" Tony said.

"Oh good," Lisa said, feeling relieved.

"You were just teasing me." Tony said.

"And that's better, how?" Lisa asked.

"No not like that. Plus, I can't even remember it all, but I remember I was chasing you, or something, and it's like you were teasing me about something, maybe because I couldn't catch you, I don't know. Like I said, I can't remember, but I really think it was you in my dream. I do remember that when I woke up I said; "that's okay I'll see you again."

"So you think it was me?" Lisa asked.

"I don't know for sure but I hadn't remembered that dream in years, until last night when I was trying to remember where I knew you from, and it just came back to me. I don't know Lisa, I'm just trying to make sense out of all of this, and all I know is man, I'm tired of being a screw up, and I feel like if I stay around you any longer, I may ruin your life too."

"My life hasn't been all that great, and I have had my share of screw ups too."

"Man, but ain't nobody as rotten as me. My divorce ain't even final yet and I feel like I have been in love with you since the day I walked into this office."

There was a long pause. Tony said, "see, man, I knew I shouldn't have said anything. I'm sorry if I made you uncomfortable. I'd better go." Tony headed toward the door.

"Tony wait!" Lisa yelled out. Tony stopped in his tracks.

"Shut the door.'

"You sure?" Tony asked.

"Yes!"

Tony reluctantly shut the door. Lisa sat up straight and took a deep breath and said "Tony I really like you, and I think you have a lot of potential. I also really think you can do better for yourself if you…"

"If I what..."

"Well, I just think you might want to find another church for yourself, it's not like you are getting fed here anyway. You know just as much bible, if not more, than most of the teachers."

"But you only know as much bible as you live, so that means I don't know nothing. Besides, God hasn't told me to leave yet, plus I feel like I would not be where I am at today if it were not for the support of the brothers. Man, I don't know, I don't think I am supposed to leave right now...are you trying to get rid of me or something?"

Lisa was silent.

"Lisa what's really going on?" Tony asked.

"Nothing Tony, I just don't want to see you get hurt."

"Get hurt! ME? Get hurt? Naw! I'd be more worried about you than me right now. Anyway, I gotta go." Tony turned to walk out the door then stopped and turned to face Lisa.

"Do you mind if I call you sometime? I mean, I really don't feel comfortable saying everything that is on my mind up here at the church and..."

"Yes, I guess that will be okay."

"Okay" Tony said, and he turned and walked out.

"Wait! Tony."

"What?"

"Don't you want my number?"

"I've got it already. You're listed in the phone book."

As Tony turned to walk out, Lisa muttered, "I knew he was a stalker." Lisa couldn't believe she told him yes, but she thought they would talk all throughout the day face-to-face anyway, so what could be the harm in talking on the phone. Lisa was torn between guilt and excitement; on the one hand he's still married, but on the other hand, she hasn't had a man call her in years, not one that she was interested in anyway.

Lisa started feeling like it was a mistake to tell him that he could call, but he said he just needed someone to talk to. What could be the harm in that? Maybe when he calls I just won't answer the phone, but then I couldn't do that, besides, the poor guy had been through enough already and she didn't want to add to the list. Well, at least he was honest with me about his feelings from the very beginning, and he really did seem sincere about wanting to do the right thing. She had never had someone be that honest before, and she remembered the very first thing out of Tony's mouth when he thought he was attracted to her was that he was no good. But he is a good man, or at least he has the potential to be someday.

That night Lisa was on edge; she tried not to be but she couldn't help it. What did he want to talk about that he couldn't say at the church? Tony wasn't afraid to speak his mind not even in the church, so what could it be? The phone rang. "It's him," she thought. Lisa dashed across the room like a little school girl in love. She snatched the phone off the hook and then as calmly as she could muster she said "Hello."

"Lisa?" Tony said.

"Yes, this is she."

"Hey man, I'm outside and I noticed that there is a park in back of your place can you come out for a minute?"

Lisa felt like someone punched her in the gut. "NO!" She roared. "Are you crazy? How did you find my house? See I knew you were a stalker, you said you wanted to talk."

"And I do; man, please just here me out." Tony said. "I know it seems crazy but I just want to show you something, and I promise I'll be good. Lisa, please trust me. I would never hurt you."

"I don't know, how would you feel if you were a single mother and some man just popped up over your house in the middle of the night, talking bout 'Can you come out for a minute?' Plus, I'm not even dressed!"

"Lisa look, if I was going to do anything foul I had plenty of time and opportunity to do it. All the days we have been together by ourselves in that church and out at Home Depot. Man, just come see what I want, I promise you I will be a perfect gentleman."

She thought about it for a moment, and thought he was genuinely concerned about her welfare, and even angry that she was at the church so often by herself. Not to mention he was always a perfect gentleman; he never let her open doors when he was around, he helped her carry her stuff in every morning and he cooked and shared his lunch every day. Against her better judgment she finally consented.

Lisa threw on her sweats over her shorts, she was always in sweats at home or in shorts and a tee shirt; she looked a mess but she thought, "oh well, that's what he gets for showing up at ten-o-clock at night." She walked outside.

"Have you been stalking me or something, how many times have you been to my house?"

Tony laughed. "No it's not like that, I only looked you up in the phone book the other day. I really don't know why I did it. One night I was just sitting up thinking about you and I wondered if you were listed, and you are. You should take it as a compliment."

"What, that you are stalking me?"

"No, that I was thinking about you."

"Tony you said you were going to be good."

"Oh, and I am."

"What do you want?" Lisa asked.

"Let's walk over to the park." Tony said.

"What's that in your hand?" Lisa asked.

"It's my journal." Tony answered.

"You write?" Lisa asked.

"Yeah, almost every night."

"Really?"

"Well yeah, mostly to God, but sometimes songs, poems, and stuff like that."

Lisa thought she'd lose her mind when he said that. She couldn't believe it, he writes letters to God. "I write to God, too," she thought to herself. Tony noticed that Lisa was distracted. "Are you alright?"

"Yes," she said but her heart felt like it would pound right out of her chest.

"Let's sit down on that bench over there. I just wanted to read something to you."

"Oh no," she thought, "he's going to recite poetry." She really didn't care for that.

"I want to show you why I think I have been trippin so hard over you. I am beginning to think that this is a God thing."

"What?" Lisa asked.

"Me and you."

"Oh, Lord." Lisa answered.

"No wait, hear me out. Man, Lisa, I have been trying to shake this thing since the very beginning. I go to sleep thinking about you. I wake up thinking about you, and I think about you all through the day."

"That sounds like torture." Lisa said.

"Oh it is!" Tony answered. "Well anyway, I was going through my journal, as I do periodically, to see how far I've come, what prayers have been answered, and sometimes just to see if I forgot anything. See, I have found out by doing so, that sometimes you can be complaining about where you're at, only to find out that you are actually experiencing answered prayer."

"What does that mean?" Lisa asked.

"I was about to tell you when you interrupted me." Tony answered.

"If you ever get to it." Lisa shot back.

"Okay, well one night I wrote a letter to God about what I thought I wanted my rib to be if I were to ever get married again."

Lisa interrupted. "And what does that have to do with me?"

"Wait, just listen."

Tony began to read.

Lord, I don't ever want to get married again, but if I do, this is what I want my rib to be: I would first of all want her to love you more than anyone or anything else in the world. I would also like her to be smart, and not a punk or a pushover. I don't want anyone that's afraid of me, or intimidated by me. I want her to be secure about herself, and I want someone who will believe in me and support me. I want someone that I can talk to, and who not only just listens, but really hears me. I want someone that I can like, as well as love. I want someone that respects me and accepts me for me. Lord, You know I have always said I like my women like I like my coffee; black, and with an attitude, however, I do want her to look good, too, but that is not as important as her relationship with you, and her wholeness. Lord you know my equation of a relationship is that two halves don't make a whole, that she needs to be complete in you, as I am in you, then together we form a relationship of three - first you, then her and me.

Lisa was stunned and could not utter a word; she could hardly breathe. Tony asked, "so what do you think?" By now Lisa was nervous, and stuttering and stammering, and trying to respond. Inside she was screaming "OH MY GOD - I AM SO DONE!"

"Wow! I'm speechless, so what makes you think that's me?"

"Man, stop playing, I can tell by the look on your face that you know it's you."

"Okay, I can't take this anymore. I will be right back."

"Where are you going?" Tony yelled, as Lisa ran toward her house.

"I've got to get something out of the house." Lisa yelled back.

"I will be right back…stay there!"

Lisa ran into the house which was only about a hundred yards away from the park. She knew from being around Tony that he would have a problem letting her go alone in the dark, he did but, since it was well lit and he could see her all the way there, and all the way back, so he stayed put. Lisa came back with a book in her hands.

"What's that?" Tony asked.

"It's MY journal." Lisa answered.

"Now, I want to read something to you."

Dear husband, I imagine you to be a six foot five, muscular built, dark skinned black man who is not ashamed to praise the Lord. You are a handyman who loves to cook, and you make me breakfast in bed. You love the arts; you take me to plays and to the museum.

We take long walks in the park as we talk. We run and work out together because you are my personal trainer. You only have eyes for me. You listen to me, you hear me, you love me, you are good in bed, and we are sexually compatible. You are my friend; nothing I can do can run you away, and you even tolerate my mood swings. You inspire me to greatness and support my dreams, and I yours. Nothing can ever come between us, because the bond that we have is stronger than a threefold cord that cannot be broken, because our relationship is God ordained.

....Lord, if I do get married again it won't be until my kids are grown. I don't want to bring a man into a relationship while I am trying to raise my kids. I don't want to burden anyone with my responsibilities, or to deal with the problems that the conflict can cause. If it is in your will for me to have a husband, I am perfectly willing to wait on

You, and who You have for me. I have chosen wrong so many times for myself, and endured so much pain because of my poor choices, that I would rather be alone than to do that to myself and my kids again, and Lord, if it is not in Your will for me to have a husband, then take these desires away from me to want someone so I don't continue to torture myself like this time and time again..."

"Wow!" Tony said.

"So do you think that sounds like you?" Lisa asked.

"Well I'm not a six foot five baldheaded dark skinned black man." Tony said laughing. Lisa laughed too. "I know, I'm talking about the rest of it."

"Not right now I don't - maybe one day, but we will just have to see."

"Well, I already know you can cook, and that you are not ashamed to praise the Lord."

"Yep," Tony answered. "Like I said Lisa, I don't know; that could have been me once upon a time, like in a storybook or something, but I am far from being that guy now, and I've got so much mess in my past that I can hardly see through a day for myself let alone any future with someone else. No, I don't think so, as bad as I want it to be, that's far from being me."

Now what Tony knew that Lisa didn't know at the time was that he was currently running from the law, and had a ton of legal issues to deal with. Tony also still drank, and pretty heavy at times, but he'd always minimize it by saying, "It's just beer." He really wanted to stop but just couldn't seem to. Tony didn't do anything in moderation, whether it was work, play, love, you name it. Tony took it over the top every time; and it was beginning to take its toll.

Tony was at a place in his life where he felt that there was no hope for him. The one thing that made him feel good and gave him any peace was if he could help someone else see the light, so that maybe they wouldn't have to experience the heartache that he had. Tony really thought at times that he must have committed the unpardonable sin and was destined for hell, and would live his life at times with reckless abandon because he felt he really had nothing to lose. He really couldn't understand why it seemed like he could help everyone else but himself, and what made matters worse, is that it seemed that all he got for all his efforts in return was persecuted and abandoned. Even if people wanted to help him, it was like they couldn't; he was already cursed or doomed or something and it frustrated him that he had helped so many people over the years, but couldn't seem to get it for himself.

Tony remembered his friend Bill once asked him jokingly "Hey Mr. Counselor, you are always helping other people, when do you get yours? Whose feet do you sit at?" Out of all the things that Tony thought he knew, he never had an answer for that. You see as smart as people thought he was, Tony could never connect the dots for himself.

Tony was now doodling something in his notebook.

Lisa asked "What's that?"

"It's a picture. It's you and me at sunset."

"Here." Tony handed her the book. It was a picture of a man and woman standing hand-in-hand watching a sunset. There were mountains and trees, even clouds and a couple of seagulls flying in the distance. Lisa noticed that they were naked and asked, "Why do we have to be naked?" she shrieked "I knew you were freaky!"

Tony laughed. "See, why you got to go there? It's perfectly innocent and it was not meant to be erotic."

"I can't tell!" Lisa answered.

"Man, look; I'm just imagining us like Adam and Eve, only before the fall, and before all the messiness of life as we know it now. You see, when I imagined my woman of God, I think of her as the rib that I woke up to once God took her out of me to form her. I imagine her standing there perfect, taken out of me just for me. MAN! What

106

it must have been like to live in that world; no drama, no sin, no curse, and no toil. It was just bliss; just you and me working in the garden."

"Working? - Doing what?" Lisa asked.

"They didn't have jobs and all they had to do was enjoy life."

"Ah, but that's where you are wrong. But that's cool because most people get that wrong, and that's why we're so twisted about what we think we know about God, the bible and what our responsibility to all that is."

"What do you mean?" Lisa asked.

"Well, what do you think God meant when he told man to have dominion over the earth and all that was in it, and to be fruitful and multiply?"

"Well, the dominion part meant that man was in charge, and be 'fruitful and multiply' meant that man was supposed to procreate and populate the earth."

"Part of that is right. You see my interpretation of it all is that in my mind, Adam was the first farmer. I imagine that he still had to tend to the garden; he just didn't have to fight weeds or deal with the soil like he had to after the fall. And as far as 'be fruitful and multiply,' I believe that he was not only to multiply his seed but the seed of the earth as well."

"How do you get all of that?" Lisa asked.

"Well, it's all right there in black and white. It's all a matter of, can you see it or not. I believe that

God purposely created things in opposition to each other, but they end up working together to create a perfect world. I think the greatest opposing forces he created were me and you, man and woman."

"Now, I don't know how you get all of that out of the creation story." Lisa said.

"It's simple, God created light and dark, water and earth, day and night, even the earth with its gravitational pull that just pulls hard enough to keep us from flying off the earth, but soft enough so that everything in space is not crashing down on us. Even if you crack open an atom you'll see it's filled with equally charged opposing forces."

"I don't know about all of that and why would you think that he created us in opposition to each other. I don't know if I believe all of that." Lisa said.

"Just because you don't believe something doesn't mean it's not true. Check this out- if you just look at us physically, we have opposite parts but they fit, and rather nicely, I might add."

"Tony!" Lisa yelled.

"Okay, okay, but you know I'm right. Also, the way we think y'all want to be loved, and the way we want to be respected. Y'all *think* y'all know everything, and we *know* we know everything."

"Wait, what is that supposed to mean? Now I know you didn't get that from the bible. Where does it say we think we know everything?"

"Wait now Lisa, just hear me out now. Okay, here's how it went down. Satan tempted Eve in the garden to eat from the tree of the knowledge of Good and Evil, two more opposites on one tree, right? And as a matter of fact, there was also a Tree of Life that brought you eternal life, which is also the opposite of the Tree of Good and Evil because it brought death."

"You're getting off the subject again." Lisa said.

"No I'm not, just wait; I'm getting to that part. Okay, so Satan told Eve that you ain't gonna die if you eat of this tree. God is just trippin cause he knows that as soon as you eat of it you gonna be like him and know good and evil. Then Eve wanting to be like God and know what he knows, she ate to become wise like God, 'cause that's what Satan said would happen if she ate, but she ate and nothing happened. Then Adam messed around, and instead of following what God had told him to do followed Eve, hence exalting her like the goddess she thought she would be, and he ate, and then their eyes were opened to good and evil, but instead of feeling like God, now they wanted to hide from him. Man, in my mind, Eve chose knowledge over life, and Adam chose the booty over life. That's why I say ever since then y'all think y'all know everything, and since we know you, we know everything because to most of us, like Adam, we will sell our soul for that tail."

"Like you wouldn't have done the same thing." Lisa said laughing.

"I wouldn't have, man, I would have been the rib-less man by the time it was all said and done." Tony answered laughing now too.

Lisa laughed. "But Tony, I don't think that is what it means at all."

"Humph, I don't see why not, what has changed? Man, God told Adam before handing out his judgment on him, 'and because you listened to this woman,' and think about it all throughout time and all through the bible, a lot of men, great and small, fell over their lust or desire for a woman."

"Okay Tony, speaking of great men why haven't you ever done anything with all that talent that God gave you?" Lisa asked.

"What talent?" Tony answered.

"Amongst the million and one other things that you have the ability to do, you write and you draw, you sing, you play instruments, shall I go on?"

"Well, a lot of people have talents; those ain't nothing special." Tony answered.

"No, people might have one or two of those talents, but I have never met anyone that could do so many things well."

Tony laughed. "Well, I don't know about all that, but when I was a kid I used to think that I would be something, but the older I got, I began to realize that it was just fantasy. The reality of life for me was that if you don't work, you don't eat, and none of that stuff ever made me any money, and I just got to the place where I didn't believe in all of that stuff anymore."

"Humph." Lisa grunted. "Well, I believe in you. Anyway, it's getting late; I really should go, and I'm starting to see that you could go on all night if I let you. Good night." Lisa said.

"Holla!" Tony said.

That night, though Lisa disagreed with, and didn't understand Tony's version of the Bible as she called it, she did realize that he may be on to something. She felt like she was in bondage and needed to get free from some things, but a lot of that had to do with the church, and the work she had committed herself to. She had always thought that it was the devil trying to distract her from doing God's work. Lisa remembered something Tony had said to someone one day when she was in earshot. Someone told him that maybe if he committed himself more to God and the church, things would go better for him. Tony replied "Why do you keep trying to get me to be where you hate to be? Besides, your brand of Christianity isn't attractive to me, and it don't look like what I read in the bible. Your brand of Christianity seems like it makes people lazy, stupid, and bitter because you are waiting on God to do stuff you are supposed to do, then you blame the devil on your circumstances, like being unhealthy, broke, unemployed, or being alone and stuff, when all you got to do is get an education, hit the gym, eat right, and treat people better; then maybe you'll start to feel better about yourself, at least enough to attract some of the things you really mad about not having. That's your stuff, and that ain't got nothing to do with God or the devil."

Lisa was beginning to think his analogy maybe fit her too, and was starting to wonder if that's why she was so miserable at times. As much as she wanted to believe, things always seemed to turn up mud! She thought to herself. "Why wouldn't it be God's will for me to buy a house for myself and my kids? And why wouldn't it be in God's will for me to finally stop buying used cars that broke down all the time. Not to mention the fact that I am overweight and been trying to lose weight for years. Lord, he is right about one thing; I am not happy where I am, and who would want to be saved like me?"

Lisa began to pray. "Lord, I don't know about Tony's interpretation of the bible, but if any of that is for me then please make it plain."

CHAPTER SEVEN

Everybody Needs an Angel

Tony couldn't sleep. He was in shock; he was simply blown away by the last statement that Lisa made to him. "I believe in you." It seemed that he had been waiting all his life to hear those words. Tony thought, *"that's what a man wants and is searching for all his life, a woman that believes in him."* He no longer believed that he was just trippin when it came to his feelings about Lisa. Now he knew why she made him so nervous at times, why he felt so compelled to tell her everything, things he'd never shared with another human soul, why he felt like he could go to the ends of the earth for her, and why it seemed he knew her from somewhere. "This is her!" he thought. "Man, this is the real deal. I think she *is* my rib!" Tony wasn't happy about it though; he thought "why now? I am in the worst state I have ever been in my life. Lord, is this a cruel joke? Is this my punishment? To show me what I could have had? I am fighting through a divorce. I am an alcoholic. I am a criminal running from the law. I have no job, no money, and I have nothing to bring to the table. By the time I get my raggedy life together she'll be gone!"

Tony was miserable that night; he didn't know how he was going to do it, but he couldn't let this one get away. He just *had* to get himself together somehow.

The next day at work, Lisa was still pondering some of the things that Tony had talked about the night before. She wondered if she had been wrong all these years about God. She wondered if she was really in God's will because she was so miserable. She began to wonder if she ever really heard from God at all. Lisa decided to ask Tony a question. "Since he knows so much about the bible, maybe he really can help me."

Just then Tony walked into the office.

"I was just thinking about you."

"Oooh!' Tony said, smiling and flexing a bit.

"Not like that silly." Lisa answered. "I have a question to ask."

"Okay, shoot."

"Okay Mr. Bible Man."

"I don't know about all of that." Tony interrupted.

"Okay, just kidding, but look; you said a lot of stuff last night and it got me to wondering if maybe I had missed God somewhere. I mean, I really thought I heard from God about working here at the church, and I really thought I heard from God when it was time to leave my job and come here and work full time for the church."

"So what's your question?" Tony asked. "Well, am I in the will of God or not?"

"Well, yes and no, and if it's no, it's still yes, so when you come to a fork in the road just take it!"

"What the heck! Can you just say anything plainly so somebody can get it?"

"Well, do you want an answer or not?" Tony asked.

"Yes." Lisa answered.

"Well, let me give it to you then, and stop fighting me."

"Then stop treating me like I'm simple minded, and stop speaking in riddles and telling stories and just spit it out!"

"Man, ain't nothin simple about you at all, and God ain't mad at you for what you don't know, and I can't really answer that without knowing a few things about how you ended up here. Now, how long had you worked at your other job?"

"About ten years." Lisa answered.

"Okay, and was there benefits?"

"Yes."

"Was the pay okay?"

"No, and I was constantly being passed over for a position that I was working in but not being paid for. I'd keep training people for the position; they would never stay and they would never give it to me, and I still ended up doing it anyway without the title or the pay."

"Okay, so what was the reason for not giving you the position."

"That I didn't have my degree. I have an Associates but I don't have a Bachelors yet."

"Okay, now we're getting somewhere. I would say that in your case you are currently in God's permissive will."

"What exactly does that mean?"

"Well, that means that you can actually choose something that is not His will. He permits it, but He doesn't provide for it or bless you in it, because it was not the path He chose for you, and because He still loves, you He won't forsake you; but it should have frustrated you enough to move over into His perfect will."

"I was frustrated alright!" Lisa answered. "So what happens is that you get so beat up, and so tired of it, that you get back in line by asking what His will is, then you do it; and after you learn from that, you are careful not to step out of line again."

"That sucks!" Lisa exclaimed; "So does that mean I have wasted all of this time?"

"No, that means you've learned something you wouldn't have learned if you had taken the other road at the fork, which should have been that in the almost ten years you were there, you could have finished your degree, only to find out after you got the position that you *thought* you deserved and wanted, that it still wasn't where God wanted you to be. That in actuality it was all about the preparation for where you are really supposed to be going next with that degree."

"That actually makes sense." Lisa said.

"So, what you waiting on?"

"What?" Lisa said.

"Have you started school yet?"

"No" Lisa said.

"Why not?" Tony asked.

"I owed a student loan, and it has taken me some time to quit procrastinating and finally pay it off. Plus I haven't been able to go back because of the job and my kids."

"You mean you choose not to go." Tony answered.

"Nobody and nothing stopped you from walking out of that job and taking this one, so how is it that anything is stopping you now?"

"You make a good point. All I can say is that it's just been so hard being a single mom, and trying to do all that you hope to do. I've had all these goals of going back to school, losing weight, and becoming a polished, well dressed woman. I have dreamed about this for years. I even have in my mind what, and how, that woman would be; it's like looking at someone else. I want to be a woman of wisdom and discipline, and I want you to only have to *look at me* and see discipline. Now I don't even want to go back to school just to get a better job, but rather it's just a personal achievement at this point. Does that make any sense?"

"Oh yes, it makes perfect sense. So, what do you have planned for this evening?" Tony asked.

"Well, like I said, I have been trying to lose weight forever, and I started jogging in the park and…" Tony cut her off.

"Man, I love to run; can I go?"

Lisa is stunned. "Well, uh…"

"What's the matter?"

"Well, I am just a little shocked. I don't find too many guys that like to run."

"Man, stop it, there's a lot of guys running and working out."

"Not in my world." Lisa muttered.

"What was that?" Tony asked.

"Nothing" Lisa answered.

"As a matter of fact, I go to the gym almost every day, and if you want, I can be your personal trainer. What kind of goals do you have for yourself? What are you trying to achieve?" Tony asked, obviously very excited.

"Well," Lisa said hesitantly, "I have been trying to lose weight forever, and anyway, what are you so excited about?"

"Man! Do you know how *long* I been looking for a workout partner?"

Lisa was stunned, because this was one of the things she had on her list to God regarding a husband. Lisa knew Tony had no idea what she was so stunned about; she had read him the letter she wrote to God, and even asked him if he thought it sounded like him, but he didn't think so.

The last thing Tony thought was that *anybody* would want him with all of the issues he had, past and present. Lisa constantly tried to reassure Tony that none of those things mattered, but all he'd say is "I can't tell, ain't nothing changed yet." Tony was real good at giving advice, but it seemed that when it came to taking any he was a brick wall. Lisa drifted off into deep thought. Now here he was, behaving just like she described in her letter to God about her husband, and Lisa feared she was really starting to fall for Tony, and she was an emotional wreck!

"Lisa!" Tony shouted. "Man, come back; I'm just standing here talking, and you are off in another world somewhere. What's up, girlfriend?"

"Oh nothing Tony; see you at six." Lisa said.

"Oh okay, so you wanna do the gym before or after we run."

"It doesn't matter." Lisa said

"Okay then! Meet me at the Y across from the park first."

"Oh, okay."

Now the church had started paying Tony for the work he was doing, and he decided to go out for something to eat instead of cooking lunch like he normally did.

"Hey I'm going out for lunch you want anything?"

"Yeah, but I'm not really sure what I want." Lisa replied.

"Typical," Tony said, laughing.

"She doesn't know what she wants, but I betcha bottom dollar she knows what she DON'T WANT." Tony said, still laughing.

"Don't start Tony!" Lisa scolded.

"Well, I know what I want." Tony exclaimed. "I want a Burger with cheese, no tomato or ketchup, plus mustard, with extra mayo!"

"Ewe, not me! You don't have to ever worry about me asking for Crown Burger. I hate Crown Burger. I can't even stand the smell of Crown Burger, so please don't ever ask me if I want anything from there. I can't stand their food!" Lisa scoffed.

Tony laughed and mumbled "Wow, I could never tell that, and, just like I said; she knows what she don't want."

"Shut up Tony. I know what I want now. I want a plain spicy chicken sandwich."

"Okay, plain spicy chicken sandwich." Tony said slowly as he wrote it down.

"Okay and what else? Want fries and a drink?"

"Nope, just a plain spicy chicken sandwich."

Tony returned in what seemed like to Lisa only in minutes. She was on guard wondering what was wrong that he came back so soon. Lisa headed to the door before Tony could ring the doorbell. She knew the sound of his car pulling into the parking lot.

"Get the food?" Lisa asked.

"Yeah"

"Well where's yours?" Lisa asked.

"I ate it on the way," Tony said grinning.

"You ate a whole burger between here and there that fast?" Lisa asked.

"YEP!" Tony laughed. "A double burger with fries and pink lemonade to be exact."

"That's horrible. That cannot be healthy, and I've watched you eat before; you don't even chew your food." Lisa scolded.

"HEY, I've still got my apple pies left though."
"Boy, gimmie my food!" Lisa said.

They walk back over to her office. Lisa sat down at her desk and opened up her sandwich while Tony was now fumbling with his pie; about to eat it. Lisa screamed and Tony dropped his pie on the floor and yelled; "what's wrong?

"See, I knew it!" Lisa screamed.

"Can't even follow simple instructions."

"What I do?" Tony asked.

"MAN, I said a plain spicy chicken sandwich!"
"And that's what I told 'em!" Tony exclaimed.
"NO YOU DIDN'T!" Lisa shouted back. "Because

if you had, that's what they would have given you. I know what I'm talking about. I go in there and order a plain spicy chicken sandwich all the time and I never have a problem. That's what I order, and that's what they give me!"

"That's what I ordered too!" Tony exclaimed as he followed Lisa down the hall, wondering where the heck she was going. Lisa marched into the kitchen snatched open one of the drawers, grabbed a knife, and proceeded to scrape everything off the bun. It suddenly dawned on Tony.

"You mean a dry chicken sandwich with nothing on it?" "That's what I said MAN! What's so hard about that! I said it like, over and over again too, to make sure you got it right, and you still didn't get it right!" Lisa said, still mumbling off down the hall back to her office.

"Can't see what's so hard about that! Plain spicy chicken sandwich is what I said." Tony stood alone in the kitchen thinking "But who eats a sandwich with nothing on it?" He could still hear Lisa fussing down the hallway and he laughed to himself.

"Oh I think I'm in love; this woman's got a lot of fire in her."

Tony headed back into office eating his pie while Lisa was still fussing.

"And didn't you just drop that pie on the floor? Why are you eating that?

"Faih secon ru" Tony said with his mouth full. "What? I didn't get that. Stop talking with your mouth full!" Lisa said.

"My bad I was too afraid not to answer; you were so angry." Tony said laughing. "Whatever" Lisa answered. "Five second rule." Tony said. "What?" Lisa said.

"That's why I can still eat this pie. It wasn't on the floor for over five seconds. Oh, and sorry bout the sandwich, but who eats a plain dry sandwich with nothing on it?"

"Apparently I do!" Lisa scoffed.

"Yeah" Tony giggled. "Apparently so." "Anyway, I'm sorry for going off on you like that. I'm surprised it didn't run you off." Lisa said.

"Run me off?" Tony laughed. "Man, naw, that just turned me on!"

"You've really got a problem, Tony Vincent!"

"Can't be delivered from what…

"I know, I know; don't exist!" Lisa answered. They both laughed.

It was happening. Lisa was starting to get attached to Tony. She liked his company, she liked his conversation, and she knew that his divorce would be final soon, but she still didn't trust it. There were a few women at the church that had their eye on Tony, and it seemed he didn't even notice; instead he spent most of his free time talking with Lisa. They had even offered Tony tickets to different events from time to time right in front of her. Tony would look at them and ask was Lisa going, they'd answer no, then Tony would say that he didn't want to go. Lisa giggled as she thought about the fact that he was the only man she knew that both women and men were attracted to, and she thought it was sooo funny. Tony didn't think it was funny at all; rather, it made him angry. It seemed like he was the type of guy, with his wit and charm; that he could have anybody he wanted, but all he wanted to do was spend time with her. She didn't get it. She thought "I am fifty pounds overweight, I wear old crappy clothes most of the time, and I know he has to notice. Tony looks good in his *work* clothes."

That night Tony and Lisa met at the gym and Tony explained to Lisa that the reason why she could only loose so much weight and then couldn't sustain the loss she had attained was because she needed to build muscle, especially in her trouble spots butt, thighs, abs, and arms. Tony explained that she could increase her ability to burn fat and keep it away by building muscle. Lisa was amazed and wondered what doesn't this man know?

That evening, while they were in the park, Lisa decided to ask Tony about what had been on her mind.

"Tony, are you attracted to me." Lisa asked

"Well yeah! You can't tell?" Tony answered.

"Well yeah, I know that, but what about me are you attracted to?"

Tony stopped running; she stopped too. "Man, are you kidding me? You are gorgeous!" Tony answered.

"I'm serious."

"And so am I!" answered Tony. "Lisa listen, from the day I laid eyes on you I could hardly stop looking at you. I think about you when I go to bed, I dream about you, and I think about you when I wake up. I think I am falling in love with you."

Lisa was shocked and speechless and couldn't believe what she heard. She liked Tony too, but love???? She wasn't sure she felt that strongly about him yet. Lisa couldn't say anything.

"That's okay. I know that was a little strong and maybe a little too fast, but I can't help the way I feel; but I can control what I do about it." Tony said.

Lisa noticed a bench nearby and sat down.

"Can we sit down for a minute?" She asked.

"Sure" Tony answered. Lisa took a deep breath. "What's wrong?" Tony asked.

"Well, it's just that it seems like to me, you are the type of guy that can have anybody he wants, and I can't understand why you would pick me, or for that matter why anybody would pick me. I'm over weight for one thing, and nobody has paid me this kind of attention in years. It's like I've been invisible."

"More like *protected!*" Tony answered.

"What?" Lisa answered.

"I said more like protected. Lisa look, I didn't really know what you were shaped like, and for one thing, the way you wear your clothes it's hard to tell. I think that the usher outfit you wear is about the sexiest and most revealing outfit I've seen you in to date. You have a waistline and it seems like you have a nice shape to me; and you have definitely got a nice booty, and if anybody should know booties, it's me. I like to consider myself a bootyologist."

"What the heck is that? That's not even a word."

"Sure it is. Look, check this out. A lot of guys fall for the booty in the jeans, but the booty in the jeans can be deceptive. Some jeans shape, tighten, lift, and even restrict the booty. I have noticed however, that if you look close enough you can see the dimples even through the jeans. Either way, the jean booty is hard to analyze. Now take the sweat pants booty for instance, no booty restriction properties; no matter how tight you wear your sweats you get the real shape of the booty."

Lisa laughed, "Tony that's the silliest thing I have ever heard. What does that have to do with me?"

"Well, *you* my dear have a well-defined, firm rounded booty with no dimples."

"TONY!" Lisa screamed in laughter.

"Well you asked the doctor." Tony laughed. "Listen Lisa, I know what you're getting at, and all my life I have had this problem. I had one girl tell me in school that her mother warned her about those light skinned curly haired Negros that ain't no good. Consequently, I spent most of my high school years without a girlfriend, because girls didn't trust me, or thought I already had a girlfriend. Lisa I am looking for the total package in a woman, and let's face it; neither one of us are spring chickens anymore."

"Speak for yourself." Lisa interjected.

"Okay, But Lisa listen; I have long since realized that the wrapper is not the most important part of a package, but rather what's in the package is what's important to me. I have fallen for the wrapper before only to finally get it home and find that the box is empty. Nope, a big butt and a pretty smile only goes so far with me. It's nice to look at but if there isn't any substance to go along with it, I'll pass. Besides, I had already fallen in love with you before I knew what you looked like."

"Is that bad?" Lisa asked.

"No actually that's good." Tony answered. "If I were attracted to you by what you look like, then when your look changes, what happens to my attraction?"

"It goes away." Lisa answered.

"Right! And that's sad, because we should be more mature than that and fall in love with the person; their character, or personality, or something with more depth to it. Who you are won't change all that much, and what does change about you will only make me love you more."

"Tony I don't know if I am comfortable with you using the word love. How can you be in love with me in only a few months?"

"I don't know, I just am." Tony answered.

"When did it happen?" Lisa asked?

"Well, it was pretty much love at first sight. Then I *really* fell in love when you went off on me about the plain spicy chicken sandwich!" They both laughed. "I knew that I was probably just trippin, and yeah it coulda been some ole rebound stuff, but Lisa, the more we talked; I thought 'yep, I'm sure of it. I'm in love and I can't shake it.' Man, and I told myself that I didn't want to get married again; I even had my bachelor pad all laid out in my head."

"MARRIED! Now we're getting married? I just met you! And you already talking about marriage! Uuh, when I do get married, IF I do get married, I already said that it won't be until my kids are grown and gone; and my youngest has got three more years to go so…"

Tony cut her off, "Whoa, killer; Man! I was just thinking out loud. I didn't mean to scare you, we've got time. MAN!"

"See, there you go, you keep talking about *we*."

"Look Tony, I really like you and everything but..."

"Man, you about to quit me." Tony said playfully.

"Tony, stop it! I'm serious, have you really thought about this?"

"Morning, noon, and night. I told you, *I can't get you off of my mind.*" he sang.

"I'm serious." Lisa said.

"So am I. Lisa listen, I've been looking for you all my life, sure, I got married, but it was outside of God's will, which then put me into his permissive will rather than his perfect will for me. Now when that thing failed I asked God for a second chance, and not just at marriage Lisa, but at life. Look man, I am almost forty years old, and I told God that I had jacked up the first forty, but if he blessed me with another forty I would give it to Him. And that if He saw fit to bless me along the way with a wife, that this is what I wanted her to be, and in my mind, I am sitting here looking at her, and have been since the first day I laid eyes on you. Now you may be a little rough around the edges, but you are the woman of my dreams; *you are my rib!*"

Lisa sat stunned in silence.

"Man come on Lisa, let's finish this run; it's getting dark." Lisa could not understand how Tony could just continue on with the workout and chitchat along the way as if they hadn't just had the deepest conversation ever.

Tony was like that though, he could be in deep debate, conversation, even a fight one minute, and joking the next. Lisa often wondered if there was something wrong with him, that he could change gears so easily. It's the same way he talks, she thought to herself. He's like all over the place, and I have to keep reminding him to stay on the subject or he'll drift. Lisa found that very annoying about him. Now he uses the L-word and marriage, and *thinks I am his wife*, and can just go on running and joking like it never happened! This man gets on my last nerve, she thought.

"Okay Lisa, now sprint!" Tony said as he jet off.

Lisa, shaken from deep thought, looked up to see Tony flying off in front of her and she began to sprint too. Out of breath now Lisa said, "Man you're fast."

Tony laughed. "No, you're just so slow it seems like I'm fast."

"Okay, good one; you got me!" Lisa laughed out of breath.

Lisa could hardly sleep, thinking about what Tony said. She was flattered that he actually found her physically attractive too. Even though it had been a little over a year, Lisa felt like things were moving too fast, or at least that he was. "I don't even know what I want for myself right now," she thought. She thought about all the things she wanted to be when she grew up and how much things had changed, and even said out loud; "What happened to all the time and what happened to my dreams?" She remembered playing typewriter with her fingers when she was a little girl. She had no typewriter, so she'd use whatever was available. One time she even remembered that she used the glass window. She remembered she used to like the way her nails sounded hitting the glass. She remembered one day while in school, the teacher asked the students what they would like to be when they grew up, and she answered gleefully "a SECRETARY!" The teacher scoffed at her and told her that she should be something more. Her feelings were hurt; she thought "what's wrong with wanting to be a secretary?" She remembered one of the things that Tony told her was that he saw more in her than just the person sitting behind that desk. She wondered what though. She once had dreams. "Tony thinks *he's* got a past," she thought to herself.

Lisa was abused as a child by a man she should have been able to trust. He touched her in ways that no child should have been touched. He robbed her of her childhood. From that time forward, every dream she ever had was just a distant memory. She was numb most of the time to any feelings, emotion, and never cried at all. She couldn't even cry in her dreams. When she was a child she remembered singing, dancing, laughing, and dreaming big. At one time she wanted to sing in a band, and at the age of about nine years old she sang in a garage band as the lead singer, and the youngest in the group; everyone else were teenagers. Lisa even played the guitar, carrying it on the bus to go downtown to go to her lessons. All that was a distant memory now, it was like looking back at someone else, she thought.

Lisa began to pray and ask God to help her make sense of everything and not to make the wrong decision again. Lisa had been here before, helping a guy out while he was going through a divorce and they ended up becoming close, even intimate. He moved in with her and even told her that once his divorce was final he wanted to marry her. She remembered the day of his divorce; he left the house that day and she never saw him again. To make matters worse he did re-marry months later and it wasn't to her. She remembered how used and humiliated she felt for years after that. Then one year she went to a singles conference. The speaker spoke about soul ties and how it was possible that everyone that you have ever had a relationship with or slept with created a soul tie. If you found yourself still thinking about that individual, or in some cases individuals, then you need to pray and ask God to break the soul tie that was created from that union so that you don't carry that with you; but also so that you do not carry it into any other relationship. It was at that conference that Lisa decided that she would stay single and celibate, even if it was for the rest of her life. The last thing she wanted to do, whether his divorce was about to be final or not, was to ever get her hopes up again just to have them dashed, and go down once again in utter humiliation. "Nope, not this time!" she thought. "Plus, he said he loves me and he's in love with me, but I can't really say I love him. I really like him, I am attracted to him, he is really funny and everything, but Lord, *why* would you send me a married man?" Lisa finally drifted off to sleep.

Tony came into the office the next day as his normal jovial self, but Lisa was not in the mood. She had not had much sleep as usual and she was just tired.

"Hey Lisa. Let's try to get along today shall we?"

"I'm not in the mood for it today, okay Tony."

"What?" Tony answered.

"You!" Lisa answered.

"Me? What did I do?" Tony asked

"You showed up; my life was fine, I came to work, I did my job, I went home, real simple!"

"And miserable." Tony murmured.

"I heard that." Lisa answered.

133

"I meant you to." Tony replied "Man listen, maybe you woke up down or on the wrong side of the bed this morning. Seem like to me you should have knelt down on the right side, and maybe you would have come up alright this morning."

"If you are referring to prayer Tony, I did that." Lisa said.

"Well look man, you can have a bad day, everybody is entitled to one, but you can't blame your whole life's problems on me; I can't let you get that off. You got problems alright and it ain't because I stepped on the scene either. Now I may have exposed what was already there and whoever it was that hurt you. It's not me and whatever it was that was done to you was done before I showed up. That's plain to see, otherwise I wouldn't have never turned this corner and seen you sitting at that desk and we wouldn't even be having this conversation. Cause if you wasn't already wounded you wouldn't feel like you owe this place anything and wouldn't be still stuck here because you would be off somewhere living your life instead of sitting here taking more abuse, and then beating people up like me for caring about you. Anyway you can't run me off. I believe you took a wrong turn at Albuquerque so you would be sitting there when I got here. I told you at the park that I believed that the reason that, as you say, nobody noticed you for years is that God was protecting you. Well the other reason is, I also believe that He was saving you for me. If that's too much for you to handle then I apologize but I ain't never sorry cause it's the truth whether you believe it or not. Now you can keep sitting there feeling sorry for yourself and beating the hell out of anyone who dares to try and get you to think any different about your existence or your future if you want to and you just may be sitting there for the rest of your life, but I think you're better than that."

"Tony that kind of talk may work for you but I'm not a fighter like you." Lisa replied.

"The hell you ain't. You don't have no problem snapping back at me. All you need is a reason to fight and soon as you find that, oh you'll fight alright. I know fighters and you are definitely a fighter. You ain't no punk that's for sure; you just got your spirit broke, that's all's wrong with you. Anyway I will leave you alone for today, but tomorrow, I'll be back."

"Whatever." Lisa said.

"See - it's a fighter in there I just know it." Tony smiled.

"Goodbye Tony."

"Goodbye my love," Tony said as he blew a kiss.

Lisa picked up a paperweight off her desk and hurled it at Tony; he dodged it and laughed and said "Ah you throw like a girl."

"GET OUT!" Lisa yelled.

Tony jumped into his car and called Lisa on his cell phone.

"Hello, Church of the…"

Tony sang, "*Have I told you I love you, have I told you, you still mean the world to me; have I told you I love you, I'll be your wishing well tell me what you want babe.* I love you Lisa," Tony said.

"I love you too Tony, now…"

"I know, I know, I'll see you tonight. Tony said.

"Tonight? Lisa replied

"Yeah, meet me at the gym. Holla." Tony said, and hung up.

"This man is impossible. What is it he doesn't get? I told him I do not want to be bothered with him today and he just won't go away! Oh, what can it hurt?" she thought; running and working out for her was always a good form of relieving stress, but how's that going to work when what was *causing* her stress would be there waiting for her.

When Lisa arrived at the gym, Tony had something to tell Lisa.

"Hey Lisa."

"Hey Tony."

"Guess what?"

"What Tony?"

"I've got some news."

"What?" Lisa asked.

"Well, looks like you got your wish because I got a job!"

"Oh good!" Lisa said, "Where at?"

"It's at the glass factory." Tony replied

"That's good! Well when do you start?" Lisa asked.

"Tomorrow."

"Good! But why would you say it looks like I got my wish, I mean I have been praying that God bless you with a job but I don't think that's what you mean." Lisa said.

"Well what I mean is you wanted me out of your hair so bad that it looks like God granted that wish."

"That's not what I meant Tony." Lisa said.

"I can't tell." Tony responded.

"Tony it's just been hard that's all."

"And you don't think it's been hard for me too? Tony asked.

"Well no, I didn't, I mean, I really can't tell what's going on with you because you are always joking and laughing all the time and nothing seems like it bothers you."

"Man Lisa, I have never been so happy and yet so miserable in all my life."

"Why? What do you mean?" Lisa asked

"Well Lisa, ever since we talked in the park that night I've been kind of tore up about some things. You told me that you believed in me."

"Yeah and I meant it. Tony you have a lot of potential."

"Yeah and I have been told that all my life and it never meant much and I have never amounted to much. However when you said it, it's like it did something to me. Something happened inside of me and I am not quite sure what, but I haven't been the same since. I'm dreaming again and I haven't done that in years. Lisa you inspire me in ways that I have never felt before. It's like I had been waiting to hear that said to me all my life."

"Oh Tony come on, I don't have all that power, that's God."

"No quite the contrary, do you know what a man will do when a woman believes in him, especially his woman? I know you are not my woman. Just hear me out. Man I felt like I could do anything when you told me that and it actually sparked some things in me that I haven't thought of in years."

"Wow!"

"Wow is right! Tony answered. "And more than that Lisa, I know you don't like me talking like this but I can't hold it any longer. I really think that we are supposed to be together."

"Tony" Lisa tried to interrupt but Tony stopped her.

"No Lisa wait and just listen! I know it's crazy. I know you wanted to wait until your kids are grown, and I know you have plans of being single for a while, and I know you wanted to get yourself together first and all that. Listen Lisa, I am still going through my divorce, I have got some past legal issues that I have got to take care of, I don't have any money, I still drink and smoke cigarettes, and the list can just go on. I told you from the very beginning that I was no good and if I was you, I wouldn't want anything to do with me, yet you have shown me the love of Christ. Despite all that is obviously wrong with me, you have not only been there for me, but you said you *believe* in me. Lisa if we are never anything but friends my life is better for just having met someone like you. Before we met, you couldn't have gotten me to believe that anyone like you even existed but I really believe that we are supposed to be more though. Now I can't ask you to wait on me until I get myself together but I plan to fight like hell to make sure that I don't lose you. Lisa I feel like you are the best thing next to God himself that has happened in my life. Furthermore, I believe that it was because of God that you happened in my life. Lisa this is more than just a line, believe me when I tell you this; I believe that you are the answer to my prayer. I really believe that you are supposed to be my wife and I your husband. Now I am not expecting you to say anything and this is not a proposal, I just really needed to get it off my chest. That's how I find out if things are live or Memorex. I speak them out and then how I know if it is God or not, is how He responds. I don't think meeting you was an accident or some cruel joke from God. At the least, he could be just showing me that there is a woman out there for me if I do the work to have something to bring to the table. Right now I don't have nothing; all I've got is me."

Lisa was stunned for a moment then responded "that's more than enough to get started with."

"What??? I just said I ain't got nothin but me."

"I know, and that's more than enough for me."

"So do we go together?" Tony asked.

"Are you asking me to go with you?" Lisa giggled.

"Yeah, I guess I am." Tony replied.

"Let me think about that." Lisa responded.

"That's good enough for me."

That night Lisa thought about what Tony said. It was not like she hadn't thought about it or been thinking about it too. In fact ever since she read her letter to Tony that she wrote to God, and he told her about his dream of being in front of all those people, she believed there was something more to it than just a casual friendship as well. She had some problems though; for one he is a married man, and second he's a drinker and she really had a problem with that. Tony would always say that it's *just beer*. Now that really bothered her because her dad died from just drinking beer and worse than that, they drank the same brand.

Lisa prayed to God about what she should do. The Lord told her to trust Him, and to trust Tony. She was puzzled about that response and she asked the Lord again, and He said "trust Me and trust him." She asked three times that night and the answer came back the same each time.

Tony was doing some talking to God as well. "Lord, you know I always choose wrong, you know that I am a career screw up, and I desperately want to do better but I just can't seem to get it right. Lord I am okay with continuing to screw up my life, but Lord the last thing I want to do is to ruin someone else's life as well. Lord if this is what I am supposed to do make it plain by Lisa saying yes. I know she is a woman of God and I know she talks to you so I will take her response to me as a yes from You. And Lord if it is no, help me to respect that and move on. But Lord PLEASE let it be yes."

The next day at church, Lisa was busy at work as usual and by the time she noticed, it was close to noon and Tony hadn't called yet. That's odd she thought, he gets three breaks a day and usually calls me on every one of them. Just then the phone rang, "Hello Lisa"

"Hey Tony, I was wondering when you were going to call, I haven't heard from you all day." "Yeah I know," Tony said. "I had some thinking to do."

"Oh? About what?"

"You know about what! Have you thought about it?"

"Yes, I talked to God about it last night."

"*Really!*" Tony replied. "Well what did He say?"

"He said to trust Him and to trust you."

"Trust me?" Tony asked with a shocked expression. "You sure that was God you were talking to?"

Lisa laughed, "Yes Tony I'm sure."

"Well, do we go together?"

Lisa giggled, "That's cute and you say that like we are in high school or something."

"I feel like a high schooler right about now. Man I've been nervous all morning about this."

"Well did you talk to God last night?" Lisa asked.

"Yeah," Tony answered.

"And what did he say to you?" Lisa asked.

"He didn't say anything. I told him that His answer to me depended on your answer to me; so what's your answer?" Tony asked.

"Well, I guess we go together."

"YES!" Tony screamed.

"Now look, I think we need to tell the pastor." Tony added.

"Why?" Lisa asked.

"Well, you are like his right hand man and he has been looking out for you over the years and I just think out of respect for his position and with all that can go on with us being together right now with me still going through my divorce and everything it would be a wise thing to do."

"I don't know" Lisa said.

"I do, without his blessing on this, this won't mean anything. Plus with your father not being here Pastor is your spiritual cover and I just think we should get his blessing about this first. Plus, I want you to meet my mom and my grandmother and I want to talk to your mom."

"Whoa! Man s-l-o-w down." Lisa replied. "I don't know if I am ready for all of that."

"Look Lisa this ain't gonna work if we don't do it right. I didn't do my first one right and I really want to do this one right."

"This one what? I just agreed to go together and you already ready to ask for a blessing? That's what you do when you ask for someone's hand in marriage, that's so old school."

"Right and that's just what's on my mind. If we talk to Pastor, my mom and granny, your mom and we don't get their blessing or approval then we don't even waste our time in going together and save ourselves some grief early in the game. You feel me?"

"Not really. Tony I don't about all that."

"Lisa trust me, I know what I'm talking about, let me handle this."

Just then Lisa reflects back on what God said to her and said, "Okay Tony."

"Anyway Lisa, I gotta go. My break is over."

"What time does Pastor leave today?"

"You want to talk to him today?" Lisa asked.

"Yeah didn't you just hear anything I said?"

"We ain't official until then."

"Okay Tony, he will be here when you get off."

"Cool, Tony said. "Holla."

"Goodbye Tony."

That conversation made Tony's day. The rest of the day at work, he was clowning and joking even more than usual but he still got his work done. Tony was a good worker, he had good work ethic, and there was no job that they put him on that he didn't excel at. Whatever Tony did he gave it 150 percent. His coworkers would sometimes get mad at him and tell him he needed to slow down because he was making them look bad. Tony would always say "mediocrity always complains when excellence shows up."

Tony was used to hard work. He remembered when he worked for a plumbing company and they had to put in a water main. They needed to dig a forty foot long by four foot deep trench to lay the pipe. Tony was standing there waiting and the boss walked up and asked "what are you waiting on?"

"Tony said I'm waiting on the trencher."

The boss laughed and said "You ARE the trencher, get to digging." Tony laughed when he thought about it now, it wasn't funny at the time but it's funny now. "Man, the things a brother's gotta do to make a buck!" he thought.

After work, Tony rushed straight to the church to meet with the pastor. Lisa dreaded it but she remembered that God told her to trust him. It all just seemed so crazy though, she had agreed to go with him but she didn't want the whole world to know about it. He was still a married man. "Lord," she thought to herself "I know what you said but why would you send me a married man?" Just then she heard the doorbell and she knew it was Tony. She went to let him in.

"You ready for this?" Tony asked.

"No, but pastor is expecting us."

"Does he know what it's about?"

"No but I am sure he has an idea."

Okay, let's do this," Tony said.

Lisa and Tony went into the pastor's office and sat down and Tony started right up.

"Pastor with all due respect, I am in love with your secretary."

Lisa gasped and the pastor laughed and said "I'm not surprised."

"Oh, why not," Tony said.

The pastor said "my brother, when I talked to you in the parking lot I kind of knew you two would end up together. Remember what you said?"

"Yeah, but that was before I knew you were the pastor." Pastor laughed.

"What did he say?" Lisa asked in horror.

"I'll leave that up to him, if he wants to tell you."

"What did you say Tony?" Tony laughed and said, "Well we were standing in the parking lot talking and it was some sistas walking across the parking lot, and I said Lord knows I love my chocolate."

"What's that supposed to mean?" Lisa asked. They just went on talking like they didn't hear her.

By then Tony and the pastor were laughing. The pastor said "Well when I walked up, the guys were talking about the kind of women they wanted and just then you and some other sisters were walking across the parking lot and,"

Tony cut him off "That's when I said it."

"When was that?" Lisa asked

"Oh it was before I met you. It was when I was just coming to the men's meeting on Thursday nights."

"But Tony was looking straight at you." They both laughed. They seemed to be having the time of their life Lisa thought, I may as well not even be sitting here.

The pastor then said "Look brother Tony, I have a lot of respect for you coming here and doing this. Tony we've talked before and I know you have been through a lot and really admire your strength for still being able to go on as well as you have, and I can tell you one thing, you must be a bad brother to get this sister's attention because she ain't no joke." They both laughed but Lisa didn't think it was funny.

"What is that supposed to mean?" Lisa asked. "Alright don't start no stuff," she said pointing her finger. They both said at the same time, "See what I mean," and continued to laugh, then Lisa laughed too.

Then the pastor looked at Lisa and said:

"Lisa you know I love you and I have a lot of respect for you too. You have been through a lot over the years and you are still standing. You are one strong black woman that's all I mean, and you don't take no stuff, and that's a good attribute to have in times like these because it's hard to trust anybody. You are a single mother and you have done a wonderful job with your kids and you do a great job here at the church. You two definitely have my blessing." Just then Pastor paused then asked "Tony what's going on with your divorce?"

"I'm still going through it." Tony answered.

"So it's not final yet?"

"No" Tony answered.

Lisa's heart was racing a mile a minute she thought for sure that this would be the deal breaker. Pastor then said "Well you are both grown adults so keep it holy, that's all I have to say; and keep people out of your business."

That was it! Lisa was in shock as he and Tony were standing there shaking hands laughing and smiling as he whispered something to Tony joking around like they were old friends or something. Tony had that effect on people, he was definitely a charmer, he had a gift with people, they either loved him or hated him. Lisa was shaken out of her shock as Tony called for her.

"Lisa"

"Yes," Lisa answered.

"Let's go girlfriend."

"Don't start."

"Black with an attitude, just like I like it," Tony said. Tony and the pastor laughed as Lisa and Tony walked off down the hall. Then pastor called Tony back and said "Hey Tony I need to see just you now."

"Okay" Tony said and they went into the office and shut the door.

"Tony, I just want to make sure you are attracted to the right thing here."

"I don't understand," Tony answered.

"Well, it's like this, some people think that they are attracted to someone, when in fact what they are really attracted to is the anointing that's on

148

them, so then when they actually get to know the person that is carrying the anointing, they find that not only are they not attracted to the person they don't even like them. You got me?"

"Yes" Tony answered

"Okay" the pastor said, "and another thing Tony, I noticed that you are a fighter."

"What do you mean?" Tony asked.

"Well, you are a warrior, a dragon slayer, and the problem with that is when you strike a dragon's head off, two more grow back and now you've made him even more powerful in that he has more mouths to breath fire at you with. Rather what I think you need to do since you can't kill the dragon is learn to tame your dragons and I think you will go a lot farther."

"You got me?"

"Yes" Tony answered, although Tony still believed the best way to handle a dragon was to kill it but he thought that he would take that into consideration. Tony left the office, thanking the pastor. When he approached Lisa he said "Well one down and three to go."

Oh no, Lisa thought.

"What?" Tony asked, as if he could hear her thoughts.

"Man it looks like you are scared to death."

"I am, I didn't know we were going to do all of this."

"Man I told you."

"I know, but I'm just uncomfortable with all this still."

"Well, why did you say yes then?"

"I didn't, God did."

"Yeah but it came out of your mouth," Tony said. "Look Lisa, it's gonna be alright trust me."

"Yeah, if I don't die first." Lisa muttered.

"What was that?" Tony said.

"Nothing!"

"Lisa, I gotta go home and get out of these work clothes and jump in the creek. I'll see you later?"

"I guess so," Lisa muttered.

"What was that?" Tony asked.

"I'm still in shock you gotta let me take all this in." Lisa said with a confused look of horror on her face.

Tony laughed "You'll be alright. Look, I'll pick you up at seven, and I got a surprise for you."

"Oh no" Lisa said "It's not a ring is it?"

Tony belly laughed. "Naw, you got a problem, I ain't that crazy, just wait and see alright?"

Lisa hated that; what she hated more than surprises was to get a tease right before.

Tony went home and showered and changed, while Lisa went home and was on pins and needles. She had to talk to somebody.

"Hello Angel?"

"Hey Lisa what's up."

"Girl, I don't know." Lisa answered.

"What's wrong girl, is it Tony? Girl did he do anything to you?"

"No"

"Well then what's going on?"

"Well ah," Lisa said.

"Oh no girl, tell me you did not do that thug."

"NO!"

"Well then what?" Angel asked.

"We going together."

"Oh no, that's worse, it would have been better if you just told me that y'all had knocked boots. How you gonna go with the thug? Girl have you lost your mind?"

"I'm starting to feel like it."

"Well girl, you ain't the only one," Angel said

"What do you mean," Lisa asked.

"Well when me and Jon met, he was still married."

"Really?" Lisa replied "Well that's a little known black history fact."

"Yeah girl, it had been over for years but she wouldn't sign the divorce papers."

"Why not?"

"Just out of spite. She didn't want him but she didn't want anybody else to have him either."

"So she knew about you?"

"She knew it was somebody but she didn't know who."

"How did she know?"

"The same way we know when there's somebody else."

"Oh, well that's what's going on with Tony. She won't sign the papers but she don't want him either, and what makes it so bad is she's got somebody and has for years now."

"Whaaaaaat?"

"Yeah girl, so you see where I'm at. And keep your mouth shut about it too!" Lisa said.

"You know you can trust me, but girrrrl all I can say is; hang in there, it gets better trust me. We went through hell too at first. We were ostracized, talked about, lied on, you name it. The funny part about it all is there was enough truth going on about it that was juicier than the lies, and they never got to the truth."

"I had forgot about all that and I know it was rough" Lisa said.

"Of course it was; but we got through it, and besides most of them were just miserable people that didn't have a life, who ten years later now are still the same lonely miserable people who don't have a life. Meanwhile all that time me and Jon have been happily married ever since. Listen girl I know I give the thug a hard time but if you like him and if you think he's alright then you have my support. Just watch your back girl, and I will too."

"So you don't think I'm wrong?"

"Lisa, girl no; at least I don't think so and I don't have no heaven or hell to put you in, so I don't think that makes me qualified to judge you either. Just keep talking to God girl, He'll let you know."

"Thanks girl, I gotta get ready," Lisa said

"For the thug?" Angel asked

"Yeah girl"

"Have fun!"

"Goodbye Angel"

"Goodbye Lisa girl, and don't let this stuff get to you girl."

"Okay," Lisa answered.

Just then Tony pulled up and blew his horn. Lisa hated that. Why didn't he get out and knock on the door.

"So where are we going?" Lisa asked.

"You'll see." Tony said.

As they got close, Lisa realized that they were headed to the water.

"Oh we're going to the water, I love the water."

"Yep, me too."

Tony parked the car.

"Come on, let's walk." Lisa jumped out of the car like a little girl. Lisa loved the water especially, at night with the city lights, moon, and stars reflecting off of it. The water was as smooth as glass. She ran down to the pier and put her elbows up on the rail and just looked at its beauty. It was so peaceful, this is perfect, she thought as Tony walked up behind her.

"It's so calm and quiet."

"I know" Tony said.

Tony was still behind Lisa as he looked at her and admired her silhouette as the light shown on her. He admired her small waist and her voluptuous hips. He liked the way she had worn her hair that night, pulled back into a ponytail with a piece hanging out in the front, not quite like a bang but just enough to drape down the side of her face. Tony could no longer resist it, slid his hands gently around her waist, stuck his face on the side of hers and kissed her on the cheek, and said "thanks for believing in me" and then let her go and backed up.

Lisa was trembling, she thought she'd loose her mind, she was speechless, she was in shock, she was in horror and she was in ecstasy all at the same time.

"I'm sorry; I just couldn't hold that any longer. Are you okay?"

"Yes," Lisa answered, it was all she could get out. Inside she was screaming. It seemed as though a lightning bolt went through her when he touched her. She couldn't understand it, it wasn't like she had never been touched before but it was something different about his touch; something special, so sweet, and sincere. It wasn't as if he was trying to do anything more than just thank me, but something happened when he touched me. *I felt something* she thought. Lisa managed to collect herself as they began to walk and talk along the pier.

"Lisa, look in a few more weeks I go to court for my divorce again and I am praying that it's final this time."

"I sure hope so, this is hell."

"I know Lisa, and look I'm sorry for putting you through all of this. Lisa I've been thinking that as bad as I want to, we really can't hook up until my divorce is final. Now even though I feel like my marriage has been dead for some time, I know that it's going to cause us some problems if we move too fast. People are already talking."

"I know." Lisa said.

"Yeah that's probably my fault. I have tried my best to be discrete about all of this but I can't seem to take my eyes off you. I follow you all over the church."

"I know!" Lisa said.

"You know?"

"Yes, I can feel you watching me." Tony laughed, "It's that obvious uh?"

"Yep, it's that obvious."

"Lisa I have screwed up so many things in my life I don't want to screw this up too. But you know, it's a whole lot of people rooting for us."

"And I also know there are even more that are against us."

"Like who?" Tony asked.

"Well just about all of the elders have approached me and had something to say about it."

"Like what?" Tony asked.

"Well one said I was deceived, one asked me if I was sure I had heard from God, and one who is a friend, just told me to be careful because they felt like you were nothing more than a predator."

"Wow, I'm honored," Tony said.

"Well, I guess I can tell you what one of the elders said to me." Tony said.

"They've talked to you too?" Lisa said with a shocked look on her face.

"No, just one."

"What did they say?" Lisa asked reluctantly.

"Well he asked me what my intentions were and I told him that right now we were just friends but that I hoped to marry you one day."

"You didn't."

"Yeah I'm sorry, it just slipped out. Well anyway he said that he was concerned for you, and that he had never seen you that open before and that he didn't want to see you hurt again."

"What did he mean by that?"

"I don't know, I thought maybe you could answer that one. But that's not all, he said that he was afraid that when this was all over, that I was going to leave you so broken and hurt and that they would be left to try and help you put back all the pieces. He even told me that I had you in sin and that pissed me off because when he told me his story about how he and his wife got together it wasn't exactly the holiest of situations. I asked him if he was worried that we are doing what he and his wife did before they got married, and if so we're not. I told him I really didn't believe he was concerned about you at all but rather just on a fishing expedition, whether sent or just out on his own. I don't know, but if he was looking for something to accuse me of, he'd better come correct! I told him that I had been through hell dealing with the thought of losing my marriage and leaving my kids and had been sitting up hurting and dang near drinking myself to death and never got one call. I feel like I am just starting to live again. I'm happy and getting better and *now* you want to call? Man, I just hung up on him. Man Lisa this has been rough and there hasn't really been many people there for me. But you best believe that the ones that had the courage to, I am eternally grateful for, and especially you. Lisa I feel like you have shown me the love of Christ. Despite the fact that you could be crucified for it, you have still remained my friend through all of this. Now to me, you are more of a Christian then every elder there. Now what make it so bad is I can tell that some people really want to come and talk to me and reach out to me but they're so afraid of persecution that they don't and that's just crazy. What's really got me, is they are all trippin over this piece of paper like it's the piece of paper that is gonna make this right."

"What do you mean," Lisa asked. "Are you saying that you can do what you want whether you are divorced or not? That's the law MAN!"

"I know Lisa and I intend to obey that law but even in doing so it won't change anybody's mind."

"Lisa listen, let's say we start over. Let's say we don't even talk to each other until my divorce was final, do you really think that these people's opinion about us will change all that much?"

"No," Lisa responded.

"And why not?" Tony asked.

"Well because I have known these people for years and I believe that all our relationship did was just bring out what was already in them."

"Now likewise, why should that same piece of paper whether it is final or not negate who we are attracted too? Now we do have the responsibility to do what is right in spite of how we feel because feelings are flaky, they have no intellect, and they are subject to change on a moment's notice and once we get our hearts involved it can get really messy -- you feel me?"

"Yes," Lisa answered.

"It's not the elders or the church that defines what's right or wrong, it's God's word that defines that. Now I am not trying to qualify our attraction by what I am about to say, however what I am about to say is a fact. There is a whole lot of messiness in the word surrounding marriage and relationships. David had a wife, Saul's daughter, then he took more wives, and two of them were previously married. Now the one woman's husband, David wanted to kill but was persuaded not to and he ended up dying anyway and he took her as his wife. The other woman's husband he did kill and took her as his wife. Now I am not saying that I want the problems that David suffered as a result of that either. Rather what I am saying is if the messiness of life never existed and wasn't recorded how would we ever know that there was life after mess. Now I asked God and you asked God, and we believed we heard from God, now peep this one out, we have both been married before right?

"Yes," Lisa answered.

"Why did you get married?"

"Well, I had got pregnant and I thought I was in love and back then if you had a kid with someone you were encouraged to marry them."

"Right," Tony responded. "You did it the right way and how did that work?"

"It didn't."

"Uhhm, I got somebody pregnant and I was taught the same thing plus I had made a promise to God that I would never leave my kids or their mother; and even though it lasted for years it eventually failed too. Now imagine how many people got married under similar conditions and are still together and miserable for it, or divorced, and alone and miserable. Now here we come along we fall in love with all these miserable people around and all hell breaks loose. Now that's not bible it's just my opinion. That's why I told you that I think it's important that we talk to our pastor and parents.

"Why," Lisa asked.

"Well back in the day, marriages were arranged."

"That wouldn't work today." Lisa said.

"I wouldn't be so quick with that assumption if I was you. See the way I see it is our parents been around longer than us and they can see in us and in a potential mate from their experience, what we could never see, so if they meet them and say no, it's no. Now I firmly believe that and I said to myself that if I ever got married again I would make sure that my mother approved of her first."

"You didn't do that?" Lisa asked.

"Man no, I just showed up to my mom's house and said I'm married this is my wife and this is my child. They never clicked either. At first I thought that is was just because of the way I did it, and they just needed time to get to know each other, but it never happened. We did it in a way that we thought was the right way and for the right reasons and it still it didn't work. So how do you really define what's right?"

"I don't know," Lisa answered.

"You ask God," Tony said. "And we did that. And as far as I am concerned, I really don't care what people think but I do care about what happens to you."

"I'm a big girl," Lisa said. "I can handle myself, besides my name has already been slandered and we haven't done anything but like each other."

"I know," Tony said.

"You need to know something Tony."

"What's that Lisa?"

"For some reason these same people we're talking about have never liked me and have been waiting for years to get something on me. I have worked for years to clean my name and reputation up and keep it clean and still I have been called stupid, slow, homely, and even told that I would always be stuck behind that desk and be alone for the rest of my life because I would never get a man.

"Are we talking about church people?" Tony asked.

"Yep, like you say, church people not God's people and there's a big difference."

"Tony my life there wasn't all that great before you came on the scene in the first place."

"Why so much hate?" Tony asked.

"Well, the position that I have, the one that they have demeaned me for and tried to make me feel like dirt in, is a coveted one."

"Why?" Tony asked.

"Because it's puts you right next to the pastor. A lot of things have to go through me to him and he has allowed me, because of our relationship, to make some calls on some things because he knows that I know what he would want in certain situations, just from working with him for so many years. So I haven't been well liked for a long time and I can't let you take all the blame for this. We may have been able to do some things better but we aren't the reason for all the hate; the situation just brought out the feelings that were already there."

"I feel you. I still think that we need to back off as much as we can to try and keep down some of the mess."

"Too late for that." Lisa said.

"Yeah, maybe you're right."

"Well Lisa, it's getting late and I had better get you home."

"Okay" Lisa said.

"Man, you don't have to be so sad about it."

"Well Tony, I have to say that you have added quite a bit to my life. You're smart, you're funny, you know the Word, even though I don't always get how you get what you get out of the bible, and you are a perfect gentleman. It's funny; you are almost the exact opposite of what people think you are."

"No, right now I think I am closer to being exactly who they think I am, but I have had a heart change and I want to change."

"I know that Tony and it's sad that the place where you came for help to change is so busy judging you that they can't help you."

"It's cool with me because it has taught me never to run to the church or a man again to do for me what only God can do for me in the first place. It should have been a place of safety, it should have been a place where I could have trusted my heart with the elder that I confided in and I shared my hurts with. Instead my business spread through the church like wildfire and someone even went to my ex-wife's house and tried to slander me there as well. What's crazy is we didn't even play that in the streets. In the streets there was a code, families were off limits; you mess with somebody's family and you could lose your life, and wouldn't nobody fault a dude for it because everybody knows you don't mess with nobody's family. These people don't go by any code."

"Nope!

Well Tony, I'm ready."

"Okay" Tony said.

Tony drove Lisa home and then he talked to Lisa on his cell phone on his way home.

"Hey Lisa"

"Yeah Tony"

"I still think we did the right thing by going to the pastor about how we feel about one another. I know in a perfect world we don't walk in and say anything until the divorce is final but what do we do about how we feel right now? It's already been obvious for some time and I'm sure to others. I am the kind of brother that's like this; since I know that stuff is already going to be thought and said about us anyway, no matter how we do it, I'm gonna be the first one to tell on myself."

"I know Tony but do we have to tell everybody?"

"No, only the people that we love and that we know love us. They are the only ones that matter because they are connected to us. But to the folks that don't care nothing about us and don't have our best interest at heart, well they're cut off. I don't deal with haters. Haters are people who are miserable about something and they are mad because you appear to be happy and they don't even want what you got, they just want you to be miserable too, you feel me?"

"Yes Tony, I feel you." Lisa muttered.

"What's the matter Lisa, are you mad at me?"

"No Tony, it's just that this is hard and I didn't sign up for all of this."

"Man, yes you did," Tony said, "as soon as you decided to live in opposition to what the rest of the crowd was doing and actually befriend me and help me and love me anyway like a good Christian should, you signed on the dotted line. Man Lisa look, I am going to keep saying this until you get it. I have seen the love of Christ through you, and not just with me either, man you always root for the underdog and are always helping people out. Man as I watched you working in that office, I was amazed at how many people you counseled throughout the week, and not just that, but helping them out with their resumes, trying to find them jobs, helping them out with resources, and even dealing with their personal stuff and matters of the heart. Man it takes an anointed person to do all that and that's what you are. As a matter of fact that's what they are after."

"Who?" Lisa asked.

"The haters," Tony replied. "What they are really intimidated by, jealous of, attracted too and want all at the same time is your anointing."

"Where do you get that from?" Lisa asked.

"Well, it was something the pastor said to me that I have been thinking about. He wanted to make sure that I was attracted to you and not just your anointing, and I got that. Initially I do believe what attracted me to you was your anointing. That's why I believe that early on I couldn't describe that thing in any other terms than it's just something about you, but over time and through conversation and watching you, I got to know you."

"I see," Lisa said.

"See that same anointing I can have too. I don't have to just desire yours because God wants to give me mine. That's what I mean when I say that two halves don't make a whole. We've all got a spot in us that only God can reach, only He can touch, only He knows where and what it is, only He can fill it, and only He can satisfy it. But instead of asking Him to do it because we don't even know what it is ourselves that we are trying to quench, we try and fill it up with stuff, like alcohol, drugs, food, and sex. When in reality, if we were to let God fill every part before we seek a relationship we would be whole, and complete. Instead, we're looking for someone to touch us in a way that will make us lose our minds." Tony said, laughing.

"Why do you always have to be so demonstrative? Couldn't you have picked another way to say that?"

"Well, if I was talking to a different audience I might, but I am talking to you and it's helping me as I say it and I just got to say it like I get it, as ugly as that is, it's the truth. Listen, ain't nothing wrong with us for wanting somebody. Everybody yearns for somebody. Well in my mind I hear God saying the same thing to us, while we running around destroying our lives, failing in relationships one after another, never being fulfilled and miserable as hell he's saying to us, 'I wish I could have a relationship with you and I promise you I'll never hurt you. If you let Me fill you, you will never be mistaken again about what goes in there. You will be so satisfied you won't desire to eat or drink in excess, and you will find that I am a perfect lover so you won't keep running to each other still ending up empty because only I can fill that place that ever yearns. I can touch what no one can see; I can mend your wounded, broken hearted spirit and make you whole.' The sad thing is there are a lot of us who don't even want to be whole; we are perfectly satisfied with being functionally dysfunctional."

"What makes you say that? Who wouldn't want to be made whole?" Lisa asked.

"Well ME." Tony answered.

"Why?"

"Well, because it's easy. My condition is what's familiar to me and by now it has become my friend, and I will actually fight you if you try and expose it or take it away."

"Sometimes I feel like God bringing you into my life saved my life!"

"Yeah, but I can't heal you," Lisa answered.

"Ah, but the process has begun because you have got me thinking about it."

"I can't tell because every time I bring it up you practically bite my head off."

"That's because I care and I do want to change, because if I didn't I wouldn't be conflicted enough about it to become angry in the first place."

"That just sounds so damn crazy. I hate it when you talk in riddles like that. So anyway; why don't you just stop? Lisa asked.

"I don't know. I tell myself every time afterward that I am not going to drink again and I really mean it too. I will go for a week or two, sometimes months and the next thing you know I end up right back doing the same things I said I would never do."

"Why" Lisa asked.

"Don't know," Tony answered.

"I guess if I knew that, I wouldn't be drinking in the first place."

"So how do you think you got like this?" Lisa asked.

"Well, it sure just didn't just happen one day like some people will tell you. I could go back to the first drink but I think it started way before then, when I was tempted by my co-workers; no even farther back than that. You see Lisa, what makes all this so crazy to me is I was an alcohol and drug counselor for almost ten years. I thought I knew this stuff inside and out. Sometimes my clients would tell me that I didn't know what it was like because I had never been through anything. I'd ask them what they meant and they would say that I had never been addicted like they had. I would try to convince them that I had and I did drugs before but they would just say 'we can tell by the way that you talk to us that you haven't. I never understood that at the time, and it was because I was the -- I can't see how guy."

"What do you mean?" Lisa asked.

"Well I would say, I can't see how a man could drink his life away. I can't see how people can smoke cigarettes. I can't see how a man could leave his wife and kids. I can't see how somebody could lose a good job. Then one night, while in my apartment alone crawling around on my hands and knees looking for something I know I hadn't dropped, I felt as if God himself tapped me on my shoulder and said, My brother, can you see how now?"

"Wow that's deep," Lisa said in amazement.

"Yeah, I had what I like to call a Nebuchadnezzar experience."

"What's that?" Lisa asked

"Well one day King Nebuchadnezzar was walking around admiring all that he had done and bragged about it and even made the statement that it was all for his glory. Man the next thing you know, he was out in the field eating grass like an animal, had hair like eagle feathers and nails like claws, with people walking by asking 'Is that the king?' I did the same thing.

One night I was sitting on my porch looking down at my car parked on the street and said, 'man I got the baddest ride on the block', which wasn't hard to do in the hood, so technically all I was, was hood rich. Not that God blessed me with a good job that would afford me that ride, no *I* did this. I tried to retract it but it seemed even then it was too late; my fate was sealed, not more than two weeks later the car was totaled in an accident and I was nearly decapitated. That wasn't it either, not too long after that, I woke up only after I had wrapped my pickup truck around an oak tree; I hit the steering wheel so hard it broke and broke up my face pretty bad too. One by one, I lost every single thing. I even took out a telephone pole with someone else's car. By the time life was done with me all I had was my work uniforms that I had on my back."

"Man it's a wonder you're still alive," Lisa said.

"Don't be for the grace of God, I wouldn't be."

"I noticed you didn't say God did this to you. Didn't you think He was punishing you?" Lisa asked.

"No and I will tell you why I think that is. I believe that he passed judgment on Nebuchadnezzar because he was a heathen king over God's people and God wanted to let him know who was God. Now when it comes to the people of God, laws were set in place, I look at it like a stop sign. Some people who run it are only worried about the consequences of getting caught, or they don't want to get a ticket or go to jail. But then there are others of us that think, *if I run that stop sign I could be killed or worse yet kill somebody else*. I see the blessings and curses written in Deuteronomy that way like that stop sign; they weren't put there to punish us but it was put there save our lives and even to show us the way to good health and prosperity. Sadly all we see are rules we're not supposed to break and are more worried bout getting in trouble or being punished. So now if we do it enough and nothing happens, we think we're cool and we got away with something. Ah, but there's a law out there that knows no time, yet somewhere in time, you run into the consequences of that thing. Not God's judgment or punishment but rather you meet up with what you've sown, and that's what you end up with. It's funny; we act so brand new every time it happens and get to crying woe is me, wondering *What did I do*? So because we don't want to fess up and be held accountable for our actions we blame it on someone or something else just like they did in the garden; so nothing's really changed. Then if it's severe enough, then that blame goes on God or the devil. No, I lived in direct opposition of what God loved me enough to write down warnings for me to help me not to go there but I did anyway. Now He is loving me enough to let it hurt long enough and hard enough that not only will I get it when it's all over, but I will never go there again, nor will I ever be deceived by it again because it will be so familiar to me; in fact it's so intimate that I will see it coming from miles away next time."

"Wow you've been through a lot, and you've got a powerful testimony."

"Yeah but I wish my testimony could have been that I got it without having to experience some things. I just wish one time I could learn something without having to dang near die first. Man! I want my life to mean more than this miserable existence that I am living in right now. I want to be whole before I die. Man all my life I been looking for what Jesus said in the bible that we can have. He said I came that you might have life and that more abundantly. I barely got life and the only thing I have ever seen in abundance is all the crap that I'm going through."

"I know." Lisa said. "It's like all my life I tried to do the right thing and I was always taught that if you do the right thing that good things will happen to you and that hasn't been the case with me. I have paid my tithes faithfully for years now and even gave when I didn't have it. One time somebody said, you ain't giving until it hurts and I tried that, not because I wanted anything in return, but I just believed that it was what I was supposed to do."

"Yeah, I have been victim of that one too. Sometimes it seemed like they want to guilt you into giving or something. Well I tell you what, though I can't really say that my whole life has been bad though because there have been times when God has really showed up for me in a mighty way." Tony said.

"Like what? Lisa asked.

"One Christmas I was out of work and as a matter of fact, it seemed like for a period of time in my life I ended up unemployed every Christmas for a while there, but anyway I was unemployed; now I hate Christmas."

"Why?" Lisa asked

"Well for one thing, to me it is a pagan, made up holiday that we as Christians have tried to make holy by saying it represents Christ birth but, it's not biblical. Then the other reason I hate it is all the commercialism surrounding it. Man when you got a bunch of kids and you never really had anything yourself all of your life and you want your kids to have some of the stuff your never had, you dread Christmas time; at least I did. It's okay if you've got one or two kids but man, I have a bunch of kids and I hated it. Then I got to thinking, I am not about to stress myself out over this pagan man-made holiday anymore, and I just didn't. I taught my kids what it was supposed to be about, and I wouldn't even have had a tree in my house if I didn't have kids and have to fight with their mom about it. Well one Christmas, I didn't have a job and the kids' mom was all worried about what we gonna do, and I'm like we're gonna live and be glad we alive; and how about celebrating it for what it is really supposed to be about instead of worrying about a bunch of stuff that will just be lying around the house broke up or in a closet forgotten in a few weeks. Well, that didn't go over too well with their mom or the kids. So I went the other way, I told them that God was faithful and that He had never let us down before, and He hadn't, and He would bless us. Now at the same time I am saying this to them, I'm thinking *Lord, I hope you back me up on this*, because what I really wanted them to see out of all of this was God. We got a free tree that year but that was no problem because the Salvation Army did that every year and we did the toys for tots thing and that was no big deal because they did that every year too. Now it was getting close to Christmas and nothing had happened yet, and they were letting me know about it too. 'We thought you said God was going to come through? Don't look like nothing is going to happen.' 'Just wait' I said, 'He ain't done yet.' Now I am really hoping that He shows up. It's now Christmas Eve and I am just done. The whole day went by and nothing. I was really disappointed and a bit confused; I thought why wouldn't God show up? He always had before. Man at about ten-o'clock at night someone knocked on the door. It was a lady at the door explaining that we had been picked by their organization off an angel tree or something and they were sorry that they were so late but they didn't know the area and had trouble finding the house. I looked outside expecting to

174

see a car or at most a pickup or something but it was a box truck! I mean a thirty-two foot box truck! So then I'm thinking, well they probably had other stops to make, so I ask are we your last stop? They said no, you are our only stop. That truck is filled with stuff for you and your family. Man Lisa, they got to unloading that truck and they had diapers, milk, toilet paper, soap, laundry detergent, I mean every practical thing you can imagine. I'm thinking, now these are Christmas presents, not some stupid toys and games, but stuff we really need! But they weren't done, man they brought in food, toys, and games. I was in tears; we were literally overflowing and couldn't fit another thing in the house. I said 'Lord this is enough make it stop.' They finally finished and I thanked them. I was overwhelmed with joy; the kids were squealing in excitement. As I was putting up the food and stuff, looking at all the stuff piled so high we couldn't see the floor or the couch, there was a knock at the door. By the time I turned around to get it, one of the kids was walking up to me handing me an envelope and said 'daddy they said they forgot to give you this.' It looked like it might be a Christmas card so I opened it and it was, but it was also filled with money. I couldn't hold it any longer I just burst into tears right on the spot; I simply couldn't believe it."

"Who were they," Lisa asked.

"Man to this day, I don't know. I tried to find out so I could send them a thank you card or something but I could never find out who it was."

"Wow that's powerful," Lisa said.

"Yeah, you telling me! I still get a little misty every time I tell the story. I have got a few stories like that where God came through for me and my family, so it hasn't been all bad."

"So do you still feel the same way about Christmas?" Lisa asked.

"Yep pretty much," Tony said.

"Even after all of that?" Lisa asked.

"Especially after all of that. Man God came through because He's real and He wanted to teach me that I could trust in Him, and my kids could too; it wasn't about Christmas, Christmas was just the conduit that He used to show up."

"You sure got a funny way of looking at things," Lisa said.

"No, just different," Tony responded. "Anyway Lisa my phone is about to die; we've been talking for hours." Tony said.

"I know."

"Do you get tired of talking to me Tony?"

"Man no, I wish I didn't have to go home sometimes so we could just sit up and talk all night," Tony answered.

"I think like that too sometimes. I was just thinking the other day how much easier it would be if we just lived with each other, I mean not like shacking up or anything I mean…"

"I know what you mean," Tony interrupted. "Okay Lisa I'll talk to you tomorrow."

"Okay Tony, goodnight."

"Goodnight Lisa."

CHAPTER EIGHT

A Fisher of Man

Now the next day at work Lisa had been thinking about all she and Tony talked about the night before. She was a little concerned about how he viewed things, but she thought he really has a lot of potential. At lunch time Tony called.

"Hey Lisa."

"Hey Tony."

"How's your day going Lisa? Tony asked.

"Same ole, same ole," she said.

"And you, Lisa asked.

"It's work," Tony said.

"Tony, I don't see you working in that factory or doing construction and hustling cars the rest of your life. I mean, I know you like fixing things and building stuff and everything, but I can just see you doing something else."

"Like what?" Tony asked.

"I'm not sure, maybe something in an office somewhere."

"Oh, I can't see that," Tony said.

"I can. Isn't there something you have always wanted to do?"

"Yeah, build stuff."

"No Tony, I mean like something else."

Tony thought for a moment and then said "Well, I did want to be an architect at one time."

"Good! See that's what I'm talking about."

"Man, you gotta go to school for like five years to do that."

"AND" Lisa said. "If you get started now you'll only have five years to go."

"Funny!" Tony said.

"What - you scared? I know *you* ain't scared," Lisa said.

"No it's not that," Tony answered.

"Well then, I'm going to a one-stop this weekend to register for school, you should go too."

"Okay" Tony said.

"You don't have to sound so excited about it."

"Oh no, I am," Tony said "Anyway, I've got to get back to work, holla."

"Talk to you later, Tony."

Tony was terrified. He had always wanted to go back to school but the only problem was he had never even finished high school. Tony was always ashamed and embarrassed about it too, and the last thing he wanted to do was to let Lisa know that he didn't finish high school.

That Saturday Tony met up with Lisa and they went together to the campus. Tony was was quiet.

"What's the matter with you Tony?"

"Nothing; I'm cool," Tony answered.

"Well you forgot to tell your face," Lisa said jokingly.

"What?" Tony said.

"It looks like you just saw a ghost or something."

"I just don't like crowds," Tony said.

It was crowded and there were people everywhere. There were no clear walking lanes and people were brushing up against them. Tony was agitated, he really didn't like crowds.

"Where are we supposed to go? Ain't no signs or nothing."

Lisa laughed, "Just follow the crowd MAN!"

"Where? Everybody is running all over the place."

"Well, see those tables over there?"

"Yeah" Tony said.

"That's where we're going,"

"But where's the line?

"We're in it," Lisa said.

"Man it's gotta be hundreds of people in front of us."

Lisa laughed, "It goes fast Tony, trust me."

"Man I don't know about this Lisa. I think I should come back when it's not that many people around."

Lisa laughed, "This is the last registration so you have to do it now. They will be registering all weekend and it's not going to get any better than this. Just be patient."

"Alright"

They made it through the line and Lisa got registered on the spot. She had her paperwork, transcripts, and everything ready and was all set to go. Tony however, was given a list of requirements that he had to fulfill, and he had to take a placement test. Tony was relieved because he figured there was no way he would be able to get all of this done in a weekend let alone that day. Tony was relieved because he thought he was off the hook.

"Well, how'd it go?" Lisa asked.

"Uh, I filled out a bunch of paperwork and then I gotta get a bunch of paperwork back and then I gotta take a placement test. Looks like I'm not going to be able to register." Tony said confidently.

"Yes you will. You take the placement test right down the hall and once you do that you can register for classes and they give you till almost the end of the semester to get all your stuff in."

"Man! I gotta take a test today?"

"Yeah but it's not a big deal, you're here now so you may as well go on and do it." Lisa said.

"Man that could take hours!" Tony said.

"You won't die! Now go on, I will be right here at the computers registering for my classes."

"Man! I wasn't trying to do all this. "

"I know Tony, now you better hurry because it looks like they're about to shut the door."

Tony walked into the testing center just in time, as they were shutting the door for that session. There was testing all day and all weekend on the hour. This was a college entrance exam to determine what level of classes you needed to start at. The testing was grueling. Tony hadn't been in school in years and the testing took hours. There were breaks in between each section but that didn't matter to Tony; it was hell for him. Tony finally finished with the testing and found Lisa still standing at the computers just like she said she would. Tony was ready to go, he'd had enough.

"You ready? Tony asked.

"For what? Are you done?

"Yeah" Tony said.

"Okay, now we've got to go to financial aid."

"ARE YOU KIDDING ME?" Tony screamed "We still ain't done!"

"Nope, now we have to go sign our FASFA," Lisa said.

"Oh that form I filled out online?" Tony asked

"Yes" Lisa answered.

"Well how long is that going to take?" Tony asked.

"You are really impatient," Lisa snapped.

They turned the corner to the hall where the financial aid office was and Tony gasped.

"Man is that the line?"

"Yes Tony! It goes fast."

Tony and Lisa arrived at the college at eight that morning and didn't leave until about four that afternoon. Tony was hungry and angry. Tony was always hungry and Lisa said that his feeding pattern was like that of a baby, every two to three hours. Tony had to have something to eat.

"Well that wasn't too bad," Lisa said.

"Man that was hell!" Tony responded.

Lisa laughed and said "Oh you'll live man."

"Not if I don't get something to eat soon," Tony answered.

"Well there's a Taco stand right there."

Before Lisa could even finish her sentence, Tony was headed to the parking lot. Lisa liked to dine in but Tony never wanted to be still long enough for that, he'd much rather eat while driving. Lisa hated that, she thought that he'd never get caught drunk driving but driving while eating he could kill somebody. Tony would drop something in his lap or on the floor and then bend down to pick it up! That horrified Lisa. He'd also be looking everywhere but in front of him, even looking at her while he was talking. They argued all the time about his driving. He drove too fast and he never paid attention to where he was going.

Lisa asked, "Tony can we eat inside?"

"Man, I don't care, I'm just hungry. Man I'm hungrier than a Lobo Wolf in the Mojave desert with no drinking water."

"I don't know what that means but it sounds like you must be mighty hungry," Lisa said as they sat down. Tony could eat! When he was ordering she thought he was ordering for the both of them.

"Tony, where do you get all those sayings from?"

Tony laughed, "Well just from being around different people over the years. I have been from the east coast to the west coast and literally around the world."

"How?"

"Well I was born in Colorado then we moved Kansas then I came back here when my mom and dad split. Then when I got grown I lived in three other different states, then I came back here to Parker. Plus I literally traveled around the world while in the military."

"YOU were in the military?"

"Yep"

"How come you never said anything?"

"You never asked."

"I've never been anywhere," Lisa said sadly.

"How come you ended up in so many different places?"

"Well some of the places that I lived, I knew someone there and they would tell me that the jobs at this or that place were good, and I would just take off and go. I did construction and you could literally walk off one jobsite and onto another in the same day."

"I think I would be scared to just pack up and go like that. Weren't you scared?"

"Man no, that's living. I like living on the edge. I am a spur of the moment kind of guy and I like to be able to just take off and go, plus I love to travel."

"I love to travel too but moving around just wouldn't work for me. I have to have stability."

"You could have stability and travel too," Tony said.

"How?" Lisa asked

"Man my granny travels every year. She plans these trips and lays them away. She's even been to Hawaii."

"Wow, I would like to be able to do that. I just don't have the money."

"Well if God says yes and we end up married I promise you an adventurous life and we'll see the world," Tony said smiling.

"I actually believe that," Lisa said.

"You do?" Tony said in surprise.

"Yes Tony. It's like I always tell you, I really believe you have a lot of potential and I think you can do anything you put your mind to. I wouldn't be surprised if you end up being a millionaire someday."

"I will at least be a thousandaire," Tony said, and they both laughed.

"So how do you like the whole school experience so far?" Lisa asked.

"Well it sucks so far and it's so dang crowded."

"I know it always starts out like that but it will thin out by mid semester."

"So did you get all of your stuff done?" Lisa asked.

"No, they need my high school transcript and some of my military stuff or something like that."

"Well good, that should be no problem you can just get that from your school; they'll send that right over. They do that all the time."

"I don't know," Tony said

"That might be a problem."

"Why?"

"I didn't finish school."

"WHAT!" Lisa said.

"I said..." Lisa cut him off. She couldn't believe what she just heard.

"I heard what you said. So do you have your GED?"

"But I thought you said you were a state certified counselor or did you lie about that too?"

"No but I am still a state certified counselor. I didn't lie!"

"Well how did you get away with all that

186

without having your high school diploma or GED?"

"They never asked," Tony answered

"So like I said; you lied."

"No, like I said no one ever asked. I'm sorry Lisa I wanted to say something but I was embarrassed. I just didn't get school and I don't know why, but I struggled with it and finally once my grades got so bad that I was ineligible to play sports I lost the desire to go all together. Then I got into some legal trouble and it was like either go to the military or go to jail, so I went into the military, and still ended up in jail."

"For what?"

"I threatened an officer. I was just playing but he was a boot, a midshipman, and he was scared.

"He reported me and I got sent to the brig."

"So you never finished school?" Lisa asked again.

"That's what I said," Tony answered, clearly agitated.

"Well, you've got to go back and make that thing right."

"How?" Tony asked.

"Take your GED test," Lisa said.

"Man how long is that gonna take?"

"I don't know but you need to get on it right away so you can make the deadline."

"What deadline?"

"The deadline you have to get all your paperwork in. Tony life is a process and you skipped some steps, so you've got to go back and complete the process. You have got to take your GED exam."

"Man I can't do that?" Tony said.

"Yes you can. It's not that hard. You can probably pass it on the first try."

"That's easy for you to say, you ain't the one that's got to do it," Tony replied.

"You can do it."

"If you say so," Tony said.

Tony did get all of his other paperwork in and started classes on time with Lisa. Tony even told the counselor that he didn't have his GED yet, they told him that it wouldn't be a problem and that they would give him the time he needed to turn it in but he wouldn't be able to start the second semester without it. Lisa was tickled. For the first time she finally saw fear in Tony's eyes. Passing the GED really worried him.

Tony spent the next three weeks studying for the GED exam. He called Lisa the night before the test. "Hey Lisa,"

"Hey Tony, you ready?"

"Man I guess so," Tony answered.

"So have you been studying?"

"Yeah, but I'm not sure I got it."

"Oh you'll do fine," Lisa said confidently.

"Man you always say that Lisa, but I don't know; this is a lot of stuff to try to remember in such a short period of time."

"Well you are the one who said that you like living life on the edge." Lisa laughed.

"Man that ain't funny." Tony said with a look of disgust.

"Yes it is! Remember, you ain't afraid of nothing. I wish you could see the look of horror on your face right now. So what time is the test?"

"It's at eight tomorrow morning."

"Oh you should do good then since you're a morning person." Lisa laughed again.

"Lisa I gotta go, I need to go over this math again."

"Oh, okay but don't study too much because it can backfire on you."

"Okay Lisa, I gotta go."

Tony studied until his eyes burned then closed the book and begin to pray.

Lord you know that people have always thought I was smart, but you and I know the real story. I am really going to need your help tomorrow with this test.

The next morning Tony was up early. He made himself a big breakfast. To Tony, that was the most important meal of the day. Tony had always thought that if there was any meal he had to miss it wouldn't be breakfast. He wolfed it down as usual;

he always ate fast. Lisa would always say, "whoa man slow down chew your food at least thirty times before you swallow." Tony would always say "man I can't hold my food in my mouth that long."

Tony went off to take the test. He didn't call Lisa that morning because he didn't want to deal with her teasing. He took the test. Tony was usually pretty sure about things but he couldn't get a feel for this one. He felt like he might have done okay on some parts of it but wasn't sure if it was enough to pass. He called Lisa.

"Hey Lisa"

"Hey Tony, how'd it go?"

"I don't know." Tony said.

"Well do you feel like you passed?"

"I don't know, I hope so." Tony said.

"I'm sure you did." Lisa responded.

"So what do you have planned for today Tony?"

"Nothing man, I'm wiped out. I just want to relax today. What I want to do is go fishing. I don't even care if I catch anything. I just want to sit by the water with my pole in my hand."

"Oh man you fish?"

"Yeah, I used to fish all the time with my kids."

"You don't anymore?"

"No, my ex won't let me see them and the ones that are grown are either too hurt over the breakup or too afraid to cross her to be around me."

"Well I wanna go," Lisa said.

"You like to fish? Tony asked.

"Yes, I used to go fishing with my dad. I wouldn't bait the hook and when I would catch a fish he'd take the fish off for me but I just like the excitement of a fish being on the end of my pole."

Tony laughed "You ain't no fisherman."

"You're right, I'm a fisherwoman." They both laughed.

"Okay then let's go." Tony said.

Tony kept his fishing gear with him at all times in the trunk of his car so all they had to do was get the bait. There was a bait and tackle shop right near the water so that was no problem. They pulled up to the bank and got out of the car but Tony didn't pull his gear.

"What's wrong," Lisa asked.

"Nothing; just thinking."

"Are you going to fish?" Lisa asked.

"Later, I need to talk right now. Can we just talk?"

"Sure" Lisa said. "Let's sit on that bench over there."

"Lisa, you know I go for my divorce next week.

"Yes, well is she going to sign the papers this time?"

"Well she said she would under some conditions but we'll see how that goes."

"Anyway Lisa, if it should happen to be final, I just wanted to be sure that you know what you are getting into."

"What do you mean?" Lisa asked.

"Well Lisa, I have got a lot of issues."

"Like what?"

"Well there's just a lot that you don't know about me that could come out, and I just thought I needed to tell you rather than you hear it from someone else."

"What?" Lisa asked, trying her best to remain calm.

"Well, uh, man, I don't know if you are ready for this,"

"Oh come on Tony, how bad could it be it's not like you're a murderer or something."

Tony didn't say anything. "Oh my God Tony what is it!" Lisa said while panicking on the inside. "Well, you are close. I was involved in a death. It was self-defense, but this was in a no self-defense state so it's ruled involuntary."

"Oh my God what happened?"

"Well it's kind of ugly, are you sure you want to hear about it?" Tony said.

"I don't want details; I just want to know how or why it happened."

"He thought I robbed him. I knew who did, but I didn't do it. The last thing he said was, "somebody ain't going home tonight!"

"Wow, that's horrible."

"You telling me," Tony said. "For the longest time I could still see his face, and I could see him slumped on the ground. I still wonder sometimes till this day if I'm gonna get mine for that."

"How did you ever get over it," Lisa asked.

"I didn't. I came back here and I started going to church. I used to go the altar every week and cry to God and ask for forgiveness and ask him to take it away, but it's like he couldn't hear me or something. Then one Sunday this sister walked up to me as I was on my way up to the alter and said 'brother Tony the Lord told me to tell you he's forgiven you, you just need to forgive yourself.' She said, if it seems like he doesn't hear you it's because he doesn't once you repented of it and asked for forgiveness. He threw it into a sea of forgetfulness'. Man I broke right there on the spot, sobbing in relief with that sister holding me in her arms. The crazy thing about it is, I don't even know who she was and I never seen her again afterwards."

"Wow that's deep." Lisa said. They sat in silence for a while then Lisa finally said,

"Man do you have ANYTHING else I should know about?"

"Yeah, I've got warrants right now and I have a pretty long rap sheet and when they catch up with me I will probably have to do some time."

"WHAT!" Lisa asked. "What did you do?"

"Well, I violated probation for one thing and the rest is just traffic stuff."

"So do you even have driver's license?" Lisa asked.

"Nope"

"What!" Lisa screamed in frustration. "You've got me riding around with you and you've got warrants, AND you don't have a driver's license. Man are you crazy!"

"Yep, Lisa I told you that I wasn't no good."

"Yeah, Tony but I didn't know that you would put my life in jeopardy."

"Man your life ain't in no jeopardy. It ain't that serious!" Tony said calmly.

"Nothing's that serious to you Tony. It's like this stuff don't faze you but this is serious to me. I could get in trouble or go to jail just for being with you!"

"No Lisa, that's not how it works."

"Well then why don't you tell me how it works MAN? Put my mind at ease."

"Well at most they stop us they and take me to jail, and bound me over for court but they'll just run a check on you, and if you come up clean they'll let you go."

"Let me go!" Lisa yelled. "I don't want them to get me in the first place."

Tony laughed, "Man you'll be alright, you're safe with me."

"I can't tell!" Lisa yelled. They were silent for a moment again.

"Well if you don't want to be around me anymore I understand."

"Well I can tell you one thing for sure, I'm driving back and I am never riding with you again not until you get your license. I hate that car anyway."

"Okay, okay!" Tony laughed.

"It's not funny Tony, have you lost your mind? You gotta go turn yourself in and clean that mess up!"

"I know," Tony said.

"Well when? Lisa asked.

"As soon as my divorce is final and I get some more money."

"What does money have to do with it?"

"Everything! That's all it's really about at this level. If you've got the money to pay, it will go easier. It ain't nothing but a few minor misdemeanors, plus the violation of probation, which I probably will do some time for that one, but since I'm working that will just be work release."

"Just!" Lisa screamed. "You act like it's no big deal. For real -- are you serious?"

"Well it's not really a big deal. I've been through all this before and I didn't die. I will just be uncomfortable for a while but I'll be alright."

"Tony this is too much."

"So you are you having second thoughts?"

"YOU THINK!! Wouldn't you?"

"Yes, I was wondering why you put up with me for this long."

"Oh believe me buddy, if it weren't for God I wouldn't be and I don't know if I want to continue this. You have been lying to me this whole time."

"Lying?"

"Yes lying!"

"Man I didn't lie; I just withheld information that's all."

"And that's another thing Tony; you really need to stop that!"

"What?"

"Tony listen, it's like with your GED... Tony you lied and you are a liar. If it's one thing I cannot tolerate is a liar."

"I'm not a liar."

"YES you are! Whether you told one or withheld information as you call it, you lied and you are a liar. You practice lying. If that's how you've been living your life and you held that all this time, then you have been living a lie and NO I do not want to even be associated with a liar, let alone friends. Tony I can't trust you. There is no telling how much I still don't know because you withhold information."

"I have told you everything."

"I can't trust that Tony."

"So we're done?"

"Yes Tony. You have to be a man and you need to go clean that mess up. I can't be with you like this."

"Okay" There was silence again.

Then Tony asked "Well can we have one more walk together along the pier."

"I guess so Tony."

Lisa was fuming mad.

Now as they walked along the pier, an elderly couple was walking in front of them headed toward them hand in hand.

"Man!"

"What?" Lisa asked still fuming.

"To think that could have been us in a few years."

"And nobody said it couldn't be Tony, you just got a lot of stuff to take care of and if you do that then *maybe* we'll see, but I have come too far in my life to go backward. I have to have peace and I value my peace over anything and I'd be crazy to let all this drama in my life right now or ever."

"Okay, okay you made your point."

'Tony if you are trying to get me to shut up, it's not going to work. You put me at risk of getting into all kinds of trouble. I let you drive the church van and everything and you never said a word about not having a driver's license. *And I know*, I didn't ask. That's just crazy; you just don't do people like that!"

"I know," Tony said.

"Then why do you do it then, if you know? You're so use to doing people; you'll probably do your own mother."

"That was uncalled for," Tony said.

"Maybe so but that's just where I am right now. I just don't know what to believe about you, or what to think. Just don't talk, just walk!"

"Okay," Tony said.

Now the elderly couple was getting closer.

"Well hello," they said, "And look at the happy couple."

Tony laughed but Lisa grunted. They began to talk. The lady asked them if they knew the Lord they said yes, she said good. "So how long have you two been married?"

"We're not," Lisa snarled, Tony chuckled; Lisa punched him.

The couple chuckled too and asked.

"Engaged?"

"No," they answered.

"Oh, I'm sorry. You just look like you should be together; so why aren't you?" the lady asked. Lisa just looked at Tony.

Then Tony said, "Well it's complicated, we do like each other and I hope we can be married one day, but I have a few issues that I have got to clean up first."

The elderly gentleman asked his wife, "sound familiar?" The couple laughed.

"Well it can't be as bad as our story," he said. The couple began to share with Tony and Lisa about how he was doing life in prison for a murder with no possibility for parole. His wife was a prison missionary that would visit the prison witnessing to inmates. The man wanted nothing to do with God, but she didn't give up on him. She'd send him letters, literature, books, and even a bible. He said he even tore a page out of the bible and used it to roll a cigarette, thinking that, that was all it was good for. Finally one day he gave his heart to God. They stayed in contact, they fell in love, and decided to get married. That's when she spoke and said "yeah and my family, especially my kids thought I had really gone insane. They wanted to have me committed, but I had prayed about it and I knew that God had really touched his heart and he really had a heart change and that I would be alright, and God said yes. We got married and months later appealed to the parole board and after much prayer and deliberation, he finally got paroled. The man spoke up and said, "now I am about to become an ordained minister."

"Wow, that's powerful," Lisa said in amazement.

Tony was speechless, plus he remembered that Lisa told him not to speak so he didn't say anything. It wasn't that he was scared of Lisa but he did respect her and he didn't want to totally blow it. The lady then told Lisa that she would be going to an event called the Great Banquet and she would like her to be her special guest. She told Tony that this was an all women's event and that they would be doing it for men soon and he could be the guess of her husband at that time. Tony said "If I'm around."

The man asked, "What do you mean?"

Tony feeling comfortable enough to share, with all they had shared with him said, "Well you wouldn't believe how similar our stories are but anyway, I will probably be away for a while; so if I am free, if you know what I mean, I'd love too." The elderly man belly laughed and said "Son you really have no idea about the power of God do you? You'll be fine, trust me," he said.

"Oh I know I will, it's not me I'm worried about."

Lisa knowing he was referring to her said, "Tony I'm a big girl and I'll be fine."

Tony hoped so; he desperately did not want to lose Lisa, at least as a friend. He felt like marriage, at this point, was probably out of the question, "but if she'll just be my friend," he thought, "that would be enough." They exchanged contact information and the elderly woman told Lisa that she would pick her up early the next morning.

Tony asked Lisa, "Can I speak now?"

"What Tony," Lisa responded, still mad at him.

"Well Lisa, I promise you that I am going to turn myself in and I am going to clean all this mess up and..."

"Tony," Lisa interrupted. "I don't believe anything you say at this point, so you are wasting your time. Instead of trying to say anything to me with your mouth, how about you just do it, okay?"

"Okay Lisa."

"Now take me home, I've got to get up in the morning."

"Okay Lisa," Tony said, "Are you going to drive?"

"NO! I told you, I hate that car, no I am not driving, and you just better be careful cause If we get pulled over..."

"Okay, okay man, let me hurry up and get you dropped off before you bite my head off, man!"

"I feel more like drop kicking you right here. I'm so mad at you right now Tony. I don't know what I'm going to do, but from what that lady said about the Great Banquet this weekend, it looks like I will have plenty of time to talk to God about it because right now, I don't want anything to do with you!"

"Okay," Tony said.

The ride home was a quiet one. Tony pulled up to Lisa's and she jumped out the car even before it had come to a full stop. Tony tried to get out to walk her to the door, but Lisa yelled "DON'T! Tony just go!"

Tony got back in the car and peeled off. Lisa yelled "Your ass needs to go to jail. You still ain't learned! I hope they take your ass to jail." She went in the house mumbling, "crazy, that man is just crazy, and I'm crazy for even trusting him. Lord what's up with that? You said trust him and trust you. Now I know I must have heard from the devil or something, unless I just wanted to believe so bad. That's it! Why do I keep doing this to myself, I'm just sick of it! He's always calling me on that damn cell phone too; he better not call me either! I'm not gonna answer the phone if he does call." Lisa went over to the phone and snatched it off the hook and threw it across the room. "NOW! Call that! You hear me? Call that! You bad, Mr. Man. He ain't no man, he's a liar. Lord You wouldn't send me no liar, You know I hate liars, he ain't from You. That man is from the pit of hell. He ain't nothing but the devil himself. I knew I shouldn't have ever talked to him. The day he walked in the church I knew it was something wrong with him, and he was a drug dealer, and he KILLED SOMEBODY! Lord, what's going on?

Haven't I had enough hell in my life that I have got to go through this too! The elders were right; I have lost my damn mind. I was deceived. Oh man! That explains a lot. I was wondering why everybody would always look at me so crazy when we were together. This is the devil himself. STUPID, that's what I am, just plain ole stupid." Lisa screamed. "I am just so done!" Lisa continued to slam stuff around as she pulled out her suitcase to pack for tomorrow's event.

Now as Tony was driving home he was nervous about being pulled over; he couldn't understand it. He was never worried about it before but after talking with Lisa he was paranoid. His phone buzzed, it was always on vibrate, and he about jumped out of his skin. It's Lisa he thought. He fumbled for it but the phone fell as he reached for it. He was so nervous. He started to bend down to pick it up then he thought about what Lisa said about his driving when they argued once about it. He pulled the car over and parked then grabbed his phone. He was even wearing his seatbelt now because of Lisa insisting he do so. "It's the law," she told him. "Why is it so hard for you to obey the law," she asked him one time. He promised her he'd do better but he knew she didn't believe him. She got so mad at him once, she told him that his actions spoke so loudly that she couldn't hear what he was saying. Tony answered his phone. "Lisa," he said excited.

"No I'm sorry; it's the lady from the park."

"Oh," Tony said.

She said "Tony I got your number from my husband from when you guys exchanged information. I hope you don't mind."

"No I'm cool, what's up," Tony said.

"Well, as you know I am sponsoring Lisa for the Great Banquet and part of what we do is ask family members to write a letter for them and at a point in the program, we present the letters from their loved ones and friend. And it just dawned on me that I don't know any of Lisa's family or friends so I am going to need your help."

"Oh, well I don't know how much help I am going to be able to be for you. Lisa's mad at me right now and I really don't know any of her family and friends like that. Her kids don't know me and don't really like me, and they don't trust me I guess, and her mother doesn't really know me either, so…"

"Oh, I'm sure you'll do fine."

Tony thought, "Why do people keep telling me that?"

"Okay I'll do my best. What are we supposed to write?" Tony asked.

"Well we usually ask that you tell her all that she is to you and all that she has been over the years and how much you appreciate her and love her for it. It's a letter of encouragement."

"I guess I can do that."

Tony didn't know how he was going to do it, but he knew he had to try. The last thing he wanted was for Lisa to get to that part of the ceremony and not have any letters to read. Tony got a hold of her daughter. She was the oldest and she lived right around the corner from her mom, so he knew where to find her. Now she *really* didn't like Tony, she didn't trust him. She had a friend that knew him from the streets and he didn't have anything good to say about Tony at all. She thought her mother was crazy and stupid not to see Tony for what he was, and she even told her so, right in front of him. Her daughter found out that he was still married and decided to confront them about it. She got her brothers to come with her to do an intervention of sorts, and she let her mother have it too. She said, "You taught us better than this. Why would you take up with this no good man? This man is a thug and on top of that he's a married man!"

Tony tried to interject and she stopped him and said, "Wait a minute playa; you don't have anything to say here, this is family business and you ain't family, and as far as we're concerned if you don't like it you can just bounce."

Tony knocked on the door remembering all of this and wondering if she would even open the door.

"Who is it she yelled."

He knew she had seen him pull up. He saw her peeking out the window at him.

"It's Tony," he said.

"What do you want?" She yelled.

"Hey, I need a favor."

"You ain't got no favors here playa; you must of thought you knocked on my mom's door or something. You can just get to stepping before I call 911," she yelled through the door.

"Wait please, not for me it's for your mom."

She snatched the door open but the chain was still on. She almost yanked it out of the wall.

"Why? What did you do to my mom?"

"Nothing," Tony laughed.

"I don't see anything funny. You've got two minutes mister."

"Man, you are just like your mom," Tony mumbled.

"What was that I heard? I ain't nothing like my mom, because I would have seen through you and dropped you a long time ago. As a matter of fact, I would have never talked to you in the first place; now spit it out before I slam this door in your face."

"Okay, Tony said. "Well your mom is going to this program tomorrow and the lady asked me to ask the family to write her some letters."

"What lady? And letters for what?"

"I'm getting to that," Tony said, struggling for words trying to get it out.

"Well make it snappy, I don't have all day and I don't want anybody to see you standing here either."

"Okay! We met this elderly couple at the pier and the lady invited your mom to this thing called the Great Banquet and she said that at a point in the ceremony or something they present them with letters from home and since she just met your mom she called me and asked me if I could..."

She cut him off, "Man you'd better be glad it's for my mom. What do we have to say?"

"Well, just that you love her and stuff, and how much she has meant to you over the years and stuff like that. It's supposed to be for encouragement or something."

"Man, I tell you, you can't be all bad because it took a lot of courage for you to show up here and think anybody would even hear anything you had to say. I started not to even open the door. Now how is she going to get them?"

"Well you guys write them and I will drop them off at the church."

"When do they have to have them?"

"Tomorrow, I think they are going to present them Sunday night."

"Alright, I'll see what I can do."

"Okay, well tell your brothers okay?" Tony said.

"I *said* I will see what I can do man, now don't press your luck. Now get away from my door before I call the police and tell them that it's a stalker outside."

"Okay," Tony laughed.

"I ain't playing," she said.

"I know you're not, and I'm leaving right now."

Tony backed away. He could see a faint smile on her face as he backed up, and he knew he had almost made her laugh, the way he was backing away but he didn't dare, as she said, press his luck.

Lisa was all packed and ready to go. She set her alarm clock and slumped down in the chair. She saw the phone on the floor across the room and thought she had better hang it up in case the lady needed to call.

"He better not call me, either," she thought.

The lady had given Lisa strict instructions on what to bring and what not to bring. No cell phone, no watches, no radios, but bring hygiene items that they would need and not to worry if she forgot anything because there would be some there just in case. Now even though Lisa had no idea what to expect, she had expectations about meeting God there. She had decided that one of the things she would definitely be talking to God about was this Tony situation. She had had enough, she had to know, like Tony always said, if it was live or

Memorex. She thought about how strange it was that they should meet that couple right at that time, right as she was having second thoughts. It hadn't dawned on her until now, because she was so angry with Tony, that she was about to get in the car the next morning and go off with a perfect stranger and go God knows where. She had never done anything like that before.

"Tony has got me losing my mind, I can't believe I am about to do this. Too late now," she thought, "I already said yes."

Lisa began to pray:

Lord, please forgive me for swearing and throwing a tantrum. It's that Tony! Lord, YOU know. Lord I pray that you show up this weekend. I don't know what's in store but I really need you to show up. I am really at my wits end. In Jesus' name Amen.

Tony got the letters and dropped them off at the church like he was asked. He only got letters from her kids, her grandson, and himself. He was hesitant about giving his letter. He really wanted Lisa to hear from God and the last thing he wanted to do was upset her in any way. The lady came out to the car to get them. Tony told her that that was the best he could do and that he wished he could have gotten more. The lady told Tony that it was okay because they also had past participants who would write them letters as well and that they also have people praying around the clock for them. She thanked Tony and said "God bless you."

The lady picked Lisa up that evening from her house just like she said she would. Lisa didn't actually know where she was being taken to and didn't care; she just needed a few days away from all the drama of Tony, the church, and her children. She left everything for some place she didn't know and would spend days with people she didn't know. The thought dawned on her that this woman could pick her up and murder her. She thought the thought came from being around Tony with all his drama. All kinds of strange things were on her mind but she needed time and real peace. When they finally pulled up to the church, there had to be at least 100 people all around, laughing and smiling and saying "God bless you." They all seemed genuine. Lisa could feel God's presence all around. Her sponsor took her bag and bedding and went inside the building where there was a button with her name on it. It felt very official. Her sponsor went on to show her where she would be sleeping. It was a room with 12 mattresses side by side. The sponsor made her bed as she watched. After making the bed, they mingled with other women who were also guests. Lisa felt totally at home. They spent time chatting with one another and then suddenly, as if there was a call or something, every man left the building. All the women were told to gather in the gym. As they started toward the gym, Lisa no longer had a sense of time. Every clock was covered up. They were then told to put all watches and cell phones in a bucket to be claimed when it was time to leave.

Lisa grew anxious and excited because she knew this would be the place where she would be able to hear a clear word from God. That's what I need more than anything; just to wrap up in His arms and cry because her life seemed to be a total mess.

She thought, "How could I allow myself to go utterly crazy?"

She didn't want to think about Tony or any other responsibilities. She thought to herself, "I just need to take care of myself. I need to be comforted, to be held by God, to be told that I'm not crazy."

After all the cell phones and watches were collected, they had a brief meeting about the rules. The rules were no outside contact with family or friends, no peaking at clocks, and to spend time getting to know each other and spend time with God.

That night they had a nice service in which they shared their burdens. It brought her to tears. The next instruction was for them to not speak a word to each other until breakfast the next morning. It was only 8:30 p.m. She was used to staying up until 1 or 2 o'clock in the morning. "Huh, don't speak, that's going to be easy," she thought.

But what happened is while she was not speaking (or begging God for something) a funny thing happened, God started speaking to her. There had been so much drama going on in her life that God's voice had been drowned out. Now, it was as if she had tuned into the right channel. She did pray that night for God to give her some understanding and some clarification as to what was going on with her. She asked the Lord why she was being treated so harshly at church. He told her that she had allowed people to walk all over her and so they did. He told her that it was up to her to say no when she needed to. He also told her that He allowed the perception of the relationship with Tony so that she could see the true character of the people that she had been with for so many years. He knew that she would not have seen it otherwise. He reminded her that during trials and tribulations, what comes out in frustration is really what's in the heart of man. The Lord reminded her about the dream she had about Tony.

She dreamed that they were married and it seemed like they were a happy couple. The Lord reminded her that only He could repair relationships, repair reputations, and hold a relationship together, if He wills. She asked the Lord, what was her ministry, and where does she

212

go from here? The Lord said, "Tony is your ministry, and I showed you the end before the beginning." She did get excited trying to figure out what type of timeline this would be, but there was only the word "wait." She said, "Lord, please give me confirmation through some woman here that I'm not having a conversation with myself but, that this is truly from you because I surely can't make sense of it myself. My flesh does not want to appear foolish and yet that is exactly what it looks like to everyone, including myself."

She finally drifted off to sleep. She slept harder than usual and woke up refreshed to the faint sound of instrumental music. It was so soothing. She felt rested, relieved, curious, and anxious to talk to the Lord some more because she felt like she had His undivided attention. Who knew that I would meet a total stranger who would bring me to a place where I could talk to the Lord? But God knew and she was ever so grateful for that.

At breakfast the group began to break the fast with talking and laughing. It seemed that each woman had had a similar experience with God that night. It was the most awesome experience she'd had in years. Just to be close to the Lord is awesome she thought. There were many group activities and singing and testimonies throughout the weekend, as well as bonding with God and the group. She had almost forgot what she prayed for until she heard one testimony that struck her to the core. This woman stood before them telling what sounded like her exact story with Tony. She thought she would pass out. She couldn't believe it. She said all the things that Lisa had been thinking, the shame, the agony, the way she was treated by her church and family but she survived it and God restored her reputation and she was six years on the other side of where Lisa was. Lisa could not believe it. She looked over at Lisa and says "God wants you to know that he loves you and you heard from Him, but there are consequences if you move too fast but He will restore you." Lisa was shaking now. She knew that God said yes, she was to marry Tony. However, she couldn't see how. She only knew for sure that he was the ministry, her ministry, the biggest ministry she had ever had in her life. Lisa knew from that day forward that Tony would always have to be in her prayers.

On that Sunday morning, the women were gathered at tables within groups when they were presented with letters. Lisa opened her bag of letters and the very first letter she pulled out of the bag was from Tony; a letter professing his love for her. He wrote that he believed that they were destined to serve together in the ministry someday, and he wrote that she had made a positive impact on his life. The next letter was from her daughter who said she admired her and loved her. The next letter from her oldest son who said how much he loved her and appreciated all that she had done for him over the years. The next letter was from her youngest son who said he loved her. Then she opened the letter that made her flow in tears, from her grandson who had drawn a picture with the words I love you scrolled across the bottom. Lisa lost it and burst into tears.

After reading letters they gathered in the sanctuary where everyone gave their testimony of what God had done for them while there that weekend. Lisa told everyone that she had come to hear an answer from God on a question that would change her entire life and God answered. Her sponsor told everyone of how they met. Everyone was in awe that they had just met, practically hours before Lisa was picked up for this event. She closed by saying that she was just being a fisher of man.

CHAPTER NINE

Sense and Nonsense

Tony was at home and he was miserable not being able to talk to Lisa. They talked every day at least three or more times a day and to be without her for that long was torture. Tony began praying that God help him to get his life in order.

Lord he said, *I know that I haven't been the best cat in the world, but You know I love You even though my actions don't show it most of the time. Lord, I want to do right, but I just can't seem to do it. People keep telling me that I will be just fine but I can't tell.*

Tony then wrote some words that came to him that he figured he might use as a song later on.

Lord who am I that Thou art mindful of me, I don't want to live like this, but I don't want to die like this, and yet why you love me so is something I will never know. You laid down your life for me, gave me a new song to sing, and in spite of all the wrong I have done, still promised you'd never let go...

Tony then stopped and began to pray again.

Lord I am just so tired. I am so sick of myself and I don't know what to do. I ruined my marriage, ruined my kid's lives, and the last thing

I want to do is to bring somebody else into my mess. Lord she doesn't deserve this, she deserves better than me. Lisa is right Lord, I am a liar. Lord, I don't want to live a lie anymore. Lord I don't even trust myself. You know Lord, I talk to You all the time, I have said every time that if You get me out of this, I will never do it again and I end up in the same crap all over again. Well Lord this time, I'm not asking for You to bail me out. Leave me in my crap. I got in it and I can find my way out and if I don't that's okay because I would rather die trying than to live like this another day. Lord I am not even going to ask You for Lisa. Do what you want with that; maybe if I lose her it will finally wake me up or something, I don't know. I don't blame her for not wanting to be bothered with me, heck I don't want to be bothered with me half the time. Lord if nothing else let my divorce be final this week. I really don't know how much more I can take of this. And Lord help me to restore my relationship with my kids, because this has been horrible on them. In Jesus' name Amen.

Now Tony was bugging out. He had to talk to someone so he called his friend Jaxon.

"Hello," Jaxon said.

"Hey Jaxon, what you doing?"

"Talking to you," Jaxon said.

"Funny! Hey, can you come and get me?"

"You okay?" Jaxon asked.

"Yeah, I'm cool I just need to get out for a minute," Tony said.

"Well what's wrong with your car?"

"Nothing, I got into it with Lisa and I promised her I wouldn't drive until I got my license back."

"What's up with that?" Jaxon asked.

"Nothing - I ain't supposed to be driving."

"I mean, I know that, but that never stopped you before. Why the change? I mean don't get me wrong I'm glad somebody finally talked some sense into you. I've been telling you that you need to slow down for years and it seems like this girl comes along and you're ready to change your whole life. Maybe I don't have the right body parts, but I am your best friend, or did she change that too?"

"Man, stop it, just come and get me," Tony laughed.

Jaxon laughed too. "Okay man, you ready right now?"

"Yes!"

"Okay let me get myself together and I'll be there in a few."

"Okay" Tony said.

Tony was thinking about what Jaxon said and he was feeling a little bit punked lately, but he shook it off and thought Jaxon was trippin. "I'm just trying to do the right thing for a change," Tony thought.

Jaxon pulled up and blew his horn and Tony went out and got into the car.

"What's up man?" Jaxon said.

"What's up Jaxon?"

"Man you alright?"

"Yeah man, why?"

"Well you forgot to tell your face. Man, you look like you lost your best friend or something."

"Naw man it's just all this stuff man, like the divorce, I miss my kids and now I may have lost the best thing that ever happened in my life."

"Whoa man, back the truck up. What you talking about? Who, Lisa?" Jaxon said.

"What? Why do I have to be talking about Lisa?"

"Because Tony, ever since you met this girl man, you been acting funny. Remember those guys you used to laugh at for acting like you acting?" Jaxon said.

"What are you talking about Jaxon?"

"Man come on Tony, you are gaga over this chick. Man every time we're together and no matter what we're talking about, you bring up Lisa."

"Man, no I don't Jaxon."

"Yes you do Tony. Man I'm telling you, if I say let's go to Crown Burger or something, you'll say something like Lisa don't like Crown Burger she likes Frenchie's chicken, just a plain chicken sandwich with nothing on it absolutely nothing, just dry. I don't know how she can eat a dry sandwich. Then she only eats one thing at a time, she won't eat her fries with her sandwich. She will either eat the fries first then the sandwich or the sandwich then the fries, then when she does she just picks pieces off and she won't just pick the sandwich up and bite it ever. She pulls pieces off of it little by little until it's all gone. It takes her about an hour to eat one sandwich and a small fry and I will be done like three times before she gets done with one meal. Now where did I get that from and how do I know all that if you didn't tell me the story over and over again?

Tony laughed, "Okay, maybe I do talk about her a little bit but I wouldn't say I'm gaga and all that."

"Man Tony trust me when I tell you, you my brother are gaga, gone, stuptified!"

"Okay man, let's change the subject," Tony said.

"Something is obviously bothering you about this girl and you need to talk about it. Now I am your friend and you called me and I came to get you because you said you needed to get out and man whenever you say that you need to talk, I'm here, cause that's what friends are for - now talk."

"I'm cool Jaxon."

"Man no you are not. Now man how long have we known each other?"

"I don't know, for some years."

"Right, a lot of years and Tony I know you. I know when something is bothering you. We are not going anywhere until you talk."

"Okay I'll talk. Man Jaxon, this girl man, it's just weird she just does something to me. I, I just can't explain it."

"Man Tony are you whipped?" Jaxon asked.

"Naw man it ain't like that. We haven't even kissed or anything. I mean I kissed her on the cheek one night but that's been about it."

"Okay Tony look, now like I said we've known each other for years right?"

"Yeah" Tony said.

"Well man look, I have never seen you as happy as you have been since you been talking to this girl, and you know we go back before there was any trouble in your marriage; now am I right?"

"I guess so," Tony said.

"Well I know." Jaxon said "Man Tony look, if you don't know that's fine, but I do know. I used to be tore up because you was tore up and I couldn't do nothing to help you. Now ever since you got out and started going to that church you started changing. Then when you moved out to Marcus' place you really started changing and I mean for the better. Man it's noticeable; ask anybody that knows you if you don't think so."

"No I know you are right," Tony said.

"So what's the problem?"

"Me!" Tony said. "Man I seem to screw everything up. I told Lisa my past last night."

"You didn't!"

"I did," Tony said.

"Well what did you do that for?"

"Well I didn't want her to be caught off guard in case she found out any other way."

"Well how did she take it?"

"Not too good," Tony said.

"Plus I told her that I didn't have a driver's license."

"Oh she didn't know that?" Jaxon asked

"No and I was driving the church van and everything."

"You didn't." Jaxon said.

"Yep I did," Tony said.

"Tony what were you thinking?"

"I wasn't," Tony answered.

"It's one thing for you to drive your own car like that but to jump in somebody else's car like that is just crazy." Jaxon said.

"Man I know," Tony said.

"So what did she say?"

"Well to make a long story short, she said I was a liar and that she hated liars and that she didn't want anything to do with me."

"Man! That's messed up."

"I know," Tony said.

"Well you can't blame her."

"I don't," Tony said.

"Well is that all she said?"

"No, she said that I needed to go clean my mess up."

"Well what did you say?"

"I said I would after the divorce and that I was trying to stack my loot."

"Oh, well don't you go to court this week for your divorce?"

"Yeah," Tony said

"Well how's that going?"

"Well it's *supposed* to be final if all goes like I hope it will."

"I hope so man," Jaxon said. "Man you really need to get free from that."

"Yeah, I know, but all I can do is leave it up to God."

"Well Tony, I wouldn't give up if I were you. Like you said, she is the best thing that ever happened in your life. Do you think you gonna find something that good and not have to fight for it?"

"No not really, but I just don't know how much fight I have left in me," Tony said.

"Man now COME ON! Now that's not the Tony I know. You are always so confident. How you gonna punk out now?" Jaxon said.

"Naw man, it's not like that. It's just that I decided to leave this one up to God man. It's in God's hands. Plus I don't blame her for not wanting me; she deserves better than me."

"WHAT?" Jaxon yelled.

"Now you trippin! Tony listen, you got a lot of potential and you have gone through a lot of stuff and you still here. I think you can do anything you put your mind to; you just never had a chance. Ever since you told me that Lisa said she believed in you, you turned into a different person, a better person. You were so angry at times that you used to scare me. There were times that I thought I would watch the news at night and find out you was dead. Now it's like I said; it's like you are a whole different person. You can do what you want but you better not give up!"

"I won't" Tony said.

"You cool?" Jaxon asked

" I'm cool," Tony said.

"What do you have planned for the day," Tony asked.

"Well right before you called, Bill called and asked me if I wanted to come over and shoot some pool."

"Aw, cool, let's go," Tony said.

"Okay but Tony you know what we do when we go over there, so are you gonna be cool?"

"Yeah I'm cool," Tony said.

Jaxon was referring to the fact that there would be a lot of drinking and smoking over Bill's house. Bill's house was what was known as *the spot*. It was where some of the guys from work would hook up to shoot pool, watch the fights, drink beer, smoke weed, and talk trash. Tony knew it and he wanted at least one beer.

"Now are you sure Tony? "Cause you been doing pretty good and I don't want you to fall off the wagon. Don't go over there if you think you can't handle it."

"I'm cool Jaxon. I've been having a beer every now and then and I've been cool."

"Alright now, cause I don't want to be the cause of no mess."

"Jaxon, I drink because I want too and I like to drink. I just need to learn how to cut it off because you know how I get."

"I know, that's why I'm asking."

"I'm cool," Tony said.

"Alright then, let's go shoot some pool."

It started out okay as it always did with Tony only having a few beers, but once he got loose it was all over. He was past the point of no return. Tony lost count of how many beers he had and now he was really drunk. Tony hadn't eaten anything in quite a while so he decided he would eat some of the spaghetti that Bill's wife made. Tony stumbled up the stairs and piled up his plate with spaghetti and headed back down the stairs. Tony made it down the stairs okay but as he began to sit down he missed the couch and spaghetti went everywhere. Tony laughed but nobody else did. Nobody thought it was funny. All the guys liked

Tony but they didn't like seeing him like that. The next thing they knew Tony was on the couch passed out. Jaxon was embarrassed and he felt horrible.

"I knew I shouldn't have brought him over here." Jaxon said to Bill.

"Hey Jaxon don't worry about it. It's cool and don't worry, he's not the first and he won't be the last."

When Tony woke up, Jaxon asked him if he was ready to go.

"Yes!" Tony said with slurred speech. Jaxon helped him up the stairs and out to the car.

"Man I'm cool," Tony said.

Tony started to head to the car on his own but he fell. He staggered to his feet laughing and stumbled into the car. Tony was a pitiful drunk and he murmured all the way home about how he did it again and that he was no good and that he was never going to change and Lisa might as well forget about him. It was three in the morning when he got home.

"Okay we're here," Jaxon said.

"Oh thanks Jaxon. Man what day is it?" Tony asked.

"Well now it's Sunday morning, why?" Jaxon asked.

"I'm supposed to go to church tomorrow and there's no way I'm going to make it to church like this."

"Well Tony just sleep it off man."

"Yeah, I just need some sleep. I'll holla!"

"See you later Tony."

Tony staggered into the house and went into his room. Bill had given Tony a plate of spaghetti to take home and Tony wolfed that down, took a couple of aspirins, and fell across the bed. Tony didn't have a headache or anything but from experience he knew that if he took them now he may not wake up feeling so horrible the next morning or in his case that same morning.

At about nine that morning Tony woke up, he looked at the clock and was shocked that he was awake. Tony thought it must really be meant for him to go to church this morning. It was a good thing he went to church with Marcus. Marcus went to church faithfully every Sunday. He sang in the choir and when needed he sometimes played the drums. Marcus could really sing too. You wouldn't know it to hear him talk, though, because he had a rough voice, but when he sang it came out smooth as silk. Marcus always wanted Tony to join the choir too, but Tony would always decline saying that he wasn't ready for all that.

Marcus was up singing around the house as usual as Tony passed through headed to the shower. "What's up big dog?" Marcus asked.

"Aw, nothing man, what's up with you?"

Marcus looked at Tony and laughed and said "rough night last night, huh?"

"Yeah" Tony answered trying to muster a smile even though his head was pounding.

"Well man, I made some shoe polish as you call it. Get you a big cup of that and take you a couple of aspirins and you'll be alright." Marcus chuckled.

"Okay" Tony said.

Now Marcus was one cool dude, Tony thought. He was really supportive of Tony. Tony had periodic drinking binges and would always apologize to Marcus for it afterwards. Marcus would always say "Man you don't have to apologize to me big dog. I know how hard it is. Man compared to me Tony you don't have no drinking problem. If I was still drinking right now, the way I drank, you'd be saying man I ain't got no drinking problem, that Negro's got a drinking problem. I drank morning, noon, and night, I'd hide a bottle under the stairs at work just so I could keep drinking, then go out and drink at lunch, and get off work and go drinking, then go home and drink myself to sleep, and wake up and start all over again. Man I would be so liquored up till if you would had struck a match around me we would all blow up!"

Tony laughed. "Man you couldn't have been that bad!"

Marcus would respond, "Man you better ask somebody!"

Now amazingly Tony actually got ready in time for church. "You ready big dog?" Marcus asked.

"Yeah" Tony answered.

"How's your head?"

"Aw, it's cool. That actually worked. You and Lisa make your coffee the same way. I swear if I take this coffee to the graveyard and pour some on the ground, all kind of people would get up!" Marcus laughed.

"Hey Tony, now when you told me that you still drank every now and then and asked me if I had a problem with that I told you no, right?"

"Yeah" Tony answered thinking, *well here it comes*, he wondered how long it was going to take before he wore out his welcome and ripped it with Marcus. "I hope he doesn't put me out," Tony thought.

"Well, now you a grown A man and you can do what you want to but Tony the men at church really look up to you and they're watching you. The young men too and well, if they see you drinking they might think that it's okay for them to drink too, and they might not be able to handle that and end up in all kinds of trouble and I know you, and I know you don't want to confuse anybody."

"Yeah you're right," Tony said, relieved that that's all it was.

"I'll try and do better Marcus. And for the record, I ain't handling it and I'm confused myself."

Marcus laughed and said "Aw, you'll be alright big dog, it takes time. Like I said, I know how hard it is. It was like losing my best friend or something. I actually went through a grieving period over it."

Tony laughed.

Marcus said, "Man you laugh, but I'm serious. Wait you'll see what I'm talking about when it's really time for that thing to go. You may even become violent trying to hold on like somebody trying to take your woman away. Watch what I tell you."

Tony was crying laughing now. "I already know what you mean, that's why I'm laughing so hard." Tony said. "Every time Lisa gets on me about it, it's like world war three or something."

"I told you dog, and that ain't nothing, wait till it's time for it to go for real. You are liable to be crying like a baby all huddled up in a corner somewhere. You might even become suicidal. I ain't playing. I was so depressed I thought I was going to have to be put on some kind of medication. But that wouldn't have worked for me because I was so bad I would have started abusing that too."

Tony knew that Marcus was serious, but Marcus had such a delivery, that even when he was telling the truth about something and even trying to be serious, it made people laugh. They laughed and talked all the way to church. As that pulled into the parking lot Marcus said, "Hey Tony, you better stay away from Lisa today if you don't want no trouble, you know she can smell alcohol a mile away."

"I know, she always says that after I've been drinking like this, that it's coming out of my pores, but I won't have to worry about that today because she's gone to this retreat thing, plus she quit me again."

Marcus laughed, "That's like the ninety-ninth time or something?"

"Naw, it's over a hundred." Tony responded.

They hopped out of the car and hurried into the church. Tony tried to sit as far away as he could from anyone so he would not offend them because he knew he reeked of alcohol. While he could never smell himself, Lisa would always tell him that when he had been out drinking like that he should stay out of people's face, because they can smell me a mile away. She could never understand how Tony could drink like that and then still want to talk about God to somebody like nothing happened. She really hated that. She'd tell Tony how hypocritical she thought it was and ask him why did it? And how can he have the nerve to. But Tony would always respond that what's really in me is what's going to come out. Like sober thoughts from a drunk mind. I'm going to keep talking it till I get it! Lisa would always say, "Yeah you keep talking and you're going to get it alright!" "Tony" she'd say, "You really do have some serious issues!"

"Yep, but you can't be delivered from something that don't exist, so I'll be the first one to admit that."

So Tony sat in the balcony that day and everyone that knew him knew that there was something wrong because Tony would sit in the same spot just about every Sunday, and that was closer to the front. This prompted some of the guys from the men's group and even a couple of the sisters to ask him if he was alright, and of course they also asked him where Lisa was. Even though they weren't married yet, when you saw one you usually saw the other. Even though a lot of people would never admit it, there were quite a few who could really see them together. It was obvious that they were good for each other.

Tony couldn't wait to get out of there, he had tried to do as Lisa suggested but he was well liked by some and they were in his face checking to see if he was okay. They said that he just didn't seem like himself. Tony said he was okay, but he did have a lot on his mind; Lisa. While he should have been more concerned with the divorce and how all of that was going to play out, he was more concerned with how all of this was affecting Lisa. *I have totally ruined her reputation in this church* he thought.

Tony went home and tried his best to watch football with Marcus and really focus on the game but all he could think about is Lisa. He wondered if she was back yet and if so, why didn't she call him. He knew why, he thought to himself; *she doesn't want me or to be around me anymore and I can't blame her either.*

Lisa did come home that afternoon but she didn't call Tony. It wasn't because she didn't want to, she just didn't think about it. She knew she had heard from God about Tony and what she was supposed to do, and that God said yes that they would be married, and that was enough for her. She just figured that she would talk to Tony tomorrow sometime.

Tony could never understand how Lisa could go all day without calling him. He'd fuss at her and tell her he'd been sitting on pins and needles wondering if she was alright. Tony would leave messages on her phone, knowing she got them, and she sometimes still wouldn't return his calls. Lisa would just laugh and tell Tony she didn't mean it like he was taking it. Lisa said she was not used to checking in or answering to anybody, having been single for so long. She said she was not used to having anybody worry over her like that except for her youngest son. If she stayed out too long or he didn't know where she was, he would be waiting up for her like he's her daddy or her man or something.

She could be gone all day and half the night with nobody hearing from her and she wouldn't even give a brother a courtesy call. Lisa promised she would, but never did, so that was the other reason why he didn't sweat it more than what he already was, because he knew that this was just how she was and she really didn't mean anything by it. Tony always tried to talk her into getting a cell phone but Lisa wouldn't hear of it. Tony couldn't see how anyone could go without one. Lisa never had one and never wanted one. She said she was on the phone all day at the church and the last thing she wanted was a way to contact her no matter where she was.

The next day Tony had divorce court.

"So tomorrows the big day huh dog?" Marcus asked.

Tony snapped out of his daydream about Lisa. "Uh yeah, yeah man that's right."

"Well what are you thinking is going to be the outcome?" Marcus asked.

"Well, it's supposed to be a done deal, but she gave me an ultimatum. She told me that if I would give her full custody of the kids she would sign the divorce papers."

"All man, now that's cold! I don't know if I would do that."

"Well, that's what I thought at first and then I thought - those are my kids no matter what a piece of paper says. Not to mention the fact that the only reason why she is doing it is number one, she wants to try and hurt me, number two she thinks if she has control over the kids then she can still control me, and finally, and you know this one, it's about the money. She knows that if she has full custody then I am obligated for the max in child support, which I don't care about and that pisses her off. She tried to throw that in my face by saying that I would never have anybody and nobody would ever want me because I had all those kids and that I was always going to be broke because of it. Plus, she is going for spousal support. Man, I laughed and said 'If you think that is a threat or a punishment to me to have to take care of my responsibilities you are sadly mistaken, because no matter what amount I am ordered to pay it still would not exceed what I would have spent and what I have spent in the past taking care of you and the kids.' And furthermore, I had promised her that no matter what happened with us that I would make sure that she was provided for. I looked at it like this: the court is just about to make sure that I am going to keep my word. Man she was salty. She knows how to hurt a brother though, because she said that if I did sign she was going to be sure to tell the kids that I chose that over them."

"Aw, man - now that's really cold, you don't do no kids like that," Marcus said, shaking his head. "Well man, she knows that if I was nothing else, I was a father to my kids and she knows that I love my kids. That's why she was able to hold me hostage as long as she did because she kept telling me that if I left I would never see my kids again, and if I were to try that she would call the police on me."

"Man that's crazy!" Marcus said.

"I know but pretty soon they will be old enough to make a decision for themselves about whether or not they want to see me again and that's the day I am looking forward to."

"Tell me something, isn't she seeing somebody?" Marcus asked with a puzzled look on his face.

"Yeah, even though she says she's not, even the kids are telling me that much."

"Well then, why didn't she just sign the papers; then she wouldn't have to lie, she could just do what she wanted to do." Marcus said.

"Now you are going to think this is really crazy, but one time I went back on one of my many 'I'm going back and trying work things out' trips, and I was laying in the bed half asleep and heard her talking on the phone to one of her girlfriends telling them, 'yeah girl he's back, girl that man ain't going nowhere, I've got him wrapped around my finger.' Then I heard her say me and, the guy's name; 'yeah we still seeing each other, we're friends,' then she laughed and said 'girl whatever, girl naw this man took twenty years of my life; he ain't going nowhere, an he's 'bout to pay for what he done.'

Marcus that was it. I had heard enough. I got up packed my little overnight bag and headed down the steps and she saw me. Man she went off. She was yelling and screaming 'where you going, come back here.' I kept going. Then she said, 'that's right run, that's what you do best, every time stuff gets hard you run like a little bitch!"

"No she didn't," Marcus said.

"Yes she did. Marcus it took everything that was in me not to turn right around and go back in there and tell her something but I knew that's what she wanted. See, we had played that game before; or rather I got played by that game before. Man I bounced and never looked back. Meanwhile, she's still yelling all outside, 'that's why he kicked your ass, cause you ain't nothing but a punk. I hope he catch you and kick yo ass again."

"Whaaaat! He beat you up Tony?"

"Yeah man! I was hanging out looking out for somebody, being the designated driver while he got his face on, and once we got to his house I got my face on. She drove my car sometimes and was at her sister's house, so he probably thought it was her there and he stopped and knocked on the door. I was pretty buzzed because I didn't even look to see who it was before I opened the door. I just thought it was family or somebody else we knew. I opened the door and it was him. Before I knew it, he had me by my throat and down on the ground choking me telling me 'see, nigga I could kill you right now if I wanted too.' Then her sister came out and screamed for him to let me up, and to get away from her house before she called the police."

"Did she?" Marcus asked.

"No"

"Did you?

"No"

"Why not?" Marcus asked.

"Man, I was humiliated that he got out on me like that. Plus I had warrants so if I would have they would have arrested me."

"Man that's messed up," Marcus said. "Well what I can't understand is now he's sleeping with your woman, so what is he jumping you for? It should have been the other way around."

"Man I know! He used to call the house all the time threatening me, and I would ask him why and he would say 'because I just don't like you,' like some kiddy mess. Then I would tell her that she'd better tell her dude to stop threatening me before I do something to him and she would take up for him and tell me he ain't nobody to mess with, and that I better not mess with him because he had a reputation. Man I was like you talking about him like he's your husband or something; if anything he should be worried about me. Man I shouldn't have to be the one watching out for my life because of somebody she's messing around with. Man I had to start carrying a pistol, because him and his boys tried to catch me sleeping a bunch of times out at the club. It just so happened somebody would always tip me off, and I would be able to get out of there okay."

"Man how long has that been going on," Marcus asked.

"Well they have been kicking it for about three years now, but him threatening me has been only going on now for the last year or so." Tony said.

"Man and that's too long. So how long does she think you need to pay?"

"According to her, twenty years."

"Man that's crazy," Marcus said.

"So you feel me now?"

"Yeah dog, I had no idea man. I'm sorry, I'd be drinking too if I had all that drama going on."

"I ain't proud of it but I would be lying if I said that didn't have a little to do with why I drink like I do. The bad part about it is that it used to help a little bit at first, but now nothing; I don't care how much I drink now, it's still there. Now it's like ever since I joined that church and met y'all, and especially Lisa, none of this bothered me the way

239

it does now. Now it's like I try to do what I used to do before, and this big ole giant spotlight shines on me; it's like I can hear somebody say 'TONY, WHAT ARE YOU DOING?'"

Marcus laughed.

"Man I'm serious, then what make it so bad is now Lisa don't never call me, but it seems like every time I am right in the middle of, or about to get into some dirt she calls and says 'Hey Tony what are you doing?'"

Marcus laughed "I bet you're looking around for the cameras."

"That really freaks me out. It blows my whole high. Or if I am about to make a hustle and where I once was pretty confident about it, now I'm all paranoid and stuff."

Marcus fell out laughing.

"I'm serious Marcus, she even got me wearing a seatbelt now."

"AW MAN, NOT THE SEAT BELT!" Marcus laughed "She got you whipped. It must be good, that's all I've got to say. I mean I ain't trying to get in your business or anything, but man…"

"Naw man, that's what Jaxon said too, but like I told him, man we ain't even done nothing yet; naw this is something else."

"Oh man, Tony you in love," Marcus said.

"Now that much I can agree with," Tony said.

Tony was thinking about calling Lisa later that night but he didn't. He really wanted to talk to her before he went to court tomorrow, so he hoped she would call him. "Fat chance of that happening," he thought.

The next day he went to work but told them that he needed to get off at lunch time so he could go to court. On the way to court Tony became increasingly nervous. He believed that the divorce would be final but he was still worried that something else would come up. Tony had filed almost a year before he met Lisa, but his ex had been fighting it ever since. He really hoped that this was it. Just then his phone rang, he thought it was Lisa but it wasn't, it was his ex. She said "Hey Tony, I just wanted to tell you something before we go to court today." Tony thought, oh no, now what? "What's up?" Tony said.

"Well, if you promise not to bring up the infidelity, I promise I won't fight the divorce."

You see, she really didn't want them to know about her part in all of this, and Tony had threatened her with it before by saying that all he had to do was to go into court and tell them about all that she had done, and they would probably not only honor the divorce but by the time it was all over with she may have to pay. She wanted to make sure that Tony didn't bring it up. Tony never had any intention to follow through with it and had only used it as a threat, hoping that it would scare her into signing. Tony told her no problem, he would do as she requested and they hung up the phone.

Tony walked into the court building and was surprised that one of his sons was there. He didn't quite know what to make of him being there, except that maybe he was there to support his mother. When Tony's ex was called into a conference room with her lawyer, Tony's son approached him and told him that he understood what he was doing, and why, and that although he was there to support his mother he had a lot of respect for his dad for doing what he was about to do. Tony's kids knew a lot about what had went on over the years. Tony apologized to his son for having put him and his siblings through this over the years. His son told him "that's alright dad," and they both went back to their seats knowing that they'd better not be seen talking to each other.

Finally they were called into the courtroom and at one point the judge asked Tony if he had anything to say. Tony looked at his ex and she looked at him as if to say - *you promised*. Tony said "No your honor," and he granted the divorce under the terms and conditions signed and agreed upon by both parties involved. It was now final.

Tony had mixed emotions over it all. While he was glad that it was finally over, he was sad that it ended the way that it did. "It wasn't supposed to end at all," he thought. He looked at his son, and his son gave him a slight head up nod, and Tony gave him one back.

On the way out of the courthouse, Tony's ex's lawyer told Tony that was a nice thing he did in there, and he told her thank you. He was always so confused why people thought it so strange that he did simply what he thought was the right thing to do. It was the same thing with his lawyer. Tony agreed to the terms of the spousal and child support, but his lawyer thought that he should have not agreed to any of the terms and waited six more months. He told Tony if he did wait he wouldn't have to pay anything. That would have put it at two years and Tony was willing to do whatever it took to get his freedom. Tony told his lawyer that he was going to take care of his children and as far as the spousal support; if that was all he had to pay for the price of freedom he'd gladly pay it. His lawyer told him he was stupid and crazy.

Tony knew that everybody thought that he would be broke or struggling over it or something, but Tony always felt like he couldn't be down forever. In Tony's mind, he'd make it, and at some point even do better than just make it. Tony always believed that there was nothing that could keep him down for long, and that one way or another, everything would be alright. He was used to being the underdog and being told that he couldn't do something, and took delight in proving people wrong.

Tony headed straight to the first store he could find and purchased three twenty-four ounce cans of beer. He knew he shouldn't be drinking especially having to work the next day but he figured that these would be all he drank, and furthermore, he deserved to celebrate. He popped one on the way home and actually drank it while driving. Not only was he back behind the wheel of his car with no driver's license, he was drinking and driving as well. He could have caught the bus or asked Jaxon because he worked third shift and was available to take him. Jaxon would have gladly given him a ride, and been there for support for him if he had he asked. Truth be told, Tony didn't want anyone to take him anywhere because he was on his *I'm a grown-A-man* trip again.

By the time Tony thought about calling Lisa he already had a pretty good buzz going.

"Hey Lisa," Tony said with slurred speech.

"Hey Tony, so what happened?" Lisa asked.

"It's final," Tony said.

"Really!" Lisa said hesitantly. "So it's done?"

"Yeah that's what I said cabbage head," Tony said.

"Oh no, you've been drinking," Lisa said in a disgusting tone.

"Why do you say that? Because I said cabbage head?"

"No Tony, it's because you're slurring."

"Yeah I had a couple."

"But why? Why would you do that especially during the week? Don't you have to work tomorrow?"

"Yeah, why?"

"Because you know how you get," Lisa said while becoming increasingly angry.

"I'm cool, I only got three and that's where I'm stopping at."

"I don't see why you had to get any at all," Lisa shot back.

"Man Lisa, don't start okay; the divorce is final and I just thought to myself, why not have a couple to celebrate."

"I can think of better ways to celebrate than that," Lisa answered.

"Well so can I," Tony said laughing.

"You know what I mean!" Lisa said

"Yeah, I know what you mean."

"But Lisa what did you do when your divorce was final?"

"I partied for like a week Tony; but I was younger, I wasn't saved, and…"

Tony interrupted, "Let me have my moment okay?"

"Okay, but if you lose your job don't say I didn't warn you."

"I know Lisa, I'm cool."

"Anyway Tony, I've got to go. You know I don't like talking to you when you're drunk."

"I'm not drunk," Tony said with slurred speech.

"Not yet, but you will be before the night is over," Lisa said.

"No, I won't! I'm stopping right here."

"I'll believe that when I see it. Goodbye Tony,"

"Talk to you later, Lisa."

As soon as Tony got done with the last of the beer, he immediately went to the store and got three more. By ten that evening he had lost count. Tony was a miserable drunk. Tony started thinking about the divorce and he wondered how he got into the mess in the first place. "I should have never married her in the first place," he thought. "She told me no when I asked her but I just *couldn't* leave her alone. I just had to marry her anyway. She's right; I took twenty years of her life. I'm selfish and all I think about is me, just like she said. She was right, I am selfish."

CHAPTER TEN

Sober Thoughts of a Drunk Mind

Tony had to talk to somebody, but he knew he couldn't call Lisa; because she wouldn't want to talk to him when he was drunk. Plus, he didn't want her to know that she was right. He called an old friend of his, a pastor. They had met each other when they were teenagers.

"Hello, Raphael?"

"Yes" Raphael said.

"It's Tony."

"Hey bro. What's up?"

"I'm divorced"

"I'm not surprised; that thing was doomed almost from the start!" Raphael answered.

"What? Why didn't you say anything?"

"Man, Tony, you were crazy when we were teenagers, and then once we got older and you started coming to my church, I was a pastor by then and forbidden to say anything about it. It was like watching a slow train wreck."

"Raphael - why did all this happen? I mean, I know why it happened; we both were at fault and…"

Raphael cut him off, "Tony, the first thing I want you to do is to not play the blame game over this. You need to understand something about all of this, and that is that this is a God thing."

"How you figure?" Tony slurred.

"Why would God want to break up my marriage and separate me from my kids?"

"Now careful Tony, God didn't do this; you two did. However, what you need to understand about God is that he is not concerned with human comfort, happily ever after, or you having a perfect marriage, or a perfect life. What God is concerned with, and only concerned with, is your salvation and your family's salvation as well. Tony you have to understand something. When it came to you and your family, you were their god, and they were yours. God is a jealous God, and now you are out of each other's way. God knew what to touch to get your attention. This happened because he loves you. Tony, you were never really in love with your ex-wife so much as you were in love with the idea of family. What you are really hurting over is not the marriage itself, but rather your image as a father; your happy family is gone now and that's what made you, not God or your relationship with God. You defined who you were and found your self-worth in your family, instead of God. That was your foundation; so now that it has been destroyed, you feel like your life is over."

"Isn't it?" Tony asked.

Raphael laughed, "Actually this is just the beginning. Tony, it's time for you to come home. I expect to see you back in ministry somewhere, and if not I don't expect to see you at all."

Raphael's words frightened Tony, because it sounded like God might strike him dead or something if he didn't get it together soon. What did he mean by - it's time to come home? Tony wondered.

"Thanks Raphael, for listening."

"Oh, no problem brother man, see you at the top doc."

"Yep" Tony answered and they hung up.

Tony passed out after that. He did, however, wake up in time to go to work the next day although he felt like crap all day. He called Lisa that day at lunch as usual.

"Hey Lisa"

"Hey Tony, so did you make it to work?"

"I'm here now." Tony said.

"Oh good! So did you get drunk?"

"Yep"

"Told you!" Lisa laughed.

"It's not funny!"

"Oh, but you DESERVED to celebrate, remember?"

"I know, I just don't want to hear it right now, alright."

"Okay Tony, but why do you continue to do this to yourself if it makes you feel so horrible the next day?"

"Man, when I figure that out I guess I will be able to stop this."

"You will never be able to stop it," Lisa said.

"Why would you say that Lisa? I would think that you would be in my corner on this; that you would want me to stop."

"Oh I do, but I just believe that you are not going to be able to stop it, because if you could, you would have by now."

"So what's going to stop it then?"

"I don't know what it's going to take Tony. I just pray that you don't die, or have to be close to dead before you get it."

"Get what?"

"That you can't have just one beer; I think once you get that, then maybe things will change, but as long as you keep thinking you can control it, you are going to continue to drink."

"I just wish you were more like Marcus. Marcus knows that he can't drink and he doesn't. Maybe you should talk to him."

"I talk to Marcus all the time and it hasn't changed anything yet." Tony said.

"That's because you haven't tried to change," Lisa answered.

"I have, over and over again, and it's not working."

"Well, you just have to keep trying until it does. I tell you what I'm going to do. I am going to pray that every time you take a drink that you get sick."

Tony laughed, "What's that going to do? I'm sick every morning after I drink now and I still drink."

"I know, but I'm still going to pray it and it's going to be more than just a hangover I can tell you that."

"What!" Tony said laughing. "Are you going to put a root on me or something?"

"No Tony, I'm going to put God on you."

"Yeah, WHATEVER!" Tony said. "Anyway Lisa, I've got to get back to work. I'll holla."

"Talk to you later Tony."

Tony laughed but it did concern him. He did fear God and he wondered what he would do to him if he kept drinking. He shook it off and got back to work.

Lisa did just what she said and began to pray as soon as they hung up, she simply said, "Lord, I pray that every time Tony takes a drink that he gets sick; in Jesus' Name, amen." And then she went back to work.

Tony didn't drink for a long while after that. He and Lisa began to spend a lot more time with each other, going to school, and also spent a lot of time talking to each other outside of school. They'd sit outside on Lisa's patio in the evenings and just talk. Tony smoked and Lisa knew it and she allowed him to smoke out on the patio since it was outdoors. Lisa's kids were around from time to time and began to warm up to Tony a little.

One night while sitting out on the patio talking, Tony was about to light up and Lisa looked at him and just said, "Forget this, I just can't take it anymore."

"What? You don't want me to light it?" Tony asked.

"No just wait." Lisa jumped up and went in the house. When she came back out she had a cigarette in her hand.

Tony asked "What's that?"

"It's a cigarette" Lisa giggled.

"Man YOU smoke?" Tony asked.

"A little" Lisa answered.

"So do you need a light" Tony asked?

"No, I have matches."

Tony watched as Lisa fired up; he couldn't believe it. "So is that the only one you have?" Tony asked. Lisa blew out her smoke after a long inhale like a pro.

"No I have a pack."

"What?" Tony asked. "So how long have you been smoking? I didn't make you start smoking did I?"

Lisa laughed, "No, I've been smoking since I was a teenager."

"That means that you have been smoking longer than me. I didn't start until I was in my twenties, then I quit for over fifteen years and only started back a couple of years ago." Tony got quiet.

"What's wrong? Lisa asked.

"Well, it's just that we have known each other now for almost two years, and I can't believe that I didn't know you smoked all this time. What else don't I know about you?"

Lisa laughed "Nothing Tony, I just don't let everybody know that I smoke, so you'd better never tell anybody either."

"So nobody else knows that you smoke?"

"No, just my family and a few close friends, that's it. So, if you tell anybody you're a dead man."

"Okay man, your secret is safe with me." Tony got quiet again.

"What?"

"Well that means that we may have more in common than what I thought."

Lisa giggled, "Like Bobby and Whitney?

"What?" Tony asked.

"I said like Bobby and Whitney" Lisa answered. "You know everybody always thinks that Bobby was the bad guy, and that he is the one that probably turned Whitney out, but I have always thought; since Whitney is older than Bobby, how do we know that she isn't the one that turned Bobby out? How do we know that she isn't the bad one?"

"Man, I never thought about it like that, but I also didn't know that Whitney was older than Bobby either."

"Oh yeah man, where have you been? Whitney had been in the business for years before New Edition came on the block. Bobby was just a kid when she started out. She is like six years older than Bobby, and you know men mature slower than we do so…."

Tony interrupted, "Whoa, so what are you saying - that we are slow?"

Lisa laughed "No, it's a fact; that's all I'm saying, and you add that together with no telling what she had already experienced, with being in the industry before he got there."

"Man I never thought about it like that before, you might have a point. Wait, so what does any of that have to do with us?" Tony asked, really concerned about what the answer could be.

Lisa saw the concern on Tony's face, and laughed and said "Well let's just say that there may be more to me than what you know."

"Like what?"

"You drink too?"

Lisa laughed and said, "No Tony I don't drink, but I used to."

"REALLY! I would have never guessed it, so what else?"

"Well, I used to hit the clubs pretty hard back in the day and I didn't take no stuff either. It didn't even matter if it was a man, especially if I was drunk. I would get in a guy's face in a minute and threaten to kick his tail."

"Wait, wait, wait, man hold on - you used to get drunk?"

Lisa laughed, "Yes, I would party even on work nights and still make it to work on time the next day. I did that for years until one day I finally got tired of it. I stopped and have never done it again since."

"Man I would have never guessed that. So what were you like when you were a little girl?"

"Oh man, when I was a little girl I was completely different. I had big dreams. I was outgoing, I sang, danced, I was creative, but as long as I could remember I always wanted to be a secretary."

"Really? Why a secretary?"

"I don't know, I just did. I liked typing but I didn't have a typewriter so I would pretend and I used whatever was around. My favorite thing to use was glass; I liked the sound my nails made when I pecked on it."

"Interesting, but what happened to that little girl?"

"What do you mean?"

"Who you described as a girl, I don't know her. Nor do I see her in there anywhere either. It's like she doesn't exist anymore or something."

"Well you're right. I was violated as a child and robbed of my childhood and it pretty much changed everything about me after that. It makes me angry every time I think about it. I once felt like I could be or do anything and now I just don't know. I second guess everything now. It's hard for me to trust. I am still continually targeted and abused just emotionally and verbally by bosses, so called friends, coworkers, and just anybody that I come in contact with. What pisses me off the most is I just take it. I want to say something but I don't. It's like I feel like I deserve it or something, I mean I know I don't but for some reason I just can't bring myself to stand up for myself."

"Man, you have got to go back and get that little girl."

"What do you mean?" Lisa asked.

"Who you were as a little girl was part of who God intended for you to be. Your growth was stunted instead of growing into your potential. Even though the devil is not omniscient (all knowing), he has watched us long enough to realize who has the potential to really be something great in the kingdom. Now this is not in the Bible, but rather what I have observed over the years while being a counselor, and just living life. I have found that it always seems like the people with the most potential, that are the most gifted and the most talented, are the ones that get into the most trouble, have the worst things happen, or end up incarcerated or dead."

"Wow I never looked at it like that, but I don't think that fits me. I can't do anything." Lisa added sadly.

"Not true. You only don't know what you can do now because what was done to you was temporarily effective, and now you're stuck there. That was the purpose of all that has happened to you in the first place. It was to make you of non-effect and to completely destroy the possibility of you ever dreaming, believing, or even living again."

"That sounds about right," Lisa responded. "My life has pretty much sucked ever since."

"Yeah but it doesn't have to." Tony said.

"How do I change it?" Lisa asked.

"Well it starts with your recognition of what happened, and since you already know what happened, it's about the task of getting back to who you were before it happened. The first step is forgiveness and not just forgiveness of the original abuser, but everyone after that. Then secondly you have to realize who the real enemy is, and we have identified him as being the devil. Then thirdly you have to come to terms with the fact that everything about you says *'come get me abusers, manipulators, and predators.'* They can see you and even smell you coming from a mile away."

"What do they see? I got saved, I believe I have forgiven everyone, I mean I can't forget about it, but I have forgiven them. I have tried to begin to live my life. I go to the movies by myself, I take myself out to eat, and I even go to concerts."

"Lisa listen, when the guys got wind that I liked you they started teasing me; saying that they were afraid of you. They said that sometimes they are even reluctant to hug you. They definitely don't ever want to work for you because they say that you are a slave driver."

Lisa laughed. "That's because I rarely get a man around there to do anything, so when I do, I make sure I get as much out of him as I possibly can, because I never know when I will have the help again."

"Okay, I'll give you that one, but what they see is that you are guarded. You say that no one has even noticed you in years but that's because you don't WANT to be noticed. It's not even a conscious act anymore you've gotten so good at it. The way you dress, the way you carry yourself, even the way you wear your hair. I'm surprised that you even have highlights."

"I hadn't for years; I just did this the weekend before you showed up at the church." Lisa said.

"As much as you want to be invisible, you only hide yourself from people that you want to take notice, but it makes you really stand out with the people that you fear the most."

"I think you're right, but how do you know all this?" Lisa asked.

"Well part of it is a gift from God, or so I've been told, but most of it is just because hurt knows hurt. I was abused myself as a child."

"Really?"

"Yeah; my story in no way compares to yours, but it was abuse."

They were quiet for a moment.

"Tony, there is something that has always puzzled me about you."

"What's that?"

"Well, you're so smart, I hear you counseling everybody, so how come you can't help yourself?"

"The same reason why you can't help yourself. We're not supposed to be able to help ourselves. If we could, what would we need each other for? Or why would we even need God? Could you imagine me if I could fix myself? You wouldn't be able to tell me nothing."

"Oh I know!" Lisa said laughing.

"Ha! Ha!" Tony said. "Listen, I have watched you help and counsel people as well, but you can't fix yourself either, can you?

"Apparently not. So are you ever going to get to how I fix it?" Lisa asked.

"Just like you told me about how to fix some stuff in my life, Lisa, it's a process; the whole way you think has got to change, but it's not your fault that you got stuck here in the first place. Now I don't think you were wrong for leaving your other job and going to work at the church. But I do think that you may have a little trouble telling when it's time to go, and maybe even where to go or what to do. I don't know what you're supposed to be doing; I just know God has got to have much more than this for you. It kind of reminds me of the story about the eagle that was raised with chickens. Are you familiar with that story?"

"No," Lisa said.

Besides, what does that have to do with me getting the little girl back?

"Plenty just listen to the story!"

"Oh brother, another story" Lisa sighed,

"There was this farmer that went out to hunt game one morning, and as he often did before he started, he would go to a cliff side and look out; admiring God's creation. Now this particular morning as he stood there he heard a faint screeching sound coming from just over the cliff. He peered down over the cliff's edge and saw an eaglet in its nest, with its mother lying slain next to the nest. The farmer carefully picked the baby eaglet up, and took it home to his farm. Not knowing what else to do, he put the eaglet in with his chickens. Now the eaglet grew much faster that the chicks of course and the farmer thought he looked so strange and out of place out there pecking with those chicks, but he knew that he was still too young to fend for himself so he let him be.

Soon he was really big and it seemed ever animal in the barnyard knew he didn't belong except him. The chickens would chase him, the dogs would bark at him and chase him, and even the other chicks that still weren't full grown yet would bully him around. The farmer thought how funny that the prey is dominating the predator. He even noticed the eaglet looking up in the sky from time to time as if he felt like he belonged there, but he just bowed his head and started pecking like a chicken again. Still he wasn't old enough yet to fend for himself, so he left him alone. Then one day when the farmer was coming in from the field he saw his wife standing outside with the broom, and she was angry; she said, 'Homer…' "Homer?" Lisa said. "Yeah I just made that part up. Anyway, she said 'Homer, you have got to do something about that eagle. I have been keeping the other animals off of him all day. It seems like everything in the barnyard knows that he don't belong here except that ole dumb eagle.' 'I know Martha,' he said, 'I've been meaning to do something about that but I just don't know what yet.' 'Well you'd better get a move on it before he gets himself hurt, or hurts one of the other animals.' 'Okay Martha,' he answered. Now that weekend he had a thought, 'I've got to teach him how to fly.' He carefully picked him up and threw him up in the air. The eagle flopped right to the ground like an ole weak chicken and started pecking on the ground. 'Not

261

high enough' he thought, so he took the eagle and climbed on top of the fence and threw him up from there but it was the same result. That ole eagle just flapped and flopped right back down to the ground like an ole weak chicken, pecking on the ground again. 'Still not high enough,' the farmer thought. This time he took him up to the hay loft and threw him off of there. Same result, 'poor ole dumb eagle,' he thought. 'Well, I tried Martha,' he said, 'that eagle just won't fly.' 'Well you'd better figure something out because he can't stay here,' she said. 'I will Martha, I will.' The next day the farmer had another thought. 'I'll take him back to where I found him, and maybe that will help'. He didn't quite know what he was going to do with him when he got there, but he knew that he couldn't stay on the farm forever either. He just didn't fit. Now once he got to the cliffs edge it came to him; 'I know what I've got to do now,' he thought. He stepped over to the cliff's edge and held the eagle up in the air and said, 'well Mr. eagle, you are going to either do one or two things today; you are either going to fly, or you are going to die, but I got no other choice.' He said a short prayer and he threw that eagle right off that cliff. Now it was hundreds of feet down, and that eagle flapped and flopped and was plummeting right down to the ground. 'Well, sorry Mr. Eagle; I tried,' the farmer said. But just then an updraft caught the eagle's wings and it stretched them wide. The farmer was amazed because the eagle had never even spread his wings before and his wings had to be at least six feet, the farmer thought. The eagle fluttered and flapped then soared allowing the wind to carry him on his wings. Now he still tumbled when he finally hit the ground but the important thing is he didn't die. The farmer thought. 'Well you might be alright after all' Homer said. Then he went back home to tell his wife the good news."

"But what happened to the eagle," Lisa asked.

"Ah, good question, grasshopper! Now most people I have heard tell this story just end the story there, and then get to hooping about don't be an eagle pecking with the chickens, you got to flyyyyy!" Tony says imitating a preacher singing a sermon.

Lisa laughed.

"Okay, anyway, what I go on to say is that eagle still had no idea of how to be an eagle or even worse, he still didn't know he *was* an eagle. Maybe he just knew that he could soar and it felt good, it felt natural, it felt like that's where he belonged. So how does an eagle learn how to be an eagle? He has to find another eagle. He has to learn how to hunt, when to hunt, what to hunt, and even how to defend himself, just to survive. If not, even though he can fly, he will still eventually die. It just won't be from the sudden quick stop at the bottom of a cliff, but rather a slow painful one from starvation, or worse; he could be killed. I think we've got to find other eagles and learn to soar, because getting saved is like that; we have a lot to learn, and we need good teachers that are seasoned enough to warn us of the dangers that they themselves have encountered during their growth period. They will teach you what to eat, what to pursue, and even what to stay away from. Then we are supposed to be able to soar on our own. Only not exactly like an eagle, because they travel alone; they mate for life, but they don't travel in packs. We are supposed to stay connected with the church body for a number of reasons. For one, to grow up we need the body in order to come to full maturity, two there is strength and safety in the body, just as there is in a herd. The devil can't go about like a roaring lion and devour you if you don't stray from the herd, and number three, the Lord is coming back for a bride that is supposed to be made up of what we now call the church. Man, I want the full experience of being a child of God, and I want the wholeness that's promised, the liberty that we are supposed to have in Christ Jesus, and the victory. I have been looking for this stuff ever since I was a small child. I don't know why, but I just believed there was a God even then and I used to talk to Him all the time. He was my friend, my closest friend. I always knew He would be there to listen to me, and even though I never heard Him talk back I just knew He was listening."

"I used to talk to God when I was a little girl like that, and he was my best friend too. I would talk to God because I knew He would keep a secret. I knew He would never betray me and go tell everybody."

"That's funny," Tony said.

"Lisa, when I was a child and going to Sunday school; I used to get in trouble for asking questions. Like one time I asked; 'Jesus said we will do over and abound the things He did. Where is that in the bible, and what did He mean' I never got that answer. Now He had raised the dead, caused the blind to see, and the deaf to hear, and all I was really wondering was if this thing called salvation is so great, then why does everybody seem so miserable about it, and broke to boot. I mean I can understand struggling a little bit, but if He said, and He did, I came that you might have life and that more abundantly, what did He really mean? Now to me, that means that even if we are never prosperous and just have enough we should at least be rich in love and joy. We should at least have an abundance of something, don't you think?"

"Yeah, I guess I never thought about it like that." Lisa said.

"I do all the time," Tony said. "The only problem is, by the time I got done learning from the church about what God was, I didn't see Him as my best friend anymore. I now saw Him as this big mean powerful giant that was always mad at me, and was just waiting for me to step out of line so He could squash me like a bug, or strike me with a bolt of lightning or something."

"Not me," Lisa said, "there have been times when I am alone, and I am lonely, and I have asked God to hold me and even rock me to sleep, and He has."

"Not me," Tony answered. "I mean come on, just think about it, does it really look and feel like your daddy is a king and your brother is a prince? Man it seems like the harder I try the farther I get away from it. I had always said that if I ever got saved I wanted everything that the Bible says I'm entitled to."

"So you're not saved then?" Lisa asked.

"Not according to a lot of church people that I have talked to over the years. According to them; the way that I been living lately, I can't be saved. They believe that if you ever go back, you were never saved in the first place."

"What do you believe?"

"The only pastor that I truly trusted with my heart, as a matter of fact, he is the only person that I ever trusted in my life, said something once. He said God isn't mad at us. Now he wasn't talking to me, but rather my clients. I had invited him to come and speak in one of my group therapy sessions. He told them that the first thing that they needed to know was that God is not mad at them.

His Son died for their sins and He judged sin once and for all at the cross. He told them that from then on, it was all about relationship with Him. He said that God is grieved over their sin because it breaks relationship, but you never stop being a son or a daughter. He can't be with you in sin. He's there, but He has to watch from afar because He cannot be part of you and sin. You part with your sin just through simple repentance, which puts you right back into His presence again. He also said something else that puzzled me, but at the same time it was quite liberating."

"What's that?" Lisa asked; wondering if Tony was ever going to get back to how she gets the little girl back, but she knew by now that once he's on a roll to just let him wind down.

"He said that God only sees us through the blood of Christ, so he doesn't even see our sin. He can't, its why Jesus, while on the cross Himself, asked His Father 'why have you forsaken Me?' You see, I think that when Jesus was in the garden, agonizing over what He was shown that He had to go through, the beating, the mocking, being spat upon, and all that; that what really grieved Him the most about the whole thing is that His Father would have to turn His face away from Him, because of the sin He carried for all of us. He had *never* been without the Father. I think the thought of that meant more to Him than life itself."

"Not that I don't agree with you, but what makes you think that?" Lisa asked "I would have been worried about the pain and suffering too."

"Oh, and so would I."' Tony said, "but Jesus knew something that we fight to believe, and have been trying to come to terms with for the whole of our miserable little lives."

"What's that?" Lisa asked.

"That this is all temporary. No matter how long you stay on this planet, and I don't care if it's two hundred years, we all have got to go. As the Word says, it is appointed to man once to die. There is however such a thing as life happily ever after or an eternity in hell. Either way it's forever. I have often thought what if I finally get all the things that I have ever desired to have in life; the house, the cars, the love of my life, and so on, and then die the very next day, and not get to enjoy one moment of it here on earth? I always thought that would really suck, yet that's what we do. I have seen people work hard all their lives to build a nest egg to retire and finally enjoy life as they know it, only to die of cancer or something a few months later. Somebody else like their kids or a wife ends up enjoying what they worked for all those years."

"Boy does that sound familiar; sounds just like where my life might be headed." Lisa lamented.

"You got that right; that could be any one of us, but I came up with a solution for all of that."

"What's that?"

"Well I don't know if it will actually work or not, because I haven't started it yet, plus part of it won't be fulfilled until I do die. That's the happily ever after part. I will worry about that later, but for now my philosophy is that I don't believe in retirement, that's number one. The other thing is that I want to live right now; none of this waiting for later stuff for me. The way things have been going in my life; there may not be a 'later' waiting for me."

"What do you mean?

"Well the way my life is going right now, I feel like I don't want to live like this, and I don't want to die like this. Does that make any sense?"

"Well let me answer you like this; like you always say, MAN I Feel you; because it makes *perfect* sense to me," Lisa said. "That's exactly where I'm at. I feel like the walking dead. Even though it sucks how we have been done and treated over our relationship, this is like the most exciting thing that has happened in my life in years."

"Really?"

"Oh sure! Tony there are a lot of things that I don't like about you, but there's a lot of things about you that I do like. Even though I don't always get you, but that's ok, because like you said; that's not the important thing; the important thing is to get God."

"By George I think she's got it," Tony said.

"No seriously Tony, it's like you have given me the will to live again. You tell me that I am beautiful even when I don't feel beautiful, and I know I look a mess. You walk and run with me, and even work out with me, and no man has ever done that with me before. You look at me, with those eyes of yours, like I am a hot babe or something. Even though I've been shedding some pounds, I'm still overweight."

"In my mind, you are a hot babe."

"Well thanks Tony, it really sounds like you are sincere."

"Oh - I am!" Tony said.

"Lisa look, just like you can see in me what other people can't, including myself, I can see in you what you can't see in yourself. I see you as the most beautiful woman that I have ever laid eyes on, and I don't mean like when people say 'beauty is in the eye of beholder' either. I really think the reason why you get so much hate from other women, and so much crap from guys, is because whether they like it or not, they can see it too. Lisa, check this out, before you and me started talking to each other, we were both miserable. Now would you say that that is a fair assessment?"

"Oh, more than fair."

"Now we started talking, became friends, we started smiling and becoming happy, and what happened."

"All hell broke loose."

"Right, so you see, I'm not talking about the superficial, skin deep stuff that most people trip out over. What I am talking about when I say beauty is that the *real* beauty is what's going on inside of you. Now as broken, or as dead, or even as miserable as you felt your existence was, the one thing that still shined bright to me was what was really in your heart. Now though your spirit may be broken, and it is, you still manage to love people. So that put you a cut above most of the people around you, and that's what they really envied about you the whole time."

"Yeah, I wasn't trying to be, and I don't feel like that most of the time." Lisa said.

"Oh I know, and that's what's so wonderful about the whole thing. It's so in you that you can do it without even thinking about it. Now that's how you know what your true calling is because no matter how low you go, or how bad you feel, you can still do it. It has become who you are."

"So I guess you must be called to preach then because drunk, sober, tired, or whatever, you are always preaching a sermon to somebody, even if it is just to yourself." Lisa burst into laughter.

"I don't think that's funny, and neither do I believe I am called to preach either."

"Why not - are you scared?

"Well yes, very scared. The Bible warns that not many of us should become preachers and teachers, saying that stricter judgment will fall on us for leading people astray."

"Ah Ha! I got you!"

"What?" Tony said.

"You said us!"

Tony laughed. "Okay - well that was a Freudian slip."

"So you don't believe you've been called?" Lisa asked.

"Oh I know that I have, but not to your traditional, or what we know of as preachers and pastors. I heard a man hooping one time and told the Lord that if I had to do all that then I don't want the job. I can't stand all that screaming and stuff. I mean don't get me wrong, I like a little flavor every now and then, and I believe it has its place, but I ain't really cut like that." Tony said.

"So how ARE you cut then?"

"Well I do believe that I have been called to be a discipler if you will, or for lack of a better term." "What the heck is that?"

"Well, it's a teacher," Tony said.

"So why didn't you just say that instead of just making up a word to call it." Lisa said.

"Because, the word teacher doesn't adequately describe it. Listen, was Jesus a preacher?"

Lisa thought for a moment and said, "Wow, I don't really know. I guess I never thought about it like that."

"Well I don't believe He was, in fact, I don't think that anyone was until after the Comforter had come, but that's a whole nother story. I also don't believe that He can be reduced to being just another one of the prophets either, and that has always been funny to me. Think about it, in the first place, the ministry of every prophet was all about the coming of Christ, or warnings from God about what was going to come. Now here we have God Himself in the flesh, in the form of the Son, and what, He is prophesying about Himself? I don't think so. No, He was, and is, the Messiah, the Alpha and Omega, the Beginning and the End, the Word itself made flesh standing among men, and He was a teacher. He discipled men, and then instructed them to go out and make more disciples. Now once you got a group that was big enough; that met regularly, they formed what we now have come to know as the church, or the body of Christ Himself. Now the Bible sometimes referred to the church as the flock, and every flock needs a shepherd. We are even depicted as sheep. Now that's really funny, because as smart as we think we are, God says that we are as sheep without a shepherd. Trust me when I tell you; that's a pretty sad state to be in."

"Why do you say that? Lisa asked.

"Well, simply because we don't have a clue what that really means, because we don't understand sheep. Listen, sheep are like the dumbest and most defenseless animals in the world. I heard a story one time, told by a real shepherd, about how two of his sheep wandered away from the flock; a lion had killed one of them and began to eat it, and the other sheep didn't even have enough sense to run away. The shepherd said that it was running around in a circle, just bahhing and making so much racket that the lion had to stop and kill it too, just to eat the other one in peace.

Take the shepherd's prayer that David prayed, being a qualified shepherd, about the part that says 'He maketh me to lie down in green pastures' well, sheep would eat themselves sick, so he literally had to make them lie down in a field full of green grass. Then the part that says 'He leadeth me beside the still waters; sheep were afraid of swift moving water. Lastly, the part that says 'Thy rod and Thy staff, they comfort me;' now there are two reasons why I believe this is made mention of. One of which is that the staff was used as an instrument of protection against predators, and the other is that the shepherd would actually use it to pull a lamb back in line, or even break a little lamb's leg to keep it from running away. Now to me, even deeper than that is the Bible also says 'My sheep know My voice.' That shepherd had to carry that little lamb until his leg healed, not to mention he would rub all of them from snout down to their hooves with some type of ointment or something, to keep parasites away from them until they were old enough to fight them off for themselves. So there was an intimacy there, unlike anything we are familiar with, when dealing with a flock or a herd. Our ideas about a flock come from maybe what we've seen in an old western or something. On a cattle drive, our herds are driven, prodded, even whipped back in line. With cattle, any experienced cowboy can effectively drive herd; it doesn't even have to be his."

"Now I heard another story once about sheep, where they tried an experiment to see if the sheep really knew the shepherds voice, or if they were they just responding to the commands. Well, to make a long story short, the sheep only responded to the voice of their shepherd."

"Tony how do you know all that stuff?" Lisa asked.

"Google, Google knows everything, plus I just always wanted to know, because the Bible never made any sense to me otherwise. I will give you a 'for instance'. Do you know what 'hoeing a row' means?"

"No, and I am almost afraid to ask," Lisa said.

"See, that's just what I mean, you don't have a clue, because where you grew up, and all you know about the word, hoe has been used in a derogatory sense as referring to a whore. However, that term would not be that foreign at all to you if you were brought up on a farm, where it simply means weeding rows of crops with a tool called a hoe. All of the Bible's references are to a whole society and culture that hardly exists anywhere today. How can anyone truly say that they have rightfully interpreted the Word if they don't understand the context; such as, in the case of Jesus making a statement, understanding who He was talking to, what He was talking about, the setting; and by setting I mean what the conditions surrounding the events, why He said what He said, when He said what He said, or for that matter, the timing of when things were said. Additionally, just because Jesus said it, or the Bible says something, doesn't mean that we can just go around saying it anytime we please, either. Even before Jesus said something, sometimes He said 'he that hath an ear to hear,' which says to me that everybody wasn't trying to hear what He had to say, and not necessarily because they didn't want to hear the truth, but because while some of them may have had hard hearts, many others just couldn't hear because God himself hadn't yet given them an ear to. They weren't ready for it yet or the conditions were not right. Now imagine how many people came to believe after the death of Christ, who couldn't believe that they didn't get it while He was yet with them. And so goes our story today. None of us were around when the Christ was on the earth, so all we have is our shepherds and other believers to model Christ before us, and as a whole

I don't think we have done so hot, largely due to our own ignorance of it all. Like the Word says, my people perish for a lack of knowledge. He said my people. Not heathens, not sinners but my people. That qualifies as what we know today as the Church, Christian folks like you and me. So I really ain't mad at the Church, or better stated, church people, because they don't know. However, what really makes me mad at them is when they act like they do know, but then when somebody like you or me comes along, really needing some answers and some help, real deliverance, or real power, ain't nothing there. Then to boot they make us feel like *we* are the ones that are stupid or something."

"I know, and I have even been told that I am where I am because I don't have faith."

"What! The only reason why you still standing and haven't totally lost your mind is *because* of your faith. Lisa, let me tell you something; you are the smartest and strongest woman I have met to date, next to my mother of course. Can't nobody top momma, but you know what I mean."

"I don't feel like it." Lisa said.

"That's cool, because it ain't based on a feeling; I mean - thank God we've got them, but man, feelings don't have intellect, and they'll have you doing all kinds of stupid stuff if you're not careful."

"Well that sucks," Lisa said. "Then what's the use in having them?"

"Well, partly for our pleasure, and in part as a warning mechanism. Our problem with feelings is that we have a hard time deciphering between what's live and what's Memorex. Now let me take you to school for a minute."

"I thought class had already started hours ago, if you ask me." They both laughed.

"Okay, now you've got physical feel and emotional feel, but with both of those you can feel hurt or pleasure. Now physical feel is a little bit easier to understand, simply because if we touch something hot and it burns us we don't touch it again, or at least we try hard not to right?"

"Right," Lisa answered.

"Now where physical feel gets a little harder to understand is when we do something that feels good or feels right, but we know is bad for us, but because of the way it makes us feel, it is a little harder for us to stay away from."

"I know! Why is that?"

"I'm not sure, but I believe I can shed some light on it with the Word."

"Never would have imagined that," Lisa mumbled.

"What was that?"

"Oh nothing Tony, go on." Lisa giggled.

"Well, I was reading something Paul said about the sin against the flesh. He said that every other sin that you can commit is done outside of the body, but that the sin of sexual immorality is a sin against the body itself. He said that you might as well be married to whoever you slept with. He had been referring to sexual relations with a harlot; in that day. It was more common for a man to go and buy a harlot than it was for a woman to be unfaithful, because she would have been stoned to death immediately. So anyway, in our day people sleep around like it's no big deal, not even realizing that they are creating a mental, and even a spiritual bond with everyone that they've ever slept with. Now that's not where I was going with that, but it's a good lead into where I'm going."

"Uh oh," Lisa interjected. "And you don't think you are called to be a preacher. You sounded just like a preacher just then."

Tony laughed. "Okay, I'll give you teacher-preacher maybe, but anyway, there are other things that I believe we do to the flesh in sin that are just as damaging. Now it's easy to just pick on cigarettes, drugs and alcohol, but what about food? Man, you don't know how many times I have wanted to say to somebody that was overweight, with high blood pressure and diabetes, when they tell me that I need to stop drinking myself to death; that I will stop drinking when they stop eating themselves to death. Man, alcohol ain't the number one killer anymore, food is! So physical feel can be just as tough to deal with as emotional feel, but they both hurt just the same. Only I think emotional feel hurts a lot deeper, and a lot longer, and it's a lot more spiritual even than physical feel. I mean, don't get me wrong, I think there is some spiritual attachments with physical feel too, but emotional feel has roots to them that run deep. Physical feel you can get hands laid on you, maybe a little oil rubbed on your forehead, and you're cool, right? Not emotional feel. You see, I believe it's that emotional feel that keeps us doing stuff like continuing to over eat, drinking ourselves to death, or even getting into unhealthy relationships over and over again. If we stay on that emotional feeling kick long enough, I believe it develops a stronghold."

"Now that sounds serious, but I thought you said it isn't based on our feelings."

"And I did, but I didn't say that they are of no effect, rather quite the contrary. You see, a lot of what we do, how we respond, and what we have done, has been based on our feelings; and that's not so bad, because for so long that's really all we've had to go on, and in some respects it has kept us out of a lot of even more trouble we could have gotten ourselves into. The problem comes in when we've learned to trust *that* over God. The problem comes when that voice is louder and more real than God's voice. So sometimes since it's so familiar to us, and we have trusted it for so long, and it's never forsaken us, and no matter how hard we have tried, we can't stop feeling it; we can find ourselves at the point where it becomes hard to tell the difference between our feelings talking to us and God."

"So how do we tell the difference?" Lisa asked

"Time and distance," Tony answered. "Now I'm not there yet, but I believe this with all my heart, and so help me God, one day I will get there. The Word says that the more and more you draw unto Me (God), the things of the world grow strangely dim. The Word also says to us, 'Be ye transformed by the renewing of our minds.' Now I don't know about you Lisa, but I could really use a new mind right now."

"Me too," Lisa said.

"And that is by reading the Word," Lisa said.

"EXACTLY!" Tony answered.

"I have found that it is no use in me trying to think stuff away, nor have I been successful at will power, or positive thinking techniques or anything like that, but what I have found that works for me is when I was reading and studying the Word on a regular basis, things just started to change for me. It was strange in that there were things that I used to do that I had just lost a desire for. Now the only thing that I can attribute that to is the fact that there really is power in the Word. God himself said that 'My words are spirit and life,' and that His Word will not return to Him void. So I say what the

Word says about me, and my life begins to change. It's how you get the little girl back," Tony said.

"Oh, you remembered," Lisa laughed.

"Yeah you've got jokes, but yes I remembered. I didn't lose my spot.

Because of what happens to us as children, it affects our feelings and emotions, so we spend the rest of our lives guarded, trying to protect them. We make inner vows like 'I'm never going to let that happen to myself again,' or 'I'm never going to open myself up again,' and even say stuff like 'I'm never going to cry, or feel again.'"

"Oh, and I've said that too. I haven't been able to cry in years." Lisa said.

"Right, and in closing out the past and the world, we also close out God, and slowly are robbed of who and what God intended us to be before the offence happened. This is because to recapture that childlike mind, once free of inhibitions, it will cause us to dream again, and believe that anything is possible with God. We have to go back through the memories of the pain we once endured. It's the only path back; and on the other side of that journey is wholeness, so 'how bad do you want it?' becomes the only question."

"That's a lot to take in Tony, and I have a question," Lisa said.

"Okay, shoot."

"Well, you have to promise that you won't get mad first," Lisa said.

"I'm not going to get mad, now ask the question."

"See, you're already getting mad, and I haven't even asked the question yet."

"Lisa, come on," Tony said.

"Okay. Well Tony, it's just that you know so much stuff about the Bible and all, and you are a wealth of knowledge about a lot of other stuff, too, that's not common knowledge to a lot of people and I, uh…"

Tony saw Lisa struggling for words. "Let me help you out. You're wondering why I'm so stupid?"

Tony laughed. "Because like I said, all I am is an ole dumb sheep."

"That's another thing; you never seem to take anything seriously," Lisa said.

"And although there are no absolutes, such as never, always, and so on and so forth, you almost always seem to take almost everything way too seriously," Tony shot back.

"Okay touché," Lisa responded. "But Tony, you know what I mean."

"Yeah and I apologize. I do still get a little sensitive about it," Tony said.

"A LITTLE!" Lisa laughed.

"Okay maybe a lot, but did you ever stop to think; and now before I finish what I am about to say I want you to know that I am in no way trying to minimize my behavior or manipulate you in any way; but did you ever think that maybe that's why God put us together in the first place. I'm not talking in general terms either, I mean me and you."

"How so?" Lisa asked.

"Well, we are at such extreme ends of each other that maybe His plan is for us to develop a healthy balance out of this in some way."

"How?"

"Man, I don't know, that's as far as I have thought about that one. Plus, I don't know everything." They both laughed.

"But Tony, you really do know a lot of stuff. I can really see now why people think that you are smart."

"Yeah, so smart I'm dumb," Tony said.

"Now what did you tell me about putting myself down?"

"That's not a putdown, that's just the honest to God truth, and you know what I say," and they both said in unison, "You can't be delivered from something that don't exist." They both laughed.

Lisa and Tony talked like that all the time. Lisa loved it!

All she had to do was ask Tony one simple question and he could go on for hours with all these stories. She enjoyed the journey most times, but there were other times she wished he'd just get to the point.

Tony really loved talking to Lisa too. They could go on for hours if they didn't have anything else to do, or have to eventually go to their separate homes. Lisa started having thoughts of wishing they lived together, because they were together all the time anyway. She kept thinking that it would make things so much easier if they did.

Lisa knew that she would see Tony that next day at school, and thought she would talk to him about it; not so they could live together, she'd never do that, she just wanted to know if he felt the same way. Oh, they had both talked about it earlier in the relationship, but that was different. "He's divorced now, so I wonder if he still feels the same way about me," she thought. She also worried about Tony, because at times he still sounded so bitter and angry. She knew that she had problems too, and she was talking to God about them, and she seemed to be getting better and even doing better, but she didn't know about Tony. "He's like a walking time bomb," she thought. "I just hope I am not around when he finally goes off, but I pray that when he does that he will be alright." She didn't know why she didn't feel compelled to pray that he not go off; she just knew that he would eventually. It's like it was his destiny or something, and nobody or nothing could stand in the way of what was going to happen with him. She knew it was a *God thing*, as she called it. In fact, she believed that what was going to happen to him had to do with what she had prayed for him.

God told her that he was to be her ministry, while she was at The Great Banquet.

"Lord, whatever it takes to get through to Tony - do it. I know it's going to take a miracle, and that's okay; just don't kill him Lord, but save him no matter what it takes

CHAPTER ELEVEN

His-Story

Tony and Lisa were still going to school. Tony tried hard to focus on his classes, but he had problems paying attention; even as a child he had struggled to pay attention at school. Lisa noticed this, and often wondered if he might be ADHD or something. He and Lisa had two classes together, and Lisa hated it. Tony was a clown, and she couldn't imagine how Tony *ever* got any work done with his constant clowning around and joking. Tony, however, thought that Lisa took things way to seriously. Lisa thought that Tony never studied, and she thought he's going to flunk the midterms and maybe then he would buckle down and start taking things more seriously.

They had a Playwriting class together, and The History of Jazz, and Tony was a wiz at both. Part of their assignment in Playwriting was to write scenes that would be performed each week in class. Every week people would *fight* for parts in Tony's play. They were really good and funny too. Writing just seemed to come so natural to him.

287

Lisa thought that if he would take things a little more seriously and maybe even study from time to time, he could really be great. As for The History of Jazz, Tony was a music person. He loved Jazz, and he knew most of the history already, so that was a no brainer. Tony had Psychology as well, and Lisa thought there was no way Tony was going to pass the class; he didn't even go half the time, or study either. "There is no way he is going to charm his way through that one," she thought.

Tony did study though, he just never let Lisa see him, because he enjoyed seeing her so angry over it. He loved to antagonize her. As far as his psychology class, he had gone once a week to get the assignments at first, but then the professor said he did not take attendance, and that he followed the syllabus to the letter.

Tony thought to himself, "man, I like this cat. He's just here for the check and he don't care if we learn anything or not." The professor even paid one of his private practice office assistants to do the test reviews.

"This dude is pimpin' this school. All he does is come in and spit rhetoric twice a week and let his assistants do the rest," Tony thought. "Now who are the real criminals?"

Tony knew that all he had to do was to show up for the review and he should be alright.

Midterms came and went, and Tony and Lisa were comparing grades.

"I can't believe it!" Lisa said.

"What?" Tony asked.

"You've got better grades than I do, and all you do is play around; you don't even study!" Lisa said in a distressed voice.

"I did study; I just didn't let YOU see me study."

"Still Tony, I really don't think this is challenging enough for you. I really think next semester you need to major in something else instead of psychology."

"Like what?"

"I don't know. Isn't there anything you always wanted to be or do?" Lisa asked.

"Yeah, an architect; but I already checked into that, and they don't have an architectural program here; just engineering," Tony said, thinking that he could change the subject.

"Well, you should look into it," Lisa said.

"I don't know Lisa; I will have to think about that. I don't think I'm engineer material."

"Sure you are Tony, you can be anything you want."

"Yeah man, but engineering? Lisa, you know I didn't even finish high school; I only have a GED, and just got that."

"I know Tony, but I believe in you."

"Man Lisa, I know, and I appreciate that, but I think it's going to take way more than just you believing in me for this one to happen. Engineering is tough."

"I know Tony, but I really think you can do it. Just think about it, okay?"

"Yeah, I'll think about it," Tony said, thinking Lisa had lost her mind.

Tony finished that semester in school with a 3.2 GPA. He would have done better but he missed his final exam for psychology, and had to take it late, causing him to drop a letter in grade, which still ended up being a B. Lisa beat him by earning a 3.8 GPA. She was still angry that he did that well without appearing to even try while she really struggled just to get the grades she got.

They decided to get together at one of their favorite coffee shops where they used to meet sometimes after school to study together; although not much studying was done because they'd spend more time talking than anything else. Now that the semester was over, they were already talking about the next year.

"Have you thought anymore about what we talked about?"

Tony knew that Lisa was referring to him changing disciplines.

"Yeah, I have been giving it some thought, and I haven't decided yet what I'm going to do."

"Are you still going next semester?"

"Oh yeah, sure," Tony answered.

"Good, the main thing is just not to quit."

"Oh I would never do that. I want to complete at least a couple things in my life," Tony replied.

"Tony, have you thought anymore about cleaning up your legal issues?"

"Nooo!" Tony said.

"Why not?"

"I just haven't, that's all," Tony said.

"Plus, I *have* been focusing on school, and all I can really think about is one thing at a time."

"Well, I think it's time you addressed that Tony," Lisa said.

"And then what? Go to jail? Because that's what's going to happen when I turn myself in," Tony said, feeling uneasy about the subject.

"Not necessarily. Tony, if you turn yourself in now, and tell them that you are in school and working and everything, you don't think they'll have leniency?"

"You haven't had much experience with a black man in court have you?" Tony asked.

"No, but what's that got to do with anything?"

"Man from my experience - everything."

"I just thought..." Lisa said.

"Look Lisa, I know you mean well and everything, but trust me when I tell you, I've got this. I am not running from it, I just know how the system works, and I'm telling you that when I do turn myself in I am preparing myself for the worst."

"And that from a man of faith," Lisa said.

"Now faith don't have nothing to do with facts. I've done what I've done, and the fact is I did it knowing that the system isn't fair when it comes to handing out sentencing to a black man. I have been in court and seen a white man charged with drug abuse; he got caught in the act with an ounce of dope, got a public defender 'cause he's got no money just like most of us, and have seen the judge reduce his charge from a felony possession down to a misdemeanor drug abuse, giving him probation. Maybe the judge sends him to a rehab facility as a term of his probation; then if he completes the rehab, he can even get his charges dropped - but not us. Man, a brother gets up there with a lesser charge, like paraphernalia with no drugs on him, and we get slapped with a felony possession and a drug abuse charge, and get *six months* in prison mandatory by state law. Now, I've seen that with my own eyes, over and over again. So, I've decided that when I turn myself in, it will be when school's out." Tony said, clearly agitated at the thought.

"Okay, okay, Tony I'm sorry. I didn't mean to make you upset. I shouldn't have brought it up."

"It's cool. I'm sorry for answering the way that I did. I do have to deal with it. I just don't like thinking about it or even talking about it."

"Tony"

"Yeah"

"You know the appreciation dinner is coming up."

"Yeah"

"Well, are you planning on going?" Lisa asked.

"What, like on a date or something? You sure you ready to show up to something like that with me?"

"No, that's not what I meant. I mean we can both go, but I don't know that we should go together. Even though you are divorced I don't know that it would be such a good idea to rub our relationship in anyone's face." Lisa said.

"Oh, I don't care about that. Talk like that only makes me want to walk in there arm in arm with you with a big grin on my face, and I dare somebody to say something," Tony said proudly.

"I know YOU don't care Tony but I do. I still have to see these people every day; you don't."

"I know Lisa, and I'm only a little serious. But, no I hadn't thought about going, and I don't know why you would even want to go. Most of them don't even care about you.

"I know, but I have to go; it's mandatory for leadership to be there."

"I know, I know, Lisa, but sometimes I just wish that you weren't so damned loyal to them."

"I'm not. I'm doing this out of obedience to God. I am being loyal to Him.

I thought about what you said the other day, about not knowing when to leave, and I prayed and talked to God about it. He told me that it is time to go."

"So why are you still there then?" Tony asked.

"Because, (and I am going to do a 'Tony' here) the Bible says to do everything decently and in order. I am in the process of putting together a manual; so that whoever they get to replace me will know what to do, and where everything is located."

"Man, that's actually kind of cool. I never would have even thought about anything like that. When it's time for me to go, I'm just like, 'I'll holla at y'all', and that's it."

Lisa laughed. "I know Tony, but I just can't do that."

"I know and it's okay. It's strange though. It's like the things that bug me about you are the things that I love about you."

"Why?"

"Well, I love that you are so dedicated and organized and all, but at the same time since I don't have that kind of patience with people and things; it bugs me."

"Oh, so now the truth comes out," Lisa said.

"What? I was never lying about that in the first place. You knew it bugged me."

"Yeah, but you never said anything. I knew that something frustrated you about me, but I just never knew what." Lisa answered.

"Yeah, but you never asked either. If you would have ever just asked, I would have told you." Tony shot back.

"Oh, I see now, you are one of those brothers that I've got to make sure that I ask the right questions to; because if I don't you will never tell me."

"Pretty much like that," Tony said laughing. "I'd like to think that I'm getting better, though."

"Oh, you are doing a little better," Lisa said.

"A LITTLE?"

"Yes, just a little. Now Tony, you never answered the question."

"What, about the dinner thing?"

"Yes" Lisa answered.

"Man, I don't know Lisa. If I can't go with you then I just rather not go."

"Why not?"

"Well Lisa, I have never seen you dressed up before. I mean, the usher uniform is nice and everything, and even the suits that you wear to church are alright. None of that stuff is very revealing; which is fine because of the setting. You are supposed to be covered up in church, after all..." Tony paused.

"WHAT?" Lisa yelled.

"Well Lisa, I have no idea what you plan on wearing to that dinner that, but I can just imagine it being something really beautiful. Plus, I have never seen you in dress or evening gown before, and I'm just afraid that I might lose my mind. Shoot, I'm trembling just thinking about it now. I just don't know if I will be able to behave myself, that's all."

"Well, I thank you for your honesty," Lisa laughed.

"Plus, Tony continued, do you remember that construction program that I was telling you about that I went to?"

"Yes" Lisa answered.

"Well, there is a graduation ceremony on the same night as your banquet, and I will be graduating from something for the first time in my life. I was kind of hoping that you would be able to go with me," Tony answered.

"I would love to do that, but I can't."

"I know, and it's cool. Anyway Lisa, if I may ask; what *are* wearing that night?"

"Well," Lisa said teasingly, "I do have this baaaad black dress that I have had for a little over a year now that I have been waiting to be able get into."

"Why wait so long?" Tony asked.

"I bought it at the size that I wanted to be, or rather the size that I was trying to get back down to."

"Well, can you fit it?" Tony asked.

"I don't know. I haven't tried it on yet. I will be putting it on for the first time the night of the banquet, and I have you to thank for that."

"Me! What do I have to do with it?" Tony said.

"Well, a lot. Tony, before you came into my life I was a mess. I was depressed, overweight, and I wanted to do something that I thought would challenge me to make a change; so that's when I bought the dress. Now, I really hoped that I could get down in size to put it on, but truth be told, even if I had, I still didn't know if I would have had the confidence to put it on."

"Why not?"

"Because I never felt worthy enough, or beautiful enough.   It's like no matter what I did to myself before you came around, I just felt so ugly. The crazy thing about it is, by the time you came around, I was the heaviest that I had ever been, wearing a size fourteen, and it's like you never noticed. You always complimented me, and the way you looked at me, like I was beautiful; it made me feel special. Not at first though, at first I didn't trust you. I wondered, 'what does this snake want? There is no way that a good looking guy like him could *ever* find me attractive. He must have something up his sleeve.' I just figured that you would play me for something. I didn't know what, because I didn't have anything; but I was convinced that once you got whatever it was that you where after, you would be gone just like the rest of them. Tony, you have inspired me, and given me the courage to really live again. Remember all those jogs in the park? All of that encouragement, and all of the *real* weight loss, meaning emotional weight loss, has created a new me. Plus, having gone through all the things we've been through, it made me really seek God. He showed me so many things about myself, and about you, and who my real friends are. He's given me direction. The dress is just an outward sign. I have been waiting to wear a dress like that; and it's a *bad* dress, too."

"What does it look like?"

"Ah, I thought you'd never ask, but I can't tell you that; you'll just have to wait and see."

"So, how do you know if you are going to be able to fit it or not?" Tony asked.

"I don't. I just hope that by the time I put it on that I will be able to fit it."

"So if you don't mind me asking, what size is the dress?"

"Oh, I don't mind at all. I told you that I used to be a size fourteen right? Well the dress is a size six."

"Wow, that's amazing, and I can't believe you used to be a fourteen. I just can't see that."

Lisa laughed, "Well, that's what I was, right in front of your eyes."

298

"Yeah but I never saw it."

"I guess you really didn't, because you never acted like it; and the fact that you had a crush on me really amazed me. It's hard for me to believe that you are even still here at times. I really thought you were going to turn out just like all the rest of the men that I had met," Lisa said.

"I kind of felt that," Tony said.

"You did?"

"Well yeah!"

"When?"

"For one thing it was written all over your face, as well as displayed in your attitude. And one day, when we were in the office talking, you said something. I don't even remember exactly what you said, but it had something to do with always being played by guys, and ending up still alone. It was something like that. Anyway, it sounded so sad to me. I had always wondered why you were the way you are, so I asked God what happened to you, and I believe that He showed me through what you said, and that you had never been around or experienced a real man before; one that would stick around no matter what. That's when I decided..."

"Decided what?" Lisa asked.

"That I would stick around no matter what. No matter what you did, or what you said, tantrums and all; I decided that I was in it for the long haul."

"The stalker," Lisa said, smiling.

"What's that supposed to mean," Tony said.

"Remember that time I was mad at you?"

"Which time?" Tony laughed.

"Okay Tony," Lisa laughed too.

"The time I got mad at you because you smelled like alcohol, and when I asked if you if you had been drinking that day, and you told me no, we argued, because I knew you were lying? Then I told you to get out of my face, and I went up to the school; thinking that I was getting away from you?"

"*Oh yeah, that time*! And for the record, I didn't lie. I hadn't been drinking that day. I did the night before though."

"Whatever Tony! Anyway, how in the world did you find me?" Lisa asked. "As big as that campus is, I could have been anywhere. I even went to a different building, and was in a study lounge that I had never gone to before, and you *still* found me. I thought for *sure* that day that you were a stalker."

Tony laughed, "Well I just asked God to show me where you were. I walked into the first building I got to, went up the stairs, turned down a few hallways and there you were; sitting right there on that couch reading."

They both laughed. "Tony, you have helped me to live again. You have given me courage, you work out with me and taught me how to lift weights, even shown me what, when, and how to eat, oh, and most of all, you have made me laugh. Tony, if this never went any farther than a friendship, I have to say that you have been, well, maybe not the best friend I have ever had, but by far the most interesting."

"Wow! I really feel honored; it's no big deal though, really, and it's nothing compared to what I wish I could, and want to be able to do for you. So if you stick around, I promise you that you ain't seen nothing yet."

"My real concern Tony is that *you* stick around."

"What do you mean by that?"

"It's just that you're so angry at times, that I feel like you are a walking time bomb. I mean you joke and play around a lot, but just below the surface it's like something is brewing; and it doesn't seem good."

"Lisa, you don't have to worry about me, okay. I am in it for the long haul."

"I sure hope so Tony."

Lisa really wanted to believe Tony, but she couldn't shake what she felt. She remembered what Tony said about feelings, and how they were also there to warn of danger; and she couldn't help but feel that whatever it was that was about to happen wasn't going to be good. Tony noticed the concerned look that came over Lisa's face.

"What's wrong Lisa?"

"Oh nothing Tony, I'm sure it's going to be fine."

"I'm sure it will too, and I look forward to seeing you in that dress."

"So you are going to come?" Lisa asked.

"No, but I'll get my chance, I'm sure."

"You sure are confident of yourself there, mister."

"That's right - I am confident! I'm so confident that I will bet you that I can tell you how much you weigh."

"How?" Lisa asked.

Tony laughed, and started toward Lisa while striking a wrestler pose and laughing.

"I'm going to weigh you right now," Tony said, as Lisa walked backwards while laughing hysterically.

"I know you don't think you can get away from me. You know how slow you are," Tony said.

Lisa squealed as Tony scooped her up.

"See you're not that heavy at all," he said.

"Okay, Tony put me down," Lisa yelled. Instead, Tony spun her around as fast as he could while holding her.

Lisa screamed "STOP TONY WE'RE GOING TO Fall!"

They fell. Tony fell flat on his back with Lisa landing right on top of him.

"Oh my stomach," Tony said laughing.

"See, I told you," Lisa said laughing.

"Tony, you picked me up like I was just a piece of paper or something," Lisa said.

Lisa sat on Tony's stomach and looked at him. He looked at her. Her hair was long, he looked at how it draped around down her face. Suddenly he had déjà vu.

"Oh my God!" Tony said.

"What?" Lisa said, pushing herself up, thinking she might have hurt him.

"It's you!" Tony shouted.

"What are you talking about Tony?"

"Well, remember that dream I told you about? Well, I couldn't remember it all then, but it just came back to me. It was years ago, and in the dream I was playing around with this girl, I mean lady, and she ended up on top of me. She was beautiful. She had this smooth skin, and long hair. I remember her smile, and the way she looked at me. It just did something to me."

"Well, what happened in the dream?" Lisa asked.

"Nothing," Tony answered "It wasn't a sex dream or anything like that. We were playing around like I said; and I fell and she ended up on top of me, and looked down at me and smiled, and I woke up. I wondered who she was. I tried to keep her face in my head as long as I could. I remember saying to myself when I woke up that I will see her again. Isn't that weird?" Tony asked.

303

"Well yeah, but what does that have to do with me?"

"Well Lisa, remember I kept telling you that it has always felt like I have known you from somewhere? Well it's because I now believe that it was you in that dream I had," Tony said.

"Oh, I don't know about that Tony," Lisa said.

"I do," Tony answered.

"Lisa, I feel like I have been looking for you all my life."

"I'm just not used to all this dream and vision stuff; sometimes it makes a little sense, but most of the time I don't know what to think about you."

"Just think of me as your 'Paladin!"

"My what?"

"Your 'Paladin. Your knight in shining armor, your…"

"Okay, okay, Tony, I get it, but that's what I mean about you; who even uses words like *Paladin*? Where do you even find a word like that today? What is that, Old English or something?"

"Yep, by way of Middle French, derived from the Italian word Paladino," Tony answered gleefully.

"See, that's what I mean. Who even knows this kind of stuff! Well one thing for sure, you certainly are 'God's special child;' that's the only way I know how to put it. This has definitely got to be a God thing that's for sure," Lisa said shaking her head.

"Yep, I'm cheese bus helmet wearing special, too!" Tony laughed.

Lisa began to laugh too.

"Tony you really got a serious problem."

"I know - that's why I'm your special project. And anyway what did you mean by 'this is a God thing?"

"Oh nothing, I shouldn't have said anything," Lisa said.

"Well, it's out there now, so you may as well spill it." Tony said.

"Well, I was praying one night, and asking God what I was supposed to do with you, and He said ministry."

"You are supposed to do ministry with me?"

"No silly, I am supposed to minister to you," Lisa responded.

"Man! That's even better! Let's get started on ministering to me then," Tony puckered up.

"Tony, stop it. You know what I mean," Lisa said pushing him away.

"Well, the Bible does say to minister to one another in love," Tony said laughing.

"Tony, that's *way* out of context, and you know it." They both laughed.

"Man, I know what you mean Lisa, and that's why I love you."

"And sometimes I do feel like I am falling in love with you, too," Lisa said.

"And...that's all I was getting at with the dream and 'knight in shining armor' stuff."

"Oh, I know," Lisa answered.

"How do you know that? I never said anything."

"Not with your mouth, anyway," Lisa said.

"Tony, you have shown me love in so many ways; whether you know it or not, and it's not just painfully obvious to me, but it's obvious to everyone else as well. That's why everybody is trippin so hard; because they can see it."

"Man, it's that obvious?" Tony said, with a puzzled look on his face.

"Yes, it's that obvious." Lisa said.

"Does that bother you?"

"Sometimes," Lisa responded.

"How come you never said anything?"

"Well, for one you can't help the way you feel. I just wish you could hide it a little better; and for another, I think it's kind of cute."

"Aw, man! That is like the ultimate insult to a man right there!"

"What?"

"Man, I've got my heart all out there like that for you to see, and worse than that, the whole world sees it. I get teased by my boy. I go home most days feeling like I am making a fool out of myself over you, and you respond with *that's cute!*"

"Oh, Tony that's not what I mean at all. All that means is I'm flattered."

"Man, what you are supposed to say is that you love me too!" Tony said.

"And I do," Lisa said, still laughing. "But just not the way you do right now."

"Man, it ain't funny Lisa. What's so damn funny?"

Lisa tried to compose herself. "Okay, I'm just saying Tony, you have got to give it some time, that's all; and you haven't even been divorced that long."

"I know, and I apologize, but I ain't never sorry; specially in regards to how I feel about you. Man, I feel like you have already been ministering to me from the very start of our just meeting each other. I wouldn't be in school if it weren't for you, *and* I wouldn't be thinking about quitting drinking, and you've even really got me thinking about changing my major next year."

"Oh I don't know if I am responsible for all of that Tony, but I am just glad that I was able to be some help to you. You are the one who is doing the work. All I did was make a few suggestions."

"If you say so, but how it's going down in my mind is that you saved my life," Tony said.

"We'll see; it's not over yet" Lisa said.

"What's that supposed to mean?" Tony asked.

"Well, have I ever told you about how I lost my father?" Lisa asked.

"No," Tony answered.

"Well, you two were a lot alike; the life of the party, you know a lot of people, and you drink the exact same brand of beer that he did."

"Really? What happened to him," Tony asked.

"He had hepatitis C, and he died of cirrhosis of the liver from just drinking beer. That's why I get so angry every time we argue about your drinking, and you say it's just beer. It's the same thing my dad used to say; that he's a grown-A man."

"Hey, I say that too! And man, I'm sorry about your dad; that explains a lot," Tony said.

"That doesn't scare you?" Lisa asked.

"What?"

"Obviously not," Lisa replied.

"Oh, that your dad died like that?

No, because that's not how I'm gonna go out."

"You don't know that," Lisa said.

"Yes I do. Man, I ain't claiming that! I rebuke that in the name of Jesus! That is not how I am going to die, and I will not live in fear over it either!"

"You need to be rebuking beer in the name of Jesus," Lisa responded.

"Don't start!" Tony responded. "Look, we better go while we are still getting along."

"You know what Tony, I'm about sick of that with you, I hate that!" Lisa exclaimed.

"What?

Lisa continued; "When something gets too close to home for you, and you have to take a look at yourself from someone else's perspective, you want to start joking; but that's running! When are you going to be a real man and face the facts?"

"I will when somebody get the facts right! You can't take what happened to your dad and transfer that on me. I'm sorry about what happened to your dad, but the Bib…"

"DON'T!" Lisa screamed,

"Don't what?" Tony laughed.

"I'm NOT playing!

If I hear one more Bible story, or Bible lesson come out of your mouth, I will just PUKE! As a matter of fact, what you do, and how you live, speaks *so loudly* I can't even hear no more Bible from you. So just STOP IT!

Now, I have patiently listened to every one of your stories, your analogies of the stories; what you gleaned from them, and how you live to correct people or *teach people*, and I have to tell you; I don't know what to believe anymore. Don't get me wrong, I believe in God; I have a relationship with God, and I read my Bible, and what's scary is I'm starting to get what you mean, or at least what you're trying to say, but the problem is I'm not seeing what you say line up with what you think you know, so DON'T say one more word to me about God, Jesus, or the Bible, cause it don't even sound right coming out of your face!"

"So why don't you tell me how you really feel!"

"You know what Tony, I'm done with this!" Lisa said in frustration.

"You mean you're done with me?"

"WHATEVER! Tony, I'm tired, I'm tired of looking like a fool for believing in you, and you don't even believe in yourself! At some point you are going to either get it or die, and if you don't care if you die or not, why should I!"

"I didn't say I didn't care…"

"YOU'VE SAID IT OUT OF YOUR MOUTH, AND IF YOU HAVEN'T, *EVERYTHING* YOU DO SCREAMS IT! Dumb! Just dumb!"

"So now you calling me dumb?"

"Oh noooo Tony, not you, me; you're anything but dumb Mr. Professor, you're smart. In fact, you're so smart you're STUPID!"

"Ok that wasn't called for!" Tony said.

"NO?" It's my turn to glean the Word for a change on YOU! Let's call it what it is. The Bible calls the man who rejects instruction and wisdom a FOOL! Argue with the BIBLE not me! The Bible also says strong drink makes a mockery of men! The Bible also says even a fool seems wise when he keeps his big fat mouth shut! The Bible also says be ye doers of the Word! The Bible also says neither drunkards, liars, and murderers will enter heaven! The Bible also says to respect the authority that God HIMSELF has placed over you! Tony you are a drunk, a liar, you are a criminal running from the law, AND you are a fool! If you think you can keep playing with people's emotions who love you like we do, and only want better for you, and you don't want it for yourself... Do you think people don't have a cutoff point or what?

"Well," Tony responded, but Lisa cut him off. "LOOK AT YOU! Got an answer for that too don't you! I bet you gonna tell me a story about, uh let's see now, Joseph, yeah that's a good one! Joseph! That's ya boy right?"

"Oh, you mocking me now?" Tony said.

"YES as a matter of fact I AM! What's the matter, you can preach it, you can bring it, but you can't receive it?"

Tony stood stunned.

"Yeah, that's it, ain't it! Oh, looky here, I've got the answer man speechless; yeah Joseph! They didn't get his dream because they weren't supposed to! It wasn't for them, NOR was it given to them; it was given to HIM by God, FOR HIM! But what did he do, oh the same thing you do; he went running his mouth to everybody bout it, just bumping them gums, and didn't even fully understand it yet himself. Yeah, he got locked up later for something he didn't do; he wasn't guilty, but you ARE! Then, you whine about it like a little girl trying to pass it off as, wah, wah, wah don't nobody understand me, nobody feels my pain. THAT'S ABSOLUTLY CORRECT! Tony, news flash; NOBODY CARES, and even if they did, God is the only one who can do anything to correct it, and you won't even let him! You know what? I'm done; I've already said too much!"

Lisa began to walk away from him.

"Lisa wait, can we just talk about this?"

"SEE!" Just DUMB! That's what we just did Tony, only you still didn't get it. I talked and your next response to me don't need to come out of your mouth, and if you can't figure that one out, you're really dumber than a box of rocks FOR REAL! UHHHH! Oh my God, how did I get myself into this same ole mess AGAIN! Oh help me Lord!" She stormed off with Tony left standing there in a stupor.

CHAPTER TWELVE

The Big Show

Saturday night was the big night for both of them. While Tony was getting ready, the phone rang. It was Jamar; one of Tony's "less than wholesome" friends.

"What's up, big dog?" Jamar asked.

"What's up with you, big dog?" Tony responded.

"Oh nothin, just wanted to see what you were getting into tonight, and seeing if you might want to hang out."

"Aw man, I was just getting ready to head out to this graduation."

"Who's graduating?" Jamar asked.

"Me" Tony answered.

"From that program at the university that you was telling us about at the shop?" Jamar said.

Tony hung out at the barbershop that Jamar owned from time to time, just kicking it, cracking jokes, and listening to all of the latest gossip. Who got shot, who went to jail, whose car got vandalized by their girl because they got caught cheating again; the normal stuff.

"Yeah man," Tony answered.

"Tony, I'm proud of you. You should let me take you out to celebrate. What time is it over?"

"Oh, like nine-o-clock, or so."

"Okay, I'll pick you up," Jamar answered, before Tony could even think about it.

Tony didn't want to go. Well, he wanted to go, but had concerns; especially after his conversation with Lisa the night before. Jamar liked to drink, and he didn't like to drink alone. He was who Tony would be with when he'd last-call the bar, and then last-call an after-hour somewhere. Lisa couldn't stand Jamar. She felt like he was the devil himself. Tony knew it too, but he was his boy, or at least one of them. Besides, he thought to himself, "I'm a grown-A man, dog!"

"Okay Jamar, but man, look; I ain't trying to hang out all night, and you don't have no off switch."

"Like you do," Jamar said laughing.

"Okay, you right," Tony responded laughing.

"But I'm serious man; I ain't trying to start no drama."

"What? I know you ain't talking about Lisa," Jamar answered.

"Whatever man; you heard what I said," Tony responded.

"Alright, talk to you later," Jamar said.

"Yep," Tony said, and they hung up.

Tony wanted to call Lisa before he took off, but he knew she was probably still pissed with him. He felt like he'd show her somehow that he was worth all the trouble, but he knew she was right and just said "ah, forget it. I knew it was too good to be true. I do what I do, and I just gotta let it do what it do." He tried to laugh it off, but he was really aching inside unlike he ever had before. It was as if something snapped the night before with Lisa, not with her, but with him. "I just couldn't figure it out," he thought to himself; and even said out loud, "well least I know what it is now, I'm so smart I'm stupid!" He tried to laugh that off too, but it just wasn't the same anymore. In fact nothing had been the same for him anymore since his encounter with Lisa, but that seemed over now, and it was time to get on with it, whatever that was.

It seemed as if hours had passed as Lisa shook herself once again from her reflections of how they met and all the things that had transpired over the year. "There I go thinking about that bum again. This is *my* night!" she thought.

Lisa arrived at the award ceremony. She walked in after tipping the valet and gasped. It was beautiful!

As she entered the room, it was as if all of the air was sucked out, the music seemed to stop, and everything looked like it was moving in slow motion.

There were roses everywhere in lavender and black. She didn't care for, or understand why anyone would ever want a black rose. It seemed so morbid; however, she found the combination of colors worked. Lisa swore she heard the cracking of necks as the men turned to see her grand entrance. She passed a group of sisters that she had seen staring at her in a bad tone of voice from the moment she walked in the door. She heard one of them say, "Oh no she didn't wear that dress!"

Lisa responded to the woman by saying "Why thank you for the compliment."

"That wasn't a compliment!"

"Oh but it was," Lisa snapped back as she kept walking with her head held high swaying her hips. It seemed that the stilettos made her switch a little, and it was just enough to turn a head or two. One of the men walked up to her who she once had a huge crush on. She thought maybe they might be married one day. They went out a few times; she had even slept with him in a weak moment thinking that maybe he'd be the one. But no, just like all the others, once he got the goodies he was gone. He said he was sorry, and that she was a good girl; but he realized that he just wasn't ready for a serious relationship, and he told her didn't want anybody that had kids.

"Hi Chuck," Lisa said.

"Hey baby. Everybody is talking about the lady in the black dress. I even said 'who is that fine sistah over there...'

Lisa interrupted him.

"Yeah, Chuck, and then you got up closer and saw it was me and said 'aw, that's just Lisa,' I know the joke."

"Aw, baby why you got to be so mean tonight I was jus..."

"Trying to get your holla on," Lisa interrupted. I'm sorry Chuck, thanks for the compliment; but I knew what I looked like when I left my mirror, so I don't need your validation furthermore tonight. I am not ready for a serious relationship, conversation, or company. I am here to enjoy myself, and I am not going to let anything, or anyone spoil it. I am perfectly fine with me, myself, and, I." Then she strutted off to her table.

While on the way to her table Lisa saw her friend Angel. "Girl, you are wearing that dress!"

"Hey Angel!"

"You said you were going to do it. Girl, you look good too," Angel said.

"You really think so?" Lisa asked.

"Honey please, girl yeah and I ain't hating on you like these other sisters up in here, either, 'cause if I had your shape, I would be rocking that dress too."

"Thanks girl, I really needed to hear that right now."

Girl, you better go on and get to your seat. They're about to start the ceremony in like two minutes," Angel said.

Lisa sat in her seat as the MC stepped up to the podium. He began speaking, telling the audience about this year's awards and why those who were selected were selected. "Same ole thing," she thought to herself, "blah, blah, blah, blah, blah".

"Your name!" She heard Angel scream.

"Girl, he said your name; you better get up there." Her heart pounded almost out of her chest, she couldn't believe they had actually called her name.

For years she had worked hard; helping out around the church, never complaining, neglecting family at times, and not even being able to enjoy the Sunday service for being called out to do something.

As she approached the podium she heard the MC say "Sister Mary twisted her ankle, and the Pastor said that Sister Lisa would be assisting me tonight with handing out the awards. Sister Lisa, if you could just stand right down here on the floor right in front and hand out the plaques for me as we call the names."

"I just be damn," she thought to herself, "that damn Tony was right again."

Lisa stopped dead in her tracks and said

"I'm sorry, that's just not going to work for me."

The whole banquet hall erupted with an almost unison gasp as she did a U-turn right in front of everyone and made a b-line for the coat check. Lisa grabbed her wrap, stormed out and yelled "Can somebody go get my car! Now please! I am not about to waste this night on people who don't give a damn about me."

Just then Angel ran up from behind. "Girl that was cold. Where you going? I want to go! Can I go? Where we going?" Angel said, and at the same time tried to keep up with Lisa.

"The hell out of here for one, and I'm about to go enjoy my life."

"Tonight?" Angel asked, all too excited.

"No better time like the present. Tony was right. I have wasted enough of my life being in bondage to this mess."

"To what mess?" Angel asked.

"Guurrl, if you don't see it then I can't tell it," Lisa responded. "Now I'm talking like Tony."

"What's gotten into you? You are scaring me!"

"Tony; Tony's what got into me."

"Girl, I knew that man wasn't no good," Angel said.

"That's not it at all," Lisa said. "From the day that man walked into my life he meant me nothing but good, but I never understood it."

"Whatever happened to Tony, anyway?" Angel asked.

"Me! That man is crazy about me, and all I can do is criticize him. I'm no better than the rest of them."

"So where are we gonna go?" Angel asked, continuing to run while trying to keep up with Lisa as she is headed for her car.

"I don't know," Lisa said.

"I want to talk to Tony right now, but I can't because he's at his graduation ceremony."

"Girl, what's that man graduating from, criminal school?" Angel asked.

"Angel, don't start, not tonight; okay girl? Let's just try to get along," Lisa responded.

"Ewe girl, you sound just like him!" Angel said.

"Angel!"

"Okay girl, but you do."

"Thanks girl. You always know how to make me laugh."

"So do you want to go to Starbucks or something?"

"You're driving," Angel answered.

"Starbucks it is!" Lisa shouted.

"Dressed like this?" Angel asked.

"Like you said, I'm the driver, and I did not get all dressed up not to do something. Plus, maybe by the time we get done Tony will be done; and I want him to see me in this dress!" Lisa said.

"You sure that's all you want him to see?" Angel asked.

"Girl shut up!" Lisa said laughing.

"Girl, I'm just looking out for you. You know it's been a long time, and if that man sees you in that dress it might turn into a booty call." They both laughed.

"I don't know Angel. The way I feel right now, that doesn't seem like such a bad idea."

"Lisa!" Angel screamed "What has that heathen done to you girl? Have you lost your mind?"

"No, quite the contrary, I think I may have found it," Lisa answered.

"What the heck does that mean girl? I told you; the more and more I talk to you, the more you sound like Tony," Angel said.

"I know, I'm just pissed is all girl. Don't pay no attention to me," Lisa said.

"So, are you really ready to let Tony knock them boots?" Angel asked.

They both laughed. "Girl no, but sometimes it does get hard," Lisa answered.

"So has he tried anything?" Angel asked.

"No, that's what's so strange about him; he's been a perfect gentleman. I mean, I can tell that he wants me, but he actually respects me."

"I remember when he was working around the church; he acted like he was losing his mind every time I even came in the vicinity. Girl, he'd start knocking stuff over and tripping down the stairs and everything."

"Ooh girl, if you ever did give him some, it would probably kill him," Angel said, laughing hysterically. That made Lisa laugh too.

"Oh buddy!" Lisa answered "They'd probably find both of us dead with a big ole smile on our faces."

"So you really like him, huh?" Angel said.

"Yeah I really do, but I sure don't want to."

"I can sure understand why" Angel said. "Girl that man is trouble with a capital T."

"I know it," Lisa answered.

"Then why do you keep fooling with him then?" Angel asked.

"It's a God thing," Lisa answered. "Remember the Great Banquet I was telling you about that I went to?"

"Yeah, what about it?"

"Well I asked God while I was there if Tony is supposed to be my husband and to give me some kind of sign before I left that He was talking to me and…"

"Girl no!" Angel exclaimed.

"Girl yes," Lisa answered.

"How does that make you feel?" Angel asked.

"Well I cried at first, because I love Tony and everything; but girl Tony is a hot mess. I know I always tell you that he's got a lot of potential, but he has also got a lot of issues too."

"Girl I knew it! Are you sure you heard from God?"

322

"I'm afraid so," Lisa answered.

"What are you going to do?" Angel asked.

"I don't know, but I can tell you one thing; if I thought I prayed a lot before, now it's like I never stop talking to God these days."

"I can definitely understand that, especially when we are talking about somebody like Tony," Angel said.

"Wow! Tony is right."

"About what?" Angel asked.

"About how people see him. Tony feels like people view him as REALLY bad, like he's a special case."

"Well isn't he?" Angel said.

"Well yeah, I guess you could say that he's special in that people seemed to isolate him and view him like he's the devil or something, and he's not."

"He's not?" Angel said, clearly puzzled.

"I am going to excuse you, because I know you don't really mean that," Lisa answered.

"I know girl, I'm sorry. I just worry about you."

"I know, and you don't have to worry about me - God has got me. All this time I thought Tony was just trippin. He always says 'sin is sin, whether you overeat or drink too much; it's all sin to God.' I just didn't get it."

"Get what?" Angel asked

"That he is being, and has been, unfairly treated by the church." Lisa said.

"Girl, you'd better watch your mouth, you're standing up for Tony over the church?"

"No, church *people*. Like Tony said, there's a difference between God's people and church people."

"What's the difference?" Angel asked.

"Church people beat the hell out of you, and God's people love the heaven in you, and the heaven in you pushes hell out of you," Lisa explained..

"Girl, did Tony tell you that?" Angel asked.

"No, I actually just made it up, but it's true. I guess I am starting to act like Tony," Lisa giggled.

"So girl, is Tony still drinking?" Angel asked.

"Girl yes and I have a feeling he's going to drink tonight."

"Why do you say that?" Angel asked.

"Because it's the weekend and 'he got to do what it do!"

"Dang girl, that's messed up. He's a hot mess!"

"He sure is, and I told him so last night too; honey I gave him an earful, you hear me!"

"So, do you really think ya'll are supposed to be married though?" Angel asked.

"Well that's what God said, but I don't know what to think right now; I surely don't want too," Lisa responded.

"Are you sure about that?" Angel asked. "Because I know I don't trust him or like him; well he is funny, so well I guess I do like him, and

324

that's why I don't trust him; because it's hard not to like him. But girl, all jokes aside; I ain't never seen you this happy, and it even seems like you are glowing and it's like you really living now. I mean, not that you didn't have a life before, but…"

"It was kind of pathetic at times," they both laughed.

"Anyway girl, you know what I mean, you gotta walk your own path on this one. Don't let anyone influence you if you know what God is saying. Bump what anybody else thinks!"

Lisa paused for a moment.

"You know, I don't know. Most days the answer would be yes, because I know what God told me, but then there are days, or rather nights like this, that horrify me. The last thing I want to do is to marry an alcoholic. Shoot, half the time I'm up at night, like every other weekend or so with him out on one of his binges, wondering if he will make it back alive."

"Girl is it that bad?"

"Girl yes, one night I called Tony's phone and somebody picked up, and I don't even know who it was; he said he was holding Tony's phone for him because he was about to get into it with somebody. I could hear all this cussing and screaming in the background, girl it was a mess."

"Well, what happened?" Angel asked.

"Oh girl, Tony ran into this so called friend of his, and he asked him if he wanted to hang out.

Tony said he was in this late model Seville, and it seemed kind of strange; because the guy normally drove a truck. So Tony asked the guy whose car it was, and he said that it belonged to a friend. Later on that night the police got behind them, and the guy said they had to dump the car. Tony said he yelled, "WHAT?" Then the guy said that the car was hot, that he took it from this fiend. Tony said he went ballistic. He said he told the guy he couldn't believe he had him riding around all night in a stolen car. Anyway, by the time I called they were in a fight over it."

"How did they get away from the police?" Angel asked.

"Girl, I do not know. Tony has had so many narrow escapes, at least according to him."

"And you believe him?" Angel asked.

"Most of the time no, but girl, some of the stuff that he says is too crazy not to be true. The next day it was in the paper that this guy with a Seville got car jacked and robbed of all his money."

"Girl! They robbed him?" Angel asked.

"No not according to Tony. Tony said that kind of thing happens all the time. He said that the guy was out smoking dope and he ran out of money, so he pawned his car. He said that if the dope boy doesn't come back when they say they will, and he said they never do, they call the police and report the car stolen. He said it is also a way for them to

326

cover their tracks for showing up at home the next day broke and car-less."

"Girl, now that's really messed up," Angel said. "So that's the kind of characters that Tony hangs out with?"

"Well he claims it's not, but every time he comes up missing or ends up in trouble, that's who he's with." Lisa answered.

"Now I understand your dilemma, and I'm so sorry. Girl, I didn't know," Angel said.

"I know it's got to be God for you to still be bothered with that. And anyway girl; ain't you afraid that your life is in jeopardy fooling around with somebody like that? He's got to have enemies, and I wouldn't doubt it if somebody ain't looking for him, and he's probably wanted by the police," Angel said.

Lisa couldn't say anything. Angel screamed. "Girl, have you lost your damn mind or something?!! Are you kidding me? You riding around with a wanted man?"

"I'm afraid so," Lisa answered.

"Girl I would be terrified."

"It's not like that."

"Well what the hell is it then, 'cause I want to hear this one," Angel yelled.

"He's got some warrants on him yes, but he says it's just traffic stuff," Lisa answered.

"Yeah whatever!" Angel responded "Girl, I think you need to have your head examined or something. Okay maybe God did tell you that he was the one for like way, way later or something, like when he gets out of jail; if he ever gets out of jail when they catch him. Girl, you don't know what that man did; for all you know he could be a murderer, or a rapist or something."

Lisa couldn't say anything again.

"Okay Lisa, I know by your silence that it's something bad, and you know it, and girl I don't want to know," Angel responded. "Shoot! Talk about why do good girls like bad boys! I just never thought I would see the day when you would flip like this. No wonder they're talking in the church and calling you stupid. I'm starting to wonder myself," Angel responded.

"Me too! This has got to be the hardest thing I have ever done in my life; to care about someone so much that has so many issues."

"ISSUES!" Angel yelled "Girl, that's a real big understatement. That brother sounds like he's got hell on his heels and death at his door, and you his faithful sidekick."

"I wouldn't go that far. It's just sin like any other sin and he needs somebody that loves him enough to pray for him anyway," Lisa answered.

"Whatever! Most people's sin won't get you killed or chased by the police. Girl, you'd better watch your back 'cause it sounds like you need somebody praying for you. As a matter of fact, that's just what I am going to be doing every time I think about it; cause girl you need all the help you can get on this one."

"I know, and thanks girl."

Meanwhile, Tony was at the university attending graduation. It was just about over and he was already tipsy. They served wine and cheese in the vestibule before it began; and as hard as it was for Tony to pass up a drink, he definitely wasn't about to pass up a free one.

As the director was giving his closing remarks, he mentioned that the engineering department would be giving scholarships to young men interested in the program. They were trying to increase their minority enrollment at the University for engineering.

After the program Tony approached the director and asked him if there were any age limits, and could a non-traditional student like himself apply. The director told Tony that there was no age limits, and that he believed that Tony would make an excellent candidate for the program and furthermore he wanted to talk to Tony about sitting on the board for the construction program. He felt like Tony could add practical experience to the board. The board was made up of mostly professional engineers and a few city officials. Tony told the director that he didn't know what he could bring to the table. He thought that was way out of his league. The director assured Tony that he believed that he would do just fine, and that it would be a good opportunity for him to network with some professionals in his potential field of study. He said that they were always looking for bright interns, and that this may be a way in for him. Tony was excited about that and agreed to meet with him to talk more about it at a later date.

Tony couldn't wait to get going. He knew that Jamar would be waiting on his call if he wasn't already at a bar somewhere getting his face on. As soon as Tony got outside he called Jamar.

"Hey Jay," Tony said.

"Hey T, you ready?" Jamar asked.

"The better question is, are YOU ready?" Tony said.

"Yeah man! I just finished doing my last head and was just about to call you. You've always had perfect timing. So are you going to drive, or am I driving?" Jamar asked.

Tony didn't have to think about that one too hard because if there was anybody that drank more that he did it was Jamar. Tony would like to be the one that drove, and just kind of hold back on his drinking as best he could, so he could make sure they both got home safely. They both drove drunk all the time, but Jamar would be sloppy drunk.

"No, I'll drive, because you know how you get," Tony said.

"Aw, you ain't much better," Jamar said laughing.

"Yeah, but I got enough sense to keep a twelve in the car for when I get home, and then I'll get sloppy." They both laughed.

Jamar sold drugs; and not kibbles and bits either, he sold weight. He was a few years younger than Tony, but they had met years earlier. Tony advised Jamar that what he was doing was not only wrong, but it was dangerous; and if he was going to continue to do it then he needed to start a business doing something so he could explain the money, and keep it in an account somewhere instead of wrapped up in a rubber band and stuck down in a sock in the back of a closet somewhere.

Tony had noticed that Jamar liked to cut hair. He cut Tony's hair and his sons' hair as well. Tony told Jamar that it seemed like every time he turned around he was on his porch cutting somebody's hair. Tony told him that he may as well go to barber college and get his license, so that he could do something legal. Jamar always said that he owed Tony for that.

Jamar and Tony hooked up that night, but they didn't stay out at the bars as long as Tony thought they would, and he was a little puzzled by that. When he asked Jamar what was up, all he said was "I've got a surprise." Once they got to Jamar's house, he went to the cabinet and pulled out a big bottle of Cognac and sat it on the table. Then he pulled out a big bag of powder and said, "now let's really celebrate."

Tony yelled "Well let's do that thing then!" They sat up till morning snorting, smoking weed and drinking. Tony couldn't even feel his face anymore.

"Ahh, I can't peel ma pace!" Tony slurred.

"Waah?" Jamar answered.

"I said I can't peel ma pace!" They fell out laughing.

"Wait, wait, wait," Tony said.

"What?" Jamar asked.

"What we laughing at?" Tony asked.

"I don't know," Jamar said, both of them laughing hysterically.

"Oh man; it's today."

"What?" Jamar asked.

"I said, it's today."

"And?" Jamar answered.

"Well, when we got started it was today, but it was still dark so it felt like it was still yesterday but it was already today, so technically it was today yesterday, but now it's today for real, so that means it's tomorrow already."

"What the hell!" Jamar said.

"Man you cut the truck off. I don't know what you just said, and don't repeat it either."

Tony laughed, "I can, too."

"I know you can Tony. Stop it, you're making my jaws hurt," Jamar said still laughing.

"Oh you can peel your pace? I can't peel my pace. Are my lips moobin?" Tony said laughing. They fell over laughing. Tony tried to collect himself.

"Oh man! We gonna feel this in the morning, or tonight, or whatever day we wake up. What's today anyway?"

"Tony, don't start that again," Jamar warned.

"No seriously what's today? It feels like I am supposed to be somewhere today."

"It's Sunday, church boy. You supposed to be at church."

Jamar often referred to Tony as a church boy. He'd even tell the females when he and Tony were out together that Tony was really a church boy turned bad; so they'd better enjoy his company while they could, because he would eventually go back to church. Everyone knew that Tony really didn't belong; everyone except Tony. Everybody always thought Tony was supposed to be doing something else. Even though they could never put their finger on what it was, they just knew that he didn't belong where he was. Tony knew it too, only he'd never admit it out loud.

Tony used to have a saying that 'ain't nothing more dangerous than a square turned cool' and of course he was referring to himself.

Tony started to feel ill. His head hurt, his heart was racing, and his stomach was upset.

"Oooh man! I think it's time for me to go lay down."

"You can lay down here on the couch if you want to, big dog," Jamar said.

"Jay now you know if I stay here we ain't never gonna stop."

"Yeah, you probably right," Jamar answered.

Tony knew that he was bad, but he really believed that Jamar did not have an off switch. Tony got in his car and drove home. He started to think about Lisa and Marcus. He knew that they would be looking for him at church, but there was *no way* he was going to make it this Sunday. He also knew that if he didn't show up what everybody would think. Everybody that got to know Tony at church knew that if he didn't show up that he had fallen off again. It happened every so many weeks, only now the weeks were getting closer together.

Lisa was at church when she had realized that Tony had not shown up yet, and she knew that he wasn't coming. She hated it too. Everyone would ask her where Tony was. Some were really concerned, but most would ask sarcastically as if to say "we told you so, stupid." Even though she was still pissed at him, Lisa began to pray.

"Lord, I don't know where this man is today or what he's gotten himself into this time, but I pray that You protect him. Lord, I pray that he get sick." Lisa prayed this prayer every time she thought about Tony drinking. She prayed that he just get violently ill every time he took a drink.

Meanwhile back at Marcus's house, Tony was just coming in, and he was sick as a dog. His heart was beating so fast that he thought he was going to have a heart attack and die. He wondered if he should call 911. He couldn't, he thought, because if he did they would probably take him straight to jail. Instead, Tony searched the house for aspirin, or something that might slow his heart down. He finally found some aspirin and took a handful. Tony tried to lie down but he couldn't rest. All he could do was fidget. He knew he had done way too much coke. He thought maybe he needed to drink it down, but he didn't have any money. He knew that Marcus kept change lying around the house and felt bad for stealing it, especially since he was about to buy beer with it. "It's an emergency, though," he reasoned; "Marcus will understand."

He drove to the store, and on the way back the police got behind him. He thought he would die right then. He had already cracked a beer open, and was drinking it while driving down the street. The police flashed his lights. "This is it," Tony thought, "I'm ready. Maybe this is what I need to finally stop."

Tony pulled over to the curb, but the police car zoomed by. Tony dropped his head and let out a deep sigh. He was shaking like a crap game. He collected himself and drove the rest of the way home. The store was only around the corner and most days he'd walk or ride his bike.

When Tony got back to the house, he had already downed one twenty-four ounce can of beer. He had gotten three, which was his usual. He preferred bottles, but he knew that three twenty fours were cheaper than a six pack, and since he was always running short on money, he went with the cans. As Tony was about to crack open the second one he got really ill. His head was swimming, his stomach was churning, and eh…he ran to the bathroom and puked his guts. It was green! He thought he was gonna die. He tried to lie down again, but he still couldn't find any rest, it felt like the bed was moving. Just then he thought about the pills Marcus told him about. Marcus had some pain pills that he got from the dentist when he had his tooth pulled. They were somewhere in the house. Marcus said they were real good, too, and that they knocked him straight out. That's what I need, Tony thought. Tony scrambled through the kitchen cabinets until he found them. Tony didn't even read the label he just took two and plopped them right in his mouth.

Tony tried to lie down again. He could hear a voice say "go." He said out loud, "Aw, I'm trippin." He heard it again; the voice said, "You need to go now."

Tony shot straight up. He didn't know how, but he knew exactly where he was supposed to go, and what he was supposed to do. Tony jumped up and drove all the way across town to the ARC. It was the Salvation Army's Adult Rehabilitation Center. Tony knew the place because he used to work there as a counselor by day, and a cook by night.

When Tony arrived, he got to the front desk and the guy made Tony blow into an alcohol tester. He knew that if he blew over a certain number he'd have to go to detox first, then come back. They only did long term in-patient but no detox. Tony blew high but he knew he would. He had not only been up drinking all night, but he had just slammed a beer. The guy at the front desk said "sorry man, I can't let you in." Tony pleaded with the guy.

"Look man, if you don't let me in now, I don't think I'll make it back!"

The guy looked at Tony for a moment, as he contemplated what to do.

"Alright! Look, go outside and smoke a couple of cigarettes or something, and then come back in and try again."

Tony did just that. Not only was Tony smoking, but he was praying.

"Lord, I'm really sick of myself. I'm tired of hurting the people who love me, and on top of that

I stole from the man who gave me a place to stay, and hasn't charged me a dime. Lord please let me pass that test so they can let me in today. I don't know if I will be here tomorrow if I don't get in."

Tony went back inside and took the test and passed.

"Well bro, looks like that worked; I told you."

"Man, it wasn't that. I was out there praying!"

The guy laughed "And I was in here praying too."

He told Tony to take a seat and the intake counselor would be up in a few minutes. It seemed like hours passed by, but it was only minutes. The counselor finally showed up and told Tony to come with him. As they walked down the hall, the counselor stopped suddenly.

He yelled to the man at the front desk. "Hey, did you test him?"

"Yeah why," the guy at the desk asked.

"Well, for one thing he reeks of alcohol," the counselor said.

"When was the last time you had a drink?" the counselor asked Tony.

"I don't know for sure but I know I drank pretty heavy last night."

"How much did you drink?" The counselor asked "You smell like you might be flammable."

"I am, so just don't strike a match." They both laughed.

The counselor did Tony's intake, and throughout the course of questioning he found out that Tony used to be a state certified counselor himself for over ten years, and clean and sober for almost twenty.

"How in the hell did you go back to stupid? What? Did you forget all of a sudden after all of those years?"

Tony didn't even know how to answer.

"Man, I don't really know. I mean, I could give you a bunch of reasons, but then none of them are an excuse. As a matter of fact, I didn't even realize how stupid it was, or how far I had come until you said it just now," Tony said.

"So how do you know you are ready to stop," the counselor asked.

"Because I'm just tired," Tony answered in a solemn whisper.

"Okay. Since you were a counselor you are going to understand why I have to ask this next line of questioning. Do you have any legal issues that will prevent you from completing this treatment, or if you do have legal issues are they your motivation for treatment?"

Tony knew that these questions were asked to find out if he was running from the law, or trying to lesson a sentence that he would receive from the law, as was a common practice. Most people knew that if you had something pending, and you showed up to court having turned yourself into a treatment facility, that you normally got leniency and would probably be put on probation.

"I have legal issues but it's just traffic stuff." Tony answered.

"Alright then, we are all done here. Are you hungry?" The counselor asked.

"Yes," Tony answered.

"Well let me show you to the kitchen, and maybe they have some sandwiches made or something."

"Thanks," Tony said.

"Is there anybody that you need to call?" The counselor asked.

"Yes, but I don't know if I am ready to."

"Well when you're ready there are two pay phones with fifteen minute limits. You can make all the calls you need to today but there is a one month phone restriction for new clients," the counselor stated.

"Oh, I have a cell phone," Tony answered.

"Not in here you don't. So if you want to use it for the last time you will have to go outside to do so, then when you are done you will need to turn it in to me. I will lock it up and you can get it back when you leave. Is there anything else you have that I need to know about?" The counselor asked.

"Well, my car is parked outside."

"You can't have a vehicle either, so you will have to have someone come and pick it up, or it will be towed."

"Oh" Tony said.

Now he knew that he had to call someone. Lisa was the only one that had a key to his car. Tony always locked himself out of his car, and gave a key to Lisa for safe keeping. He wasn't ready to talk to anyone, especially not Lisa.

It was late in the evening by then, and Tony couldn't figure out where the day went. It seemed like it was just morning when he left Marcus' house to come to the center. He remembered the counselor saying to him that he had just missed supper, but he knew that some people called lunch supper, so he could have meant that, or maybe he just made a mistake and meant lunch. It was getting dark as Tony went outside to use his phone. This frightened Tony, because he seemed to have lost some time somewhere. Tony called Lisa.

"Hello?" Lisa said.

"Hey," Tony said in a somber tone.

Lisa was still quite angry with Tony, but she did want to know if he was alright, and was still curious to know what had happened. "Tony, where have you been?" she asked; "I was worried about you." She hadn't meant to say the last part, but it was what was in her heart.

"I messed up!" was all Tony could say.

"Are you alright?" Lisa asked.

"I will be alright, I guess."

"Well, where are you at?" Lisa asked.

"I turned myself in to a treatment center," Tony answered.

"You turned yourself in, or did the police make you go there?" Lisa asked.

"No, I turned myself in. The police would have taken me to jail. I would have gone to court, and the Judge could have ordered me to treatment or something, but not the police," Tony answered.

"Well, good," Lisa said.

"Good?" Tony asked.

"Yeah, that's good. I have been praying for you for two days; ever since you came up missing Saturday night."

"TWO DAYS! It's just Sunday," Tony said, still dazed and confused.

"You must really be messed up, because it's Monday all day."

"WHAT!" Tony answered "What happened to Sunday?"

"I don't know what happened to your Sunday, but my Sunday was spent at the church with everybody asking me where you were."

"I'm sorry, and I know how you hate that."

"I can't tell! You keep doing it over and over again."

"You're right," Tony answered.

"Look Lisa, I didn't call to argue. I just wanted to let you know that I am alright."

"Oh, I know you are now, because you are finally admitting that you need some help, and that's the first step right there," Lisa answered.

"Yep, I know. And you won't be hearing from me for thirty days." Tony said.

"Why not?" Lisa asked.

"Well, there is a thirty day restriction on the phone and visitors for new intakes."

"Oh, that's smart. That way you don't have no outside interferences, and can focus totally on God. Will they let you go to church?"

"Well, it is a Christian program, and they have their own church, and it is mandatory for everyone to go."

"Oh good," Lisa said, becoming more and more excited.

"I'm proud of you and I know you can make it," she said.

Tony was choked up and he didn't know what to say. He felt like he was at the lowest point in his life, and here Lisa was saying that she was proud of him? It just didn't make sense.

"Goodbye, Lisa. I will see you or talk to you in thirty. Oh, I almost forgot; I need you to come and pick up the car. I can't have it here."

"Oh, God is good!" Lisa exclaimed. "I will be happy to pick it up; just tell me where."

"It's at the corner of J Street and 17th. Do you know where that's at?"

"Yes, that's right around the corner from the post office downtown. I have to go there every day, so I know where that's at."

"Okay, good," Tony answered.

"Will I see you when I pick up the car?" Lisa asked.

"No" Tony answered.

"Do you still have the key?"

"Oh, yes. I just thought you might need something."

"No, I'm cool and I apologize in advance for anything you may find in the car." Tony said.

"Oh my God, is it anything illegal?" Lisa asked.

"More than likely, and I know there is definitely beer and empties in there. That's why I am apologizing in advance; just throw whatever it is away."

"That will be my pleasure," Lisa answered.

"Well Lisa, I have to go; and I just wanted to thank you for all you have done for me, and thank you for believing in me when nobody else did."

"It almost sounds like you're signing off. Don't sound so morbid. I'll be talking to you again in thirty days."

"I didn't think you would even want to be bothered with me; considering all the drama I have caused in your life. I would have thought that you would have been glad to have gotten rid of me."

"I prayed for this, for you to finally go get some help, and admit that you've got a problem. This is an answer to prayer. And you're right about one thing; with all the hell you have put me through, if you think you are going to get off that easy mister, you got another thing coming. Buddy you owe me, I will be sitting outside waiting to collect in thirty days." They both laughed.

"Tony, I know you feel messed up right now because I can hear it in your voice; but I want you to be encouraged. I think you should use this time to talk to God. And for the record, you haven't been all that bad to my life. You have brought out some things that I think I may have needed to look at in myself anyway. I wasn't very compassionate with my father and his drinking. Plus, I still hurt over the fact that I couldn't seem to get him to stop. I feel like God may have given me a second chance with you; I don't know. I just want to let you know before you go that I do love you, and I will be praying for you night and day."

"Thanks Lisa, and again Lisa, I am truly sorry for all that I put you through."

"It's okay Tony; really, just focus on getting better right now, and who knows, one day you might get to see the lady in the black dress."

"Man, at one time that's all I dreamed about, but today it's one of the farthest things from my mind."

"Wow, God really is working on you," Lisa said.

"Okay Tony, see you later."

"Okay Lisa."

After he hung up the phone with Lisa, Tony went back inside the building. He was shown his bunk area, and he fell across the bed and passed out.

Lisa had her daughter take her downtown to pick up Tony's car. The car was a mess, just as Tony said it would be. It smelled like beer, weed, and God only knows what that other smell was that she couldn't quite make out. She wished she could just have set the whole car on fire. Lisa took the car home, and cleaned it out and parked it. She went in her house and sat down with a sigh of relief, and began to write.

Lord today Tony went to rehab... she stopped, and began to wonder if her job was complete. Would she and Tony still be as close once he got out? Once he is clean and sober for a while, would he see things differently? The only thing Lisa knew was to trust God and to trust him.

Lightning Source UK Ltd.
Milton Keynes UK
UKOW07f1935141214

243121UK00013B/168/P